CALICO SPY

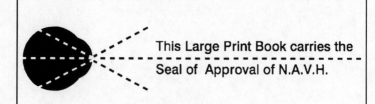

CALICO SPY

MARGARET BROWNLEY

THORNDIKE PRESS
A part of Gale, Cengage Learning

GALE
CENGAGE Learning·

Farmington Hills, Mich • San Francisco • New York • Waterville, Maine
Meriden, Conn • Mason, Ohio • Chicago

GALE
CENGAGE Learning·

LIBRARY OF CONGRESS CATALOGING-IN-PUBLICATION DATA

Names: Brownley, Margaret, author.
Title: Calico spy / by Margaret Brownley.
Description: Large print edition. | Waterville, Maine : Thorndike Press, 2016. | © 2016 | Series: Thorndike Press large print Christian mystery | Series: Undercover ladies ; book 3
Identifiers: LCCN 2015047605| ISBN 9781410487766 (hardcover) | ISBN 1410487768 (hardcover)
Subjects: LCSH: Pinkerton's National Detective Agency—Fiction. | Women detectives—Fiction. | Murder—Investigation—Fiction. | Large type books. | GSAFD: Mystery fiction. | Christian fiction.
Classification: LCC PS3602.R745 C35 2016 | DDC 813/.6—dc23
LC record available at http://lccn.loc.gov/2015047605

Published in 2016 by arrangement with Barbour Publishing, Inc.

Printed in Mexico
1 2 3 4 5 6 7 20 19 18 17 16

The LORD is good, a strong hold in the
day of trouble;
and he knoweth them that trust in him.

NAHUM 1:7

CHAPTER 1

Calico, Kansas
1880

Katie Madison tied the black satin ribbon at her neckline and frowned. The lopsided bow wouldn't do. She yanked the ribbon loose and tried again. Today she was all thumbs, and everything that could go wrong, did. Already she'd broken a shoelace, snagged a stocking, and torn the hem of her dress.

Just as she finished tying the bow for the third time the bedroom door flew open and her roommate's brunette head popped inside. "Katie! Hurry or you'll be late."

"I'm trying, I'm trying."

Mary-Lou's green eyes narrowed, and her Southern drawl grew more pronounced. "Pickens has a burr in his saddle. Said if you don't hurry he'll have your head!"

Katie's stomach knotted. She was already in trouble with the restaurant manager. "I'll

7

be there in a minute."

"A minute might be too late." The door slammed shut, and Mary-Lou's footsteps echoed down the hall as she yelled for the other Harvey girls to make haste. "Y'all better hurry now, you hear?"

Katie whirled about for one last look in the mirror and hardly recognized the image reflected back. The black dress with its high collar, starched white apron, and black shoes and stockings made her look more like a nun than one of Pinkerton's most successful female detectives.

Even her unruly red hair had been forced to conform to Fred Harvey's strict regulations. Parted in the middle, it was pulled back in a knot and fashioned with the mandatory net. The rigid hairdo did nothing for her, appearance-wise. All it did was make her eyes look too big and her freckles stand out like brown polka dots.

Wrinkling her nose, she turned away from the mirror. It was a good thing she'd chosen to be a detective as she had neither the looks nor housekeeping skills needed for landing a husband.

Not that she was complaining; two Harvey girls had been found dead, and it was her job to find the killer. The assignment of a lifetime had landed in her lap.

Working undercover was never easy, but so far this particular disguise was proving to be the hardest one yet, even harder than last year's job as a circus performer. At least here she didn't have to hobnob with lions, and for that she was grateful. All she had to deal with now was a possibly deranged killer.

Pausing at the door, she checked that her leg holster and gun were secured beneath her skirt. The pocket seams had been ripped open for easy retrieval. Hand on the doorknob, she braced herself with a quick prayer. God knows, she needed all the help she could get.

Leaving the room, she raced along the hall and sped down the stairs. Just as she reached the bottom tread the heel of her shoe caught on the runner. Arms and legs flailing, she hit the floor facedown, and the wind whooshed out of her like juice from a squashed tomato.

Momentarily stunned, she didn't move. Not till noticing the polished black shoes planted in front of her did she gather her wits. Looking up, she groaned.

The manager, Mr. Pickens, glared down at her, hands on his waist. A large, imposing man, he looked about to pop the buttons on his overworked vest. Judging by his red face and quivering mustache, his patience was equally tested.

"Miss Madison. You're late!"

Her mouth fell open. Was that all he cared about? No concern for her welfare? No thought that she had injured herself?

"Well, are you going to lie there all night?"

"No, sir." She scrambled to her feet and smoothed her apron.

His eyebrows dipped into a V. "Shoulders straight, head back, and for the love of Henry, smile! I want to see some choppers." He spread his thin lips to demonstrate but did a better impersonation of a growling dog than a friendly waitress. "Do you hear me?"

"Yes, sir," she said. "Choppers."

"Tonight you're the drink girl. Do you think you can handle that?"

Plastering a smile on her face, she nodded. How hard could it be to pour tea?

He gave her a dubious look that did nothing for her self-confidence. "We'll soon see. Follow me."

He led her to the formal dining room where tables were already set for the supper crowd. The room was decorated in shades of brown and tan. Floor-to-ceiling windows overlooked the railroad tracks. Beyond, fields of tall grass and wildflowers spread a

10

colorful counterpane beneath a copper sky.

The restaurant was shorthanded, and she had been handed a uniform the moment she stepped off the morning train. After that she'd hardly had time to catch her breath. So many rules and regulations to remember. No notepads or pencils were allowed. That meant she was expected to memorize the menu. She was also instructed to radiate good cheer to even the most difficult of patrons.

Her chances of lasting through the night didn't look promising, and that was a worry. The investigation depended on her keeping her job as a waitress. No one at the restaurant knew her legal name or real purpose for being there. As far as anyone knew, she was simply a farm girl who traveled all the way from Madison, Wisconsin, looking for adventure and a better life.

Pickens quickly pointed out the silver coffee urns and teapots. He stared at her with buttonhole eyes. "You do know the cup code, right?"

"Uh." There was a code for cups?

"Cup in the saucer means coffee." He demonstrated as he spoke. "A flipped cup *against* the saucer is for iced tea. A cup *next* to the saucer — milk. Is that clear?"

"Yes, sir, next to the saucer."

"As for hot tea," he continued, and her heart sank. "The cup will be flipped *upon* the saucer." He then explained how to tell if the customer wanted black, green, or orange pekoe tea by the direction of the cup handle. "Any questions?"

She had plenty, but he didn't look in any mood to answer them, so she shook her head no.

Satisfied that she had donned the proper attitude or at least a Harvey-worthy smile, he turned. Giving three quick claps, he called the workers front and center. "All right, ladies, take your stations!"

"Don't be nervous," her roommate, Mary-Lou, said as they strode side by side to the back of the room.

Easier said than done. Katie stopped to stare at the cups on the table. She'd come face-to-face with some of the most ornery outlaws in the country, and she wasn't about to let a china cup intimidate her. On second thought, maybe just a little. Did the cup handle facing right mean green tea or pekoe?

Already her cheeks ached from smiling, but that was the least of it. Her collar itched, and the stiff starched apron felt like a plate of armor.

As if to guess her rising dismay, Mary-

Lou said, "You'll like it here once you get used to it. You just have to work fast, be polite, and smile."

"Nothing to it," Katie muttered. She only hoped she had enough energy left at the end of the workday for sleuthing.

A loud gong announced the imminent arrival of the five-twenty-five. Windows rattled, and the crystals on the chandelier did a crazy dance as the Atchison, Topeka, and Santa Fe train rumbled into the station. With a blare of the whistle, it came to a clanging stop in front of the restaurant.

Moments later, the door flew open and travelers filed into the dining room like a trail of weary ants. Only thirty minutes was allowed for meals before the train took off again. The Harvey House restaurants took pride in the fact that no one had ever been late boarding a train because of inept service.

Katie planted a smile on her face and a prayer in her heart. *God, please don't let me be the one to break that record.*

CHAPTER 2

Sheriff Branch Whitman looked up just as the door to his office flew open. A cultured but no less commanding voice shot inside.

"Sheriff! I need a word with you!"

Branch lifted his feet off the desk and planted his well-worn boots squarely on the floor. He recognized his fastidiously dressed visitor at once, though they'd never been formally introduced.

"What can I do for you, Mr. Harvey?"

The renowned restaurateur stabbed the floor with his gold-tipped cane. He was somewhere in his midthirties, but his meticulous dark suit and Vandyke beard made him appear older.

"You dare to ask a question like that!" Harvey pushed the door shut and gazed at Branch with sharp, watchful eyes. "You know as well as I that someone is killing off Harvey girls." His British accent grew more pronounced with each word. Even his bow tie seemed to quiver with emotion. "And what, may I ask, are you doing about it?"

Branch slanted his head toward the chair in front of his desk. "Have a seat and —"

"I don't want a seat. I want to know what has been done to find the killer!"

Branch indicated the stack of files in front of him with a wave of his hand. "I can assure you that I'm doing everything in my power —"

"Balderdash!"

Harvey's impatience was no worse than Branch's own. The killings had turned into one of the most puzzling crimes he'd ever worked on. Despite weeks of investigation, he still didn't have a single suspect. Given the nature of the town, that was odd.

If a youth took a fancy to a pretty girl, or a married man so much as thought about straying, the locals knew about it. Somehow folks even knew that a young one was on the way before the expectant mother. Yet two young women had been murdered, and no one saw or heard a thing.

"I can assure you," he said, "that the person or persons responsible will be brought to justice."

Before Branch took over as sheriff three years ago, Calico was, by all accounts, the roughest, toughest, and wildest place in all of Kansas, rivaled only by Dodge City. But he'd single-handedly changed all that, and it was now a right decent town — or was before the two recent murders.

Harvey's eyes glittered. "It's been six weeks since Priscilla's death." Priscilla was the first woman to die. Less than three weeks later, the girl named Ginger was found dead in an alleyway.

"These things take time."

Harvey straightened a WANTED poster on the wall with the tip of his cane. The man was as fastidious with his surroundings as he was in dress and speech. No doubt he took issue with the stack of folders and papers strewn haphazardly across Branch's desk.

"Too much time if you ask me. So what have you got so far?"

"Right now, nothing." Branch's jaw clenched. He suspected the killer was a Harvey employee, but he wasn't ready to reveal that information. Not yet. He couldn't take the chance of word getting out that the crime was an inside job.

"This is no less than what I expected from local authorities." Harvey leaned on his cane, and his eyes hardened. "That's why I hired the Pinkerton National Detective Agency. Your services will no longer be needed."

Branch glared at him. Services? Harvey acted like he was firing one of his employees. "What happens in this town is my responsibility, and any outsiders —"

"Will report to me!" Harvey snapped his mouth shut and leaned over his cane as if to challenge Branch to disagree.

"Now wait just a minute."

Harvey's expression darkened. "No, *you* wait. We've wasted enough time and now a second girl is dead."

"And I will find her killer — both their killers." He didn't know Priscilla all that well, but Ginger was his favorite waitress. She'd often brought his evening meal to the office if she knew he was working late. Since he refused to adhere to Harvey's unreasonable regulations — particularly the *no coat, no service* rule in the main dining room — she did him no small favor.

"I'll have something to report to you soon." He sounded more certain than he felt. Each day that passed made finding the killer that much more difficult. Trails grew cold. Clues were lost. Memories faded. Even more worrisome was the possibility that the killer would strike again.

"Not soon enough." Harvey swung his cane under one arm and pulled his watch out of his vest pocket. "I'm sure the detective has arrived by now. If not on the morning or noon train, then on the five-twenty-five." He flipped the case open with his thumb. "I trust you'll give him your full cooperation."

Branch stiffened. Over his dead body. "Now see here —" The last thing he needed was some inept detective running loose in his town. Last time the Pinkerton operatives were involved in one of his cases they let the bad guys escape and almost got him killed. And look at the mess they made with the James gang. They could deny it all they wanted, but everyone knew the Pinkertons blew up the outlaws' house, killing Frank and Jesse's young half brother. No surprise there. The Pinkertons were known for their bullying tactics and underhanded methods, none of which Branch would tolerate.

Harvey replaced his watch and tipped his bowler. "Have a good day, Sheriff." He left with less fanfare than when he arrived.

Branch pounded his fist on the desk. "Dash it all!" The town was his responsibility — no one else's. The very thought of an undercover detective sneaking around like a mole in the ground set his teeth on edge.

Came in on today's train, did he? If the Pink was like most other passengers, he'd appreciate a good meal. Was probably at the Harvey House restaurant chowing down at that very moment. That was as good a place as any to intercept him. He pulled out his watch. He'd have to hurry if he wanted to reach the restaurant before the train left the station.

Decision made, he shot to his feet and plucked his Stetson off the wall.

One thing was certain. The man better enjoy his meal because if Branch had his way, the detective would be back on that train before he could say cock robin.

CHAPTER 3

The woman glared at Katie. "You gave my son hot coffee!" The notch on her front tooth pegged her as a seamstress who bit off thread rather than cutting it with scissors.

Katie looked down at the pudgy face of a two-year-old and whisked his cup away. "Oops, sorry."

"I ordered *iced* tea," the man Katie pegged as a banjo player groused. She guessed his profession based on the callus on the side of his right thumb. "You gave me *hot* tea."

"Milk? You gave me milk?" This from a gray-haired woman who stared at her cup with the same look of horror one might regard a rattler. Hands and neck dripping with jewels, she acted like a rich widow used to having servants answer her every whim.

By the time Katie straightened out the drinks, she was ready to call it a night, though none of the other girls seemed so inclined. Instead they darted around tables like lively balls in a game of bagatelle.

To outward appearances the smooth flow of dishes, which came and went with nary a spoken word, seemed like magic. In actuality, it was all part of a carefully orchestrated plan.

The train porter had taken travelers' food orders at the last stop and telegraphed the restaurant. This allowed cooks to prepare meals in advance. Supper was seventy-five cents and after each passenger paid, he or she was directed to the table where soup or salad waited.

While the diners worked on the first course, Katie followed Mary-Lou into the kitchen to refill her coffeepot.

Praying that the night would soon end, she spread her mouth in what she hoped would pass as a smile. A Harvey girl must never look dowdy, frowzy, or tired, even if her feet were killing her or her thoughts less than charitable.

On the way back to the dining room she bumped into the dark-haired waitress named Tully. "Why you . . ." Tully snapped her mouth shut and threw her shoulders back in an attempt to regain a positive, upbeat appearance. She might have succeeded had it not been for the Long Island

(Rhode Island?) hen on her tray drowning in coffee.

"You'll pay for this," she muttered under her breath. With a smile that was more lethal than friendly, she did a dainty pirouette and returned the drowning hen to the kitchen.

Katie stiffened at the sound of her name. She turned and found Mr. Pickens practically breathing down her throat.

"Miss Madison! A word with you. Now!"

After Pickens finished chastising her for working too slow, Katie straightened out the beverage mess and returned an empty teapot to the counter in back of the room.

The ten-minute warning for boarding the train had sounded, but time had never passed more slowly. Katie wasn't certain she could hold out for another minute, let alone ten.

Tully whispered something to her roommate. Tully was tall and willowy with skin as smooth as honey. Katie envied the woman's ability to look graceful in the rigid uniform, while she felt awkward and out of place. But then, that was how she'd always felt, even back home.

The shadow of growing up in a family of beautiful women seemed to follow her wherever she went. Her four sisters all took after their mother in looks and had landed successful and well-respected husbands. Katie had the unenviable distinction of being both the black sheep of the family *and* the ugly duckling.

Tully's voice brought her out of her reverie. "Why not let the new girl do it?"

"Do what?" Katie asked, keeping her tone neutral. Alienating the others would only make her investigation more difficult.

Tully pointed to the tall, lean man who had just walked into the dining room. Katie guessed from the badge on his vest that it was Sheriff Whitman. That was a surprise. Everything she heard about the man indicated he was an old crank, set in his ways and unwilling to listen to reason or work with Pinkerton detectives.

In contrast, this man was somewhere in his early to midthirties and didn't look like any crank she'd ever met. He wasn't bad to look at, either. Not bad at all.

"No one is allowed to eat in the dining room without wearing a coat," Tully explained. "You need to escort him over to the coatrack to borrow one."

"Even the sheriff is required to wear one?" Katie asked. She knew that such rules applied to the hoity-toity restaurants in some

23

of the large cities, but here in Kansas?

"Harvey rules," Tully said with a smile that seemed a tad too sweet for Katie's peace of mind.

"I'll see what I can do."

"You better," Tully said, "if you want to keep your job." It sounded like a warning.

Katie set her mouth in a determined smile and threaded her way through the dining room toward the sheriff. She was an expert in putting men in jail. How hard could it be to put a man in a coat?

CHAPTER 4

Branch scanned the crowded dining room. No sign of Harvey. Good. The last thing he wanted was another encounter with the Englishman.

He was here for one purpose and one purpose alone: to pick out the Pinkerton detective in time to escort him onto the train before it took off again.

Three possible suspects immediately caught his attention. One was a young man in a checkered coat with the eager look of a detective on his first case. Another was an older man whose interest in the attractive waitresses was probably personal but could just as easily be professional. A third man was doing a bad job of pretending to read a newspaper. Instead, his gaze kept darting around the room as if he was either looking for someone or suspected that someone might be looking for him.

Branch was just about to mosey over to

the newspaper guy when he spotted a young woman barreling toward him like a missionary targeting a possible convert. Since he didn't recognize her, she had to be new. So they sent a greenhorn to do the job, did they? *This should be interesting.*

She greeted him with a smile — and no Harvey girl smile was prettier. Hers was as wide as the Kansas prairie. But something about her didn't add up. Even as she tried to conform he sensed her resistance, sensed her sizing him up like a general planning an attack.

"Sheriff." She was a wee bit of a thing, barely reaching his shoulders. Never had so much feminine charm been packed into such a small package. Her big blue eyes almost seemed too large for her delicate features. A thin veil of freckles bridged her nicely shaped nose. The dazzling red hair didn't seem to belong in the rigid knot at the back of her head. Instead, it looked like it should fall down her back as free as the wind.

The smooth, graceful movements of her slender hips seemed to challenge the rigid confines of the black-and-white uniform. Yep, she was a looker all right. Not the conventional type by any means, but that's what made her stand out from the others.

Where did Harvey find these girls?

He held his hat in his hand and nodded politely. "Howdy, ma'am," he drawled. "Guess you're new 'round here." Must have been hired to take Ginger's place, but he didn't want to say as much.

She nodded. "My name's Miss Madison." She lifted her voice to be heard over the buzz of chatter and clank of dishes. "Miss Katie Madison."

"Mighty pleased to meet you, Miss Madison. Sheriff Whitman here, but my friends just call me plain ol' Sheriff."

"And your enemies, Sheriff? What do they call you?"

"There're some things I'd rather not say in the company of a lady such as yourself."

Something like annoyance crossed her face, though he couldn't imagine what he'd said to offend her.

"If you'll step over to that rack, I'll help you pick out a dinner coat." Her calm, casual voice seemed at odds with her sharp-eyed regard.

"Don't have much use for dinner coats," he said. "Same for neck chokers." Why any man would submit to wearing a tie was beyond his comprehension.

Her smile faded, and she glanced over her shoulder where the other three Harvey girls watched, along with their boss, Pickens.

She turned back to him, and he could see the wheels spinning in that pretty head of hers. "What a pity," she said. "A handsome man like you."

"The other girls tried flattery, too. It didn't work for them, either."

She lowered her head and glanced up at him through a fringe of lush lashes. Eleven. She had eleven tiny sun dots on her nose. Startled to find himself counting freckles, of all things, he drew his gaze to her pretty eyes, which looked blue as the wildflowers that grew alongside the railroad tracks. Chiding himself for being so easily distracted, he glanced at the newspaper guy.

"If you'll excuse me, ma'am —"

"I really need this job," she said. "And if I don't get you into one of those coats I could be fired."

Something in her voice made him hesitate. "That seems a bit drastic. Far as I know, none of the other girls lost their jobs because of me."

"I'm afraid I'm not in my boss's good graces at the moment." Her cheeks grew a pretty rose color. "I messed up the drink orders something awful and drowned a Rhode Island hen."

"You did that?" he said, feigning shock.

Her brow furrowed. "It might have been a Long Island hen."

"That's even worse," he said lightly, hoping to tease another one of her brilliant smiles from her.

She hesitated a moment as if trying to decide if he was joking. "So, please. Will you help me?"

He was so caught up with the hen business — or maybe it was the intriguing way her eyes flashed as she talked — that he momentarily forgot what she wanted him to do.

"So will you?" she pleaded when he failed to respond. "Wear a coat?"

"Oh, that." Opposed to wearing a dinner coat on general principle, he grimaced at the thought.

Unfortunately, he was also opposed to turning his back on damsels in distress. The look of dismay on her face meant the job was important to her. No surprise there. Until Harvey and his restaurants came along, few legitimate jobs existed for women, especially in this town. The work was hard and expectations high, but the job allowed a woman to earn a fair living and still stay in God's good graces.

He followed her worried glance to the back of the room. Pickens was no friend of

29

his, which meant cultivating one in Miss Madison might not be such a bad idea. Especially since his investigation into the Harvey girl murders was going to the dogs faster than a flock of fleas.

"What do I get if I put on one of them there straitjackets?"

She laughed, a musical sound that was as infectious as it was pleasant to hear. "A *straitjacket* will earn you a second helping of pie."

He grinned. "Well, ma'am, I don't suppose I can turn down an offer like that."

Relief flickered across her face. "I don't suppose you can," she said. "Follow me and I'll set you up."

With a rueful glance at the three suspected Pink detectives, he followed her.

She led him over to a rack where a dozen or so coats hung. Quickly riffling through them, she settled on a black frock coat that would have been right at home at a funeral, preferably on the guest of honor.

She met his gaze with a look of apology. "I'm afraid this is the closest we have to your size."

She held the coat up for him with a beseeching smile. As much as he wanted to, he didn't have it in him to deny her request. Swallowing his protests, he turned and slipped his arms through the sleeves. The coat barely fit his wide shoulders and stuck out over his holstered guns.

She covered her mouth and her eyes rounded in dismay as she watched him try to button it. The sleeves hit him at least six inches above the wrists.

"I can see why you're opposed to wearing a coat."

"Straitjacket," he said. "Let's hope I don't need to make a quick draw." He could hardly move his arms, let alone reach for his guns.

Her eyes softened as she studied him, allowing a glimpse into their very depths. "Thank you for helping me." He had a feeling she wanted to say more. But after a quick glance around, she fell silent.

He lowered his head next to hers, and a sweet lilac fragrance filled his head. "Perhaps you can do me a favor," he said, his voice low. "I'm looking for a man. Don't know his name. Don't know what he looks like. All I know is that he's a stranger in town."

"As you can see, Sheriff, we have a whole room full of strangers," she said.

"Yes, but this one plans to hang around."

"I see." She tilted her head to the side. "I'm new myself, but I'll ask the other girls if they know of any recent arrivals."

"Appreciate that, ma'am."

A blast of the train whistle created a flurry of activity. Passengers grabbed their few belongings and rose from their seats, chair legs scraping the wooden floor. The throng of diners streamed outside, some holding small children by the hand. Soon the buzz of excited voices faded behind the closed door, and only Branch and the restaurant workers remained.

He peered out the window and watched as all three men pegged as possible Pinkerton detectives boarded the train.

Blast it. That could mean only one thing. The detective had arrived earlier and was already checked in at the hotel.

He whirled about and practically bumped into Miss Madison. "Sorry, I have to go," he said, wiggling out of the coat like a moth from a cocoon.

"But your pie —"

"Another time." He really wanted to stick around if for no other reason than to get to know the pretty waitress better, which struck him as odd. Since his wife's death he hadn't really noticed other women. Work, church, and parenting his seven-year-old son took up all his time, and that was how he wanted it. Opening up his heart meant having to accept the possibility of loss again, and that he could never do. Once was enough.

More than enough.

He shoved the coat into her hands and, with a doff of his hat, quickly left the restaurant.

CHAPTER 5

That night after the Harvey House was closed for business, Katie ate a late supper with the other three Harvey girls. They sat at a long wooden table set aside for employees just off the kitchen. Tully and Mary-Lou were all atwitter over the restaurant owner's unexpected visit earlier that day.

Dubbed Transcontinental Fred, Mr. Harvey had single-handedly made rail travel more bearable by providing fine food and good service for weary Kansas travelers. Rumor had it that he planned to build his train station restaurants all the way to California.

"He's so handsome," the girl named Abigail exclaimed with a sigh. "And so tall."

"He's also terribly married," Tully said.

"Yes, but don't you just love the way he speaks?" Mary-Lou imitated his English accent which, given her Southern lilt, was no easy task: "How dare you call them waitresses. I won't have it. They're Harvey girls."

That brought a round of laughter from the others.

Katie's interest in the man was strictly out of curiosity. Most of the renowned people she'd had occasion to meet were bank robbers, counterfeiters, or con artists, not legitimate businessmen like Mr. Harvey. So that alone made him a novelty.

After the evening meal had been cleared away, the stations left spotless, and the tables set for breakfast, the Harvey girls clambered upstairs to their rooms.

Never had Katie known such luxurious surroundings. Her job as a detective required her to spend much of her time in cheesy, flea-ridden hotels. The last one she'd stayed in caught fire in the middle of the night, obliging her to stand outside in her nightclothes while the two-story building burned to the ground, taking her few belongings with it.

But the room she shared with Mary-Lou was fit for a queen. It was decorated with floral wallpaper, lush wine-red carpet, brocaded draperies, and fine oak furniture. Each of them had their own beds with thick mattresses, soft pillows, and satiny quilts.

She threw herself facedown on the bed, letting her feet dangle over the end, and it felt like she had landed on a cloud. "Whoopee!"

Mary-Lou laughed. "You'll never be able to sleep in a regular bed again."

Katie turned on her side. Leaning on her elbow, she rested her head on her hand. Recalling the demise of the young woman who had formerly occupied this very bed, she quickly apologized.

"I'm sorry. How thoughtless of me." No visual reminders of Mary-Lou's previous roommate remained, but somehow her presence could be felt. Probably because Katie had committed to memory the Pinkerton file on the latest victim. The woman was only nineteen, which made her death seem all the more tragic.

Facing the mirror, Mary-Lou drew the hairbrush through her hair. She wore a white linen nightgown that reached all the way to her bare toes, and her long brunette tresses hung to her waist in lush waves.

What Katie wouldn't give to have hair the color of Mary-Lou's. She would even settle for her roommate's smooth, creamy complexion that knew no freckles. Or even her delicately shaped mouth and perfect teeth. Katie felt an unwelcomed surge of envy.

The Bible warned against such feelings as it indicated a lack of gratitude and appreciation for how God had made her, but she couldn't help herself. Would it have ruined some divine plan if God had given her, say, blond hair or brown?

Irritated by such distracting thoughts, she forced herself to concentrate on the reason she had been sent to the Harvey House, which wasn't to feel sorry for herself.

"You must miss your former roommate," she said.

"I miss her something awful." Mary-Lou worked the brush through the length of her hair. "She was like a sister to me."

It was the opening Katie had hoped for. "Do you know who would have done such an awful thing?"

"I can't imagine." Mary-Lou set her hairbrush down on the dressing table and turned. "Everyone liked her."

"What about the other woman, Priscilla? Did everyone like her, too?"

"Oh yes. She was one of the nicest people you'd ever hope to meet."

It wasn't what Katie wanted to hear. Nothing she hated more than a well-liked murder victim with no enemies. And here she had two. It made her job that much more difficult.

She let the silence stretch between them before asking the next question. Show too much curiosity and she could blow her cover. "Did Ginger have a beau?"

Husbands and beaus were always suspects in such murder cases — often for good reason.

Mary-Lou finished braiding her hair into a single plait before answering. "She took a fancy to a local railroad worker. His name is Charley. She wanted to marry him but, of course, we Harvey girls aren't allowed to wed."

After a moment she continued. "They were saving up enough money so she could quit her job." She sighed. "He waited for her outside every Friday night after lights were out. Ginger would sneak out to be with him."

Katie stiffened. "Sneak out? You can do that?"

"Sneaking out isn't the problem. Sneaking back in is. She bribed one of the cooks into letting her borrow his key."

Katie made a mental note of this information. That explained why the bodies were found outside the house. That had puzzled her at first, mainly because the house was supposedly locked up tight as a fiddle at night and the girls not allowed out past curfew.

Her investigation now became more complicated because it meant that the killer could be an outsider and not a Harvey House employee as originally thought.

"Her beau must have taken her death hard."

"Hard doesn't begin to describe it." Mary-Lou reached for a blue ribbon and wrapped it around the end of her braid. "Poor man. He wept like a baby at her funeral. He still waits for her at night."

"What do you mean?"

Mary-Lou tied the ribbon in a bow and tossed the braid over her shoulder. "Every once in a while I see him standing under the lamppost after curfew watching the house. It's as if he still expects her to join him."

Katie could think of another possibility. It wasn't unusual for criminals to return to the scene of the crime. Maybe this Charley fellow was feeling guilty. Maybe that's why he returned to the house. She didn't want to think he was looking for a new victim.

"What about Priscilla? Did she have a beau, too?"

Before Mary-Lou could answer, the door flew open and the dorm matron, Miss Thatcher, walked in. "Lights out, ladies," she snapped.

From what Katie had heard from the others, the woman ran the house like a general at war. She lacked the proper uniform, but no general's scowl could compare.

Stick thin with a long, pointed nose, straight mouth, and what looked like a perpetual frown, she was apparently one of the few employees not required to smile.

Regarding Katie with an icy stare that sent chills spiraling through her, Miss Thatcher picked up, with thumb and forefinger, the white apron carelessly tossed on a chair.

"Is this yours, Miss Madison?"

Katie swung her feet onto the floor and sat upright on the bed. "Yes, ma'am. I was just about to take care of that." Dirty clothes were to be placed in the hamper in the hall. The laundry was sent to Newton, Kansas, to be washed, but each girl was responsible for ironing and starching her own uniform.

Miss Thatcher let the apron drop like one might release a dead rat. Her gaze settled on Katie. "You're still in your uniform."

Feeling like a schoolgirl caught stealing, Katie rose to her feet. "Yes, ma'am."

"You do know the rules of the house."

She wasn't sure which rule Miss Thatcher referred to as there were so many, but to be on the safe side she threw her shoulders back and smiled. That failed to lessen the scowl on Miss Thatcher's face. If anything, it made it worse.

"Do I amuse you, Miss Madison?"

"No, Miss Thatcher."

"Then take that silly grin off your face."

"Yes, ma'am."

The dorm matron's dark eyebrows drew together. "For your insubordination, you will report to kitchen duty at five a.m. Do I make myself clear?"

Insubordination? Katie glanced at her roommate, who shrugged. Since she was pretty sure that making a face would not earn her any favors, she kept her expression composed.

"Yes, Miss Thatcher."

Without another word, the woman turned off the brass kerosene lamp, throwing the room into darkness. She stopped in the doorway, her figure outlined in the soft glow from the hallway light. The way her ears stood out made her head look like a sugar bowl.

"Good night, ladies." With that she swept out of the room with a rustle of silk, the door closing with a quiet but no less commanding click.

"What a witch," Katie said, plopping down on her bed to pull off her shoes and stockings.

Girlish giggles rose from Mary-Lou's side

of the room.

"What's so funny?"

"You." Mary-Lou burst into another round of laughter. "Your first day here and already you're in trouble with Mr. Pickens *and* Miss Thatcher. It takes most girls at least a week to accomplish that feat."

Katie hadn't meant to antagonize anyone. Certainly not the dorm matron. The woman probably knew more about the girls in her care than anyone else.

Katie grimaced. Somehow she would have to find a way to get back in the woman's good graces. The manager's, too.

For Mary-Lou's benefit, she breathed out an audible sigh. "I tend to get off on a bad foot at times." Perhaps her roommate could give her some pointers on how best to handle Miss Thatcher.

"You can't say that about the sheriff," Mary-Lou said.

"What do you mean?" The memory of the lawman's intriguing dark eyes and crooked smile surprised her with its intensity.

"No one, and I do mean no one, ever persuaded Sheriff Whitman to wear a coat. You're the first."

For some unknown reason, that brought a smile to Katie's face — the first heartfelt smile since arriving in town.

CHAPTER 6

As much as Katie enjoyed the soft, luxurious bed, the stress of starting a new job in an unfamiliar place kept her tossing and turning.

Now as always when she couldn't sleep, she turned to the Lord. *God, don't let me mess up this job. You know how my mouth gets away from me and I say things I shouldn't. You have my permission to bang me on the head if I don't curtail my tongue. And please forgive my envious heart. I'm sure You had a good reason for giving me hair the color of a rooster's comb, and maybe one day You'll let me know what that reason is.*

She ended her prayer with a sigh but was no closer to falling asleep than before. As much as she needed the rest, everything she'd seen and heard since arriving in Calico kept running through her head. A surreptitious look or hasty conversation might or might not mean much, but no detective could afford to discount anything.

Somehow she had to find a way to talk to the sheriff in private. She only hoped her boss had exaggerated Whitman's dislike of Pinkerton operatives. He was nothing like what she'd expected. A man willing to help out a poor waitress he'd only just met couldn't be all that difficult to deal with, could he?

She'd considered identifying herself earlier, but too many people were present. She didn't want to take a chance on blowing her cover.

The memory of the sheriff in that too-small coat made her giggle, and she quickly covered her mouth so as not to waken Mary-Lou.

Turning over, she pounded the pillow with her fist and closed her eyes. Startled by the vision of the sheriff's handsome square face, she flopped on her back and stared at the ceiling.

Reading faces was a necessary part of her job, and she was better at it than many of her colleagues. The sheriff had strong features — a sign of integrity. Though he seemed outgoing and friendly enough, she'd nonetheless sensed his reserve. It was as if he'd purposely held part of himself back, the part that most intrigued her.

The thought made her groan. Homing in on a criminal's deepest secrets was her job. Prying into the sheriff's private life was absolutely off-limits, no matter how much she was tempted. Her Pinkerton boss expected results, and he expected them fast. She had no time to lose, and working with the sheriff might save her precious time.

He knew things about the victims and crime scenes that were not in the Pinkerton report. That made him a valuable resource.

She turned to her side. *"Report to kitchen duty at 5:00 a.m."* What time was it now? It seemed like she'd been twisting and turning all night.

She reached for the mechanical clock on the bedside table. Quietly she slipped out of bed and tiptoed to the window. Between the full moon and gas streetlight there was just enough light filtering through the lace curtains for her to read the hands on the clock. Much to her surprise, it was only a little after eleven.

Someone had described insomnia as twisting and turning all night for an hour, but this was ridiculous.

Nudging the curtain aside, she gazed down at the moonlit street, and a movement caught her eye. A man stood next to the lamppost gazing up at the house. She quickly drew back. Was that the dead girl's beau, Charley? She glanced outside again.

There was only one way to find out. Dropping the curtain in place, she felt in the dark for her clothes.

Branch picked the stranger out the moment he walked into the Silver Spur Saloon. The detective sat at a table by his lonesome. Probably trying to familiarize himself with the town before starting his investigation.

He definitely acted like a Pinkerton detective. No question. Not only was the man new in town, he huddled over his drink as if trying to make himself small and invisible.

If Branch wasn't so incensed at the thought of having to deal with the private detective, he might have laughed. The man in his Monkey Ward clothes — new denim pants, shirt, and boots — stood out like a sore thumb. And that wasn't even mentioning the barely creased hat.

If the Pinkerton agency insisted upon sending its city-slicker detectives here, the least they could do was learn how to dress them properly. Most of the cowboys and railroad workers in town hadn't seen a pair of new trousers or boots for a dozen or so years, not since Andrew Johnson was in office.

Branch had expected the detective to check in at the hotel or, at the very least, Miss Grayson's Room and Board that day, but he'd done neither. Puzzled, Branch did a methodical search of saloons, and the Silver Spur was the fourth one he'd visited that night.

The place was in full swing. Old man Taylor played a lively tune on the mouth organ, which he blew with great diligence. Along one side of the saloon a faro game was in progress.

Branch walked up to the stranger's table, pulled out a chair, and sat.

Monkey Suit looked up, revealing an ugly man with pockmarked skin, broken nose, and small, beady eyes. If it was possible to scare a criminal into going straight, that was the face to do it.

Branch wasted no time on introductions. "I know who you are and what you're doing here."

The words were barely out if his mouth before the man tossed his drink at Branch and took off running.

On his feet in a flash, Branch gave chase. The Pinkerton detectives might not know how to dress, but they sure did know how to run — his opinion of the organization went up a begrudging notch.

Shouldering his way through the crowd, Branch rushed through the swinging doors. He looked left, right, and straight ahead before spotting the man halfway down the street already.

"Stop!" he yelled.

The man ran fast as cannon fire, and Branch had a hard time keeping up. For the love of Pete, how was it possible to run that fast in a new pair of boots? Much as he hated to think it, maybe it was time to get him some of that there *Monkey Ward* leather.

CHAPTER 7

Katie let herself outside, careful not to make a sound. The front of the restaurant faced the railroad tracks, and the back faced Front and Main. Charley stood on the street side.

After wedging a wooden spoon in the doorframe to keep the door from closing and locking, she ran along the alley. Mindful that the bodies had been found here, she kept her hand on her gun and her senses alert. The alley separated the restaurant from the baggage room, ticket booth, and waiting room. In light of the recent crimes every shadow suggested danger.

The scent of cattle from the nearby stockades made her nose pucker. Somewhere in the distance a dog barked, but otherwise all was quiet. She reached Front Street, but Charley was gone.

Disappointed, she turned back to the house but then changed her mind. She couldn't sleep, so maybe a brisk walk would do her a world of good. If nothing else, it would give her a chance to get the lay of the land. She certainly wouldn't have time during the day. Sticking the gun in her waist for easy retrieval, she crossed Front to Main and stepped onto the boardwalk.

Many Kansas towns had grown in leaps and bounds in recent years due to the long cattle drives, but the railway was making such drives unnecessary. Some small towns had already suffered economic hardship as a result, but not Calico. By all appearances, it seemed to be thriving.

Walking quickly, she passed rows of shops and businesses built from brick and native limestone. A large general store took up one corner, the Calico Bank another. A barber, gunsmith, saddle shop, seamstress, bakery, and bookstore stretched along Main Street in orderly fashion.

A doctor shared an office with an undertaker, which seemed like a conflict of interest.

She reached the sheriff's office, and her pace slowed. Though the lights were off, a black horse was tethered in front. The horse nickered softly and pawed the ground.

"What do I get if I put on one of them there straitjackets?"

His voice sounded so clear and distinct in

her head that for a moment she imagined she'd heard the real thing. Startled by the pleasant shiver that ran down her spine, she quickly moved away.

At least now she knew where the sheriff's office was located. A dim light shone through the window of the *Calico Gazette* next door. A bespectacled man was bent over a long table, painstakingly placing type onto a metal-framed stick.

She was just about to return to the Harvey House when the sound of running feet stopped her. She turned but not soon enough to step out of the way. A man barreled into her and knocked her down.

Landing on her fanny, she yelled, "What do you think you're doing?"

The man kept running without as much as a backward glance.

"Of all the —"

A second man suddenly bounded around the corner. Before she could pull in her legs he tripped over her foot and fell facedown on the wood plank sidewalk in front of her. His hat landed several feet away.

Katie gasped, and her hand flew to the gun at her waist. "Are . . . are you all right?" she squeaked out.

The man pushed himself upright on his hands, the badge on his vest winking in the street light.

"Sheriff?" She pulled her hand away from her waist.

He squinted at her. "It's me, all right." He climbed to his feet and his full six-foot-something height towered over her. "You're the new Harvey girl. Miss Katie Madison."

For some reason it pleased her that he remembered her name. A ripple of awareness reached all the way to her toes. "The coat girl," she said and smiled.

One corner of his mouth lifted upward. "Fancy meeting you here."

"I was just about to say the same thing," she said.

He frowned. "What happened? Why are you sitting there? Don't they let you sit at the house?"

She gave her head an indignant toss. "I was knocked down by a very rude man."

His jaw hardened. "I'm afraid I'm to blame for that." He took hold of her hand and pulled her to her feet with one easy swoop.

Concern suffused his face as he looked her up and down. Had she only imagined that his gaze lingered longer than necessary on her tiny waist and soft, rounded hips?

"He didn't hurt you, did he?"

The smell of alcohol was overwhelming,

and she pulled her hand away. The odor brought back too many unhappy memories of the past. "No," she snapped. "He didn't hurt me."

He inclined his head as if puzzled by her abrupt reply. "That still doesn't explain what you're doing out at this time of night." Bending, he scooped up his hat. "Don't you Harvey girls have a curfew?"

She glanced at him askew. "Are you going to report me?"

The glow from the gas streetlight turned his eyes into two golden stars. "No, but it will cost you another piece of pie."

She studied him. He might smell like a whiskey barrel, but he sure didn't look inebriated. Didn't act like it, either. "You strike a hard bargain."

The corner of his mouth inched upward. "Those are the only bargains worth strikin'."

Though she'd resolved not to be distracted by his masculine good looks, his crooked smile kept getting in the way.

Noticing the dark wet spot, she pointed. "Your vest."

His hand flew to his chest. "We have our friend to thank for this." He inclined his head in the direction of the vanished runner.

Now that she knew its source, she was no

53

longer put off by the strong alcohol smell. Overhead, the big full moon looked as large and round as a Harvey House pie, reminding her of their deal.

"So what is your pleasure?" she asked. "Apple, mince, raisin, or coconut cream?" There was a fifth choice, but she struggled to think beneath the intensity of his gaze, and her mind went blank.

"Yes to all," he said, and she laughed. "I'll be happy to pay to have a whole pie delivered to my office," he said.

"I'm sure that can be arranged." He had no way of knowing it, but delivering food to his office could turn out to be a blessing. It would allow them to exchange information without arousing suspicion. It would also give her a legitimate excuse for leaving the Harvey House during daylight hours.

She swiped at a strand of loose hair. Convinced she looked a fright, she lowered her lashes and tried to decide how best to announce her true identity.

"So are you going to tell me or not?" he asked.

She looked up. "Tell you?"

"What you're doing out here so late?"

"Oh, that." She weighed her answer and decided to stick with the truth — part of it, anyway. "I couldn't sleep. It seems like you keep late hours, too."

"Not by choice." He slanted his head. "I apologize for the man's ill manners, but it's no more than can be expected."

"You know him?" she asked.

"No, but I will. I have reason to believe he's a Pinkerton detective."

"A Pink—" She stared at him. Far as she knew, she was the only one sent here to work on the Harvey girl killings. Of course, someone from one of the other offices could be here working on another case.

He nodded. "Yes, and it's been my experience they think nothing of breaking the law for their own nefarious purposes."

His harsh tone left her momentarily speechless. The Pinkerton agency had received much in the way of criticism in recent years. She couldn't argue with him there. But nefarious? That was a new one. Unfortunately, some detectives did use questionable tactics to get their man. But most, like herself, were law-abiding citizens who had helped capture some of the country's toughest and most notorious criminals.

"I take it you don't much care for Pinkerton detectives," she said, choosing her words with care. Better find out his true feelings before revealing too much information.

He placed his hat on his head and adjusted

the brim. "That's putting it mildly."

What a pity he felt that way; and to think she had looked forward to working with him. "Why do you suppose he's in town?" Since he brought the subject up first, she felt comfortable pursuing it.

"Your boss sent him," he said.

"M–my boss?" she stammered.

"Mr. Harvey came to my office to tell me to expect a Pinkerton on today's train."

Oh, *that* boss. "I would think you would welcome the help." She didn't mean to sound critical, but she couldn't help it.

The Pinkerton National Detective Agency had resources not available to local lawmen. Not only did the arm of the agency have a long reach, the Pinkerton files contained an astounding amount of information on many known criminals in the country. Instead of complaining, the sheriff should be thanking the Lord for his good fortune in working with such a well-run organization.

"It can't be easy tracking down outlaws way out here," she said. Most small towns couldn't afford the money or manpower to chase down criminals much beyond town limits.

"Nothing's easy, but I'd sooner work with a snake than work with a Pink."

His biting words made her cringe inside.

He sure didn't mince words. Still, she sensed that had she been a man he would have stated his opinion even more strongly. So everything she'd heard about Sheriff Whitman was true. What would he say if he knew he had *two* detectives in town? Better not break the news to him until after she contacted St. Louis headquarters. Her boss didn't like his female employees working alone without local backup, but maybe he would make an exception in this case. Especially if a second operative was nearby.

She gestured over her shoulder. "I better get back before I'm missed."

"Allow me to see you home."

She eyed him thoughtfully. "Don't you have a detective to catch?"

"He'll wait till tomorrow." He shrugged. "It's a small town. No one can hide from me for long."

That's what she was afraid of. "I — I hate to take you out of your way."

"Actually, you're not. I live on Front Street just up the road from Harvey's. If you don't mind, I need to pick up my horse on the way."

"Is that the black one in front of your office?"

He nodded. "Name's Midnight." He crooked his elbow. "Shall we?"

Despite his disagreeable stance in regard to the company she worked for, he had a way about him that was irresistible. His smile alone could melt the hide off a steer.

She slipped her arm through his, not because she thought she needed protection, but because of the role she played. Dark night. Strange town. Recent murders. Under those circumstances any Harvey girl would welcome the sheriff's presence. Turning down his offer might seem odd if not altogether suspicious.

Upon reaching his office, she pulled her arm away.

"Here he is," he said, untying the horse from the hitching post.

"Pleased to meet you, Midnight." She ran her hand along the gelding's smooth nose.

They started along the deserted street toward the restaurant. He led his horse by the reins as they walked.

"From now on I insist you stay inside after dark. Least till I catch the killer and we know the town is safe again."

"Is that an order, Sheriff?" she asked.

"Nope. Just plain good advice. Same advice I gave all the Harvey girls. Even Ginger."

His words hung between them like a funeral wreath, and a cold shiver ran down her spine.

In contrast, the restaurant's brick building loomed in front of them as big and happy as some of its regular customers. The slogan FRED HARVEY MEALS ALL THE WAY was painted onto the side of a covered wagon.

"Thank you," she said, stifling a yawn. It had been a long, hard day. Sleep. She needed sleep.

The sheriff perused the imposing two-story building with a rueful look. "How do you propose to get back in? Through a window or down the chimney?"

She smiled mysteriously. "I have my ways."

He leveled his gaze on her. "New in town and already you know all the ins and outs, do you?"

"Not all of them," she said with meaning. "But I will. Good night, Sheriff."

She hurried down the alleyway, stopping once to look over her shoulder. He had mounted his steed, and, outlined against the moonlit sky, horse and man melded into one.

He seemed trustworthy enough. Not that she could or would trust him. Not completely, anyway.

Putting her trust in men had gotten her nothing but heartache. First, her father had let her down with his drinking. Then Nathan

59

Cole, the man she had loved and hoped to wed. He'd led her to believe he cared for her. He'd escorted her to dances, took her on hay rides, and made her laugh. But it turned out he'd only used her to get to her sister Belle, whom he eventually married.

Swallowing the rocklike lump in her throat, she ran around the building and pushed against the dining room door. Much to her relief, the wooden spoon she'd jammed in the sill was still in place, and the door swung open to her touch.

She felt her way through the dark dining room, moving silently from chair to chair. A soft scraping sound made her reach for her gun. She froze in place and waited.

"Anyone there?" she called.

When no one answered, she quickly exited the dining room and took the stairs two at a time.

CHAPTER 8

There ought to be a law against starting work at 5:00 a.m. Having precious little sleep, Katie stifled a yawn as she made her way down the stairs, through the still-dark dining room to the brightly lit kitchen.

Never had she seen such a place. Harvey had spared no expense in making his restaurant as modern and efficient as possible, complete with running water, gas lighting, gleaming wood cabinets, and soapstone counters.

The chef greeted her with a pointed look at the clock on the wall. She was five minutes late.

His name was Chef Gassée — an unfortunate name for a cook, no matter how elegant he pronounced it. He was a high-strung man with a pencil-thin mustache and tea-strainer nose. His healthy crop of curly black hair was topped by a white linen toque, the height and pleats giving it the appearance of a Roman column.

He pointed in the direction of the plucking station where a dozen or more chickens waited to be undressed. Small rounded heads hung over the side of the counter, the beady eyes all staring at her.

Stomach churning, Katie looked away. She pretended to be a farm girl, but in reality she had been born and bred in the city. She was used to buying her tin goods from a grocer and meat from a butcher. Criminals she could handle, dead animals . . . not so much.

How does one say "I don't pluck chickens" in French?

The chef took a hen by the feet and dipped it into a large pot of boiling water. After a few seconds, he lifted the fowl out of the pot and tugged on a feather. Not satisfied with the ease by which the feather came out, he dunked the bird into the water again. He then flung the dripping chicken onto the counter and gestured for her to get to work.

She cleared her throat and shook her head. "Me" — she pointed to herself — "no pluck chickens!" She waved her hand sideways in what she hoped was a universal gesture for the word *no*.

"Well," he said, arms folded. Only it

sounded like *vell.* *"Le poisson."* He pronounced the word *poison,* pwasson.

"Yes, yes, *oui, oui.* Chicken . . . uh . . .
poison. *Pwasson.*"

He pointed to another table — this one
filled with dead fish waiting to be scaled
and gutted. The staring eyes and gaping
mouths made the chickens look almost
friendly in comparison.

"No, no." She gasped. "Pwasson," she
said, careful to pronounce it the French
way. *Fish are poison.*

"Oui, oui." He gestured wildly and confused her by nodding. His toque teetered
back and forth like a tree that couldn't
decide which way to topple.

He handed her a knife that could, in a
pinch, pass as a saber. "Le poisson!"

His scowling expression told her he meant
business and no amount of pleading would
make him change his mind. Taking the knife
in hand, she clenched her teeth and turned
to face the silver-scaled corpses. Zeroing in
on the largest, she afforded the creature that
same fish-eye stare it gave her.

Here goes nothing. Holding the handle of
the knife with both hands, she raised it over
her head. At the count of three she brought
the blade down, and it hit the body hard.
The fish popped up, head still attached, and

zoomed across the room. It plopped tail first into a pan on the stove, splattering grease everywhere. Flames shot up like orange streamers dancing in the wind.

Gasping, Katie sprang into action. She grabbed the pan of water off the chicken table and tossed it onto the blaze. The instant the water hit the stovetop it burst into an inferno. Orange flames scaled the wall and lunged at the ceiling like fiery swords.

Letting out a howl that sounded more animal than human, Chef Gassy yelled something in his mother tongue that needed no translation.

Fist pumping the air, he chased her around the counter twice before deciding that his efforts would be better spent putting out the fire. Cursing in French, he tossed an entire five-pound bag of salt on the stove and whacked the wall with a dish towel.

The moment the flames died and it looked like things were in control, Katie made a hasty retreat. She ducked out of the kitchen and ran up the stairs to her room.

Gee whillikens! There had to be an easier way to earn a living.

CHAPTER 9

Sheriff Branch Whitman sat at the kitchen table drinking his morning coffee. He was still annoyed at himself for letting that detective get away last night. No matter. The man couldn't stay hidden for long.

His thoughts were interrupted by the voice of his seven-year-old son. Andy was talking to the housekeeper. Hard to believe that the boy was about to turn eight. It seemed like only yesterday that Branch had dug through the rubble left by a deadly tornado and found the newborn infant stuffed in a cast-iron stove, umbilical cord still attached.

The thought brought a wave of memories crashing down on him. Even now, after all this time, he couldn't forget the horror of that long-ago day. There'd been tornados since, of course, but none as powerful. No one could live in Kansas for long without seeing the destructive force of a twister. But the one in '72 was the granddaddy of them all.

Thirty seconds and his life had changed forever.

The cyclone pretty much destroyed the town, along with several farms. His house was spared, and had his wife been home where she belonged, her life would have been spared, as well.

A midwife by trade, Hannah Whitman insisted upon working even after their marriage. Call him old-fashioned, but he hadn't wanted her to work. A man's job was to support his wife, and her insistence upon working made him feel like a failure in that regard. But that wasn't the only reason he'd wanted her to quit. Hardly a week went by when someone hadn't banged on their door in the middle of the night wanting her services, and he'd worried about her safety.

She was at the Clayborn farm delivering Dorothy Clayborn's firstborn when the tornado struck. The only one to survive was the infant. Somehow Hannah had the presence of mind to place the newborn babe inside the cast-iron oven before the tornado hit. The entire house had collapsed around it. The baby's frantic cries had let Branch and the other rescue workers know where to dig. They found his wife's body draped over the stove.

Hannah had saved the child's life, and it seemed only right that he keep the boy and raise him as his own. In all the confusion following the twister, no one questioned his right to do so. And why would they? The baby's mother was dead. His father had died months before the tornado. Far as he knew, the boy had no other relatives.

It seemed that Hannah had wanted to give him the son in death that she could not give him when she was alive. Her final gift to him. In return, he loved and cared for the boy as if he were his own flesh and blood.

His housekeeper, Miss Chloe, walked into the room, and his thoughts scattered like feathers in the wind.

"Law sakes, Sheriff," she began, white teeth flashing against her dark skin. "That boy of yours will be the death of me yet." She always called him Sheriff even though he'd asked her to call him Branch.

Sheriff was a whole lot better than master, which is what she called him all those years ago when he first hired her to help with the baby. Having grown up on a Georgia cotton plantation, she wasn't used to being treated like a member of the family. But she sure did learn and now thought nothing about giving him a piece of her mind should the occasion call for it.

"What's he doing now?" he asked.

"Says he doesn't need to go to no school. Says he knows everything." She laughed that big belly laugh of hers, and her brown eyes shone with humor. "Lawdy, don't we wish we could all say that?"

In a way, Branch envied the boy. It had been a long time since he thought he knew it all. He was . . . what? Seven or eight at the time, and that was way back when his mother was alive and the world still made sense.

"I'll talk to him."

"Nah." Her face grew serious. She wore a red kerchief over her kinky black hair and a bright floral dress that circled her full figure like a lampshade. "You got other things on your mind. I'll set him straight. Don't you worry none about that."

Andy walked into the room looking all spiffy for school. Smelled good, too. He wore knee-high trousers with red suspenders, long black socks, and a blue-and-white-striped shirt. Somehow Miss Chloe had even managed to corral the boy's stubborn cowlick.

Curbing the impulse to ruffle Andy's hair as he was prone to do, Branch gave him a stern look. "You're not giving Miss Chloe a

68

hard time, are you, Son?"

"No, sir."

"Good. See that you don't." Softening his tone, he asked, "Have you had your breakfast?"

"Yes, sir."

"Humph." Miss Chloe folded her arms across her ample bosom. "You call that breakfast? A half a sausage and a spoonful of eggs. That's not enough to feed a hummingbird."

Andy's picky eating habits were a bone of contention with his housekeeper, who considered any food left on a plate an affront to her cooking.

Branch pulled the watch out of his vest pocket and flipped the case open with his thumb. "You better get a move on or you'll be late for school."

Andy reached for his books on the table, held together with a leather strap. "Bye, Pa. Bye, Miss Chloe." With that he ran outside, slamming the door shut behind him.

Miss Chloe poured herself a cup of coffee. "That's some boy you got there."

Branch smiled. "You won't get any argument from me there."

"Want some breakfast?"

"No, I'll get something in town." He gulped down the last of his coffee. He was anxious to track down that annoying Pink detective. The man deserved to spend the day behind bars. Assaulting a sheriff. Knocking a woman off her feet. No less than two days in jail would be sufficient. Make that three.

The thought brought another one, equally disturbing, though far more pleasant. The vision that came to mind of Miss Madison sitting on the boardwalk made the corners of his mouth twitch.

Come to think of it, she never did tell him what she was doing out so late. In light of the Harvey House killings, traipsing about at night was a fool thing to do.

She was new in town, so it seemed unlikely she was meeting a beau. And why did he have the feeling that there was more to her than met the eye?

The last thought brought back a flood of memories. She sure didn't look like a Harvey girl last night. Not with her hair falling down her back and skirt in disarray, allowing a tantalizing glimpse of lace petticoats beneath the hem.

Good thing her English employer was nowhere around. No doubt he would have sent her packing. Fred Harvey kept his female employees on a tight rein. Miss Madison didn't strike him as one who could

70

be easily controlled. It would be interesting to see how long she lasted.

Snapping his mouth shut, he carried his cup and saucer to the sink.

"Andy's birthday is only a couple of weeks away," Miss Chloe said. "Do you want me to plan something special?"

"Yeah, we need to do something," he said. "Maybe the three of us can have dinner at the Harvey House." The thought popping out of nowhere surprised him. It obviously surprised Miss Chloe, too.

"You got a problem with my cooking?" she asked, sounding insulted.

"I like your cooking just fine." No one could fry chicken better than she could, and her corn bread was out of this world. "I just thought you'd appreciate a night off."

"Well, if it's all the same to you, I'd rather spend my time off with my husband."

"He's welcome to come."

"Thank you, but after putting in a full day at the shop there's nothing he likes better than to stay home and put his feet up on the hassock."

Branch nodded. Miss Chloe was so much a part of his and Andy's life that sometimes he forgot she had a home of her own. Her husband was the local blacksmith, and they had raised three strapping sons.

71

Whenever Branch worked late or was called out of town on county business, Miss Chloe simply took his son home with her and bedded him down. She lived a stone's throw away, so Andy was never that far away and felt as much at home at her house as he did in his own.

"Take the night off," he said. *Come to think of it, Andy might like eating in a restaurant for a change. A new experience like that might do wonders for the boy's appetite.* The idea had nothing to do with the new waitress in town — not a thing.

He grabbed his hat and headed for the door. "Got to get to work." If he was lucky, he'd catch that Pink detective before he caused any more trouble.

"Will you be home for supper?" she called after him.

He almost said no, but he'd missed a couple of meals with Andy already that week. "Count on it."

"Phew!" Mary-Lou held her nose. "Don't know what smells worse, the horrid smoke or the smell of burned fish," she said. They had finished serving breakfast to the locals and were now waiting for the morning train to arrive.

"Le poisson," Katie said.

"What?"

"Le poisson. That's how you say 'fish' in French."

"I didn't know you could speak French." Mary-Lou looked impressed.

Katie shrugged. "You'd be amazed what you can learn at five in the morning."

Okay, maybe she panicked a bit upon seeing flames shoot up from the iron cookstove. Any emergency that didn't require the use of a gun tended to floor her. Outlaws she could handle. But grease fires? Not so much. How was she to know that throwing water on one would make it worse? Homemaking was not her strong suit; catching bad guys was.

If having the manager and dorm matron breathing down her back wasn't worrisome enough, her name was now mud to a certain temperamental French chef.

A series of sneezes preceded the entry of the man who had been introduced to her the night before as Stanley Culpepper, the Harvey House bookkeeper. Sneezing into his handkerchief, he took his place at the table by the door, his eyes and nose red. He handled all restaurant finances, which included collecting meal money from customers, paying vendors, and writing employee paychecks.

"Hay fever's killing me," he muttered to no one in particular and sneezed again.

His shoe–polish–dyed hair offered a startling contrast to skin as white as a newly peeled potato. Next to the leather-faced railroad workers and cattlemen, he looked like he'd just emerged from a cave. His John Wilkes Booth–type mustache seemed almost too thick for his face and his nose too short.

Frayed cuffs told her he wasn't married, but the bruises on his knuckles puzzled her. Had he been in a fight?

"Good morning, ladies," Mr. Pickens said, drawing Katie's attention away from Culpepper's hands.

The manager perused the dining room, his gaze flicking from table to table. He pulled out a measuring stick and checked that the silverware at one table was placed the same distance from the edge. Dishes had to be correctly positioned, the two birds on the Blue Willow bread plates at precisely twelve o'clock.

Satisfied that all was in order, he then turned his attention to the four girls who stood like wooden ducks at a carnival waiting to be knocked over.

It was the second inspection of the day, and Mary-Lou assured her there were more to come. The first one had been done by the dorm matron, who wiped their faces with a damp sponge to make certain no one wore face paint.

"Miss Madison! Is that a spot I see?" Pickens pointed to her apron.

She looked down. "It's just a speck of water, sir." The starched aprons had to be spotlessly clean at all times, and already she'd changed hers twice that morning. The starched fabric seemed to attract the least bit of dust or moisture.

Pickens stared at her like a bug to be squashed.

Refusing to be intimidated, she lifted her chin. "It will dry."

"Yes, it will, Miss Madison. But not on you." He pointed to the kitchen. "You have twenty-nine seconds to change into a fresh one."

"But —"

"Twenty-*eight* seconds!"

CHAPTER 10

Branch swung the door of the empty cell open to let the man named Woody Baker walk in.

A grizzled man in his sixties, Woody had a wooden leg, a toothless smile, and a scar on his forehead. He probably wouldn't be alive if it wasn't for Branch arresting him with clocklike regularity for loitering. The town had no ordinance against lounging by public buildings, but jail was the only way of keeping him from starving or, during winter months, even freezing to death.

The widow Bisbee provided the jail food for a stipend. The meals weren't fancy, but they were nourishing and the cot reasonably comfortable. A couple of days of food and rest and Woody would be good to go again. That is, until next time.

After getting Woody settled, Branch sat at his desk, his chair squeaking beneath his weight. So far he'd failed to find the detective. The man was as slippery as a wet bar of soap. But not for long. Every saloon and businessman in town had been told to be on the lookout. It was just a matter of time. Meanwhile, he might as well work on the Harvey case.

Though he had his notes memorized, he went over each handwritten notation in the thick Harvey file word for word. Had he missed something? Overlooked an inconsistency? Failed to put two and two together?

Weeks of investigation had failed to turn up a single suspect. With an audible groan, he scrubbed his hands over his face in frustration. He was no closer to finding the Harvey killer now than when he'd first begun the investigation.

He'd questioned everyone in town at least twice, and the railroad workers many times more. He'd gone over the victims' rooms with a fine-tooth comb and checked the background of each Harvey House employee for former criminal activity. He'd even cabled the French military police force gendarmerie asking for information on Chef Gassée.

All he had to show for his work was a file full of worthless information.

Much as it went against his grain, maybe he should step back and let the Pink take over. See if the hired detective could do any better at solving the crimes. Two young women were dead, and as much as he hated to admit it, he was stymied. So far his prayers for God's help in arranging a break in the case had not been answered.

Or at least not in the way he'd hoped. He pinched his forehead. Why did help, if that's what it was, have to come in the guise of an organization for which he held nothing but disdain? Was this God's idea of a joke?

The front door swung open, and he dropped his hands to his desk. The widow Mrs. Bracegirdle stepped into the office, cane first. He stood ready to help her to a chair if necessary. As if to guess his intent, she motioned for him to stay where he was.

Obstinate as a barn full of mules, she hadn't aged in thirty years. She looked eighty when he was knee-high to a milk stool, and she looked eighty now. Thin white hair framed a face as wrinkled as an old peach pit. Skin hung from beneath her chin and shook like a turkey's wattle when she spoke.

Still, he had a soft spot for her. Not only had she given him candy when he was a youngster and remained his most avid supporter through the years, she was one of only two people in town who knew the truth about his son.

After swearing her to secrecy all those years ago, he hadn't mentioned it since and neither had she. He'd hoped that somehow she'd forgotten and accepted Andy as his own flesh and blood, but that was probably only wishful thinking on his part.

The only other person who knew his secret was Reverend Bushwell. That was because everyone else who knew the truth had either left after that terrible tornado wreaked havoc in the town or had since passed away. At one point it looked as if the town would die with them. Then along came the railroad, bringing with it new families, new life, and a whole set of new problems.

He waited for Mrs. Bracegirdle to settle herself in the chair in front of his desk before seating himself. She leaned her cane next to her side and smoothed her purple skirt.

He knew Reverend Bushwell wouldn't reveal his secret and until recently hadn't worried about Mrs. Bracegirdle. Lately, though, she'd been given to strange hallucinations and wild imaginings. He never knew what she would come up with next.

Last month, she claimed to have been abducted by a man on a white horse. The month prior, she claimed that she found a stranger in her bed. No one was there, of course, and he had a hard time convincing her of that, but he was beginning to see a pattern.

"Hi, Woody," she called to the man in jail. Everyone in town was on a first name basis with his resident prisoner.

Woody rolled over on his cot. "Howdy, Miz Bracegirdle."

"Who's been in your bed this time?" Branch was teasing her, but one wouldn't know it by the serious look on her face.

"No one." She regarded him with faded blue eyes. "The reason I'm here is that there's a strange noise coming from next door."

"From next door, do you mean the bank side or the barbershop?" She lived on the second floor over her son's dry goods store.

"From the apartment over the bank," she said. "And it keeps me awake at night."

"Sorry to hear that." Out of respect for her, he would have to check it out, of course. Just as he'd checked out the marmalade cat that screeched like a bad opera singer and interfered with her sleep. The animal's owner didn't take kindly to having her cat's tonal deficiencies compared to opera, saying no cat of hers would put on such airs.

"What kind of noise?" Branch asked. "Can you describe it?"

"It's a tapping sound. And sometimes I hear a scraping. Occasionally there's a bang."

"Sounds like a ghost to me," Woody called from his cell.

She pulled a lace handkerchief from her sleeve and daintily dabbed her nose. "Whatever it is, it's a nuisance. How's a body to sleep with that racket? That's what I want to know."

"How long has this been going on?" The bank closed at 5:00 p.m. and didn't open until nine in the morning.

"For several weeks."

He raised his eyebrows. "And you're just getting around to telling me about it now?"

"It stopped for a while but then started up again. The sound was particularly loud early Sunday morning."

"Maybe it's a church mouse," Woody called and laughed at his own joke.

Ignoring him, Branch folded his arms across his chest. "Okay, I'll check with the bank president and get back to you."

"That would be very nice." Today her eyes looked clear and focused. Maybe there really was something to her complaint.

"It looks like I'm not the only one who didn't get any sleep," she said.

"What?"

"You look like you missed a few winks yourself."

Branch raked his hair with his fingers. Looked that bad, did he? Small wonder. He hadn't had a good night's sleep since the first Harvey girl was found dead. Since he'd failed to find Priscilla's killer, he blamed himself for Ginger's death. If the killer wasn't found soon, he might kill again.

"Just working hard," he said.

Tucking her handkerchief into the sleeve of her dress, she reached for her cane with a gnarly hand and rose from her chair, bones creaking. "You know what they say about all work and no play."

"Makes a man rich," Woody called.

"Don't I wish?" Branch said and grinned.

Fearing she was about to get started on his nonexistent love life again, he stood and walked around his desk. Work and his son took up all his time. He didn't want to think about anything else.

Taking her by the arm, he escorted her to the door. "I'll let you know what I find out at the bank."

Just as soon as he tracked down that Monkey Ward detective.

CHAPTER 11

Katie paused outside the kitchen door.

Sneaking away from the Harvey House was no easy task, especially during the morning hours. It had been two days since the fire, and Katie hadn't been able to escape Pickens's watchful eye. Today, however, he was nowhere in sight.

The timing couldn't be more perfect. Fortunately, Chef Gassy was busy yelling at the man hired to paint the smoke-stained wall and ceiling. Unfortunately, the painter dripped white paint into the chef's prized English pea soup.

"Balourd!" Gassy yelled, and the man turned almost the same color as the newly painted wall.

While the two were going at it tooth and nail, Katie snatched an entire apple pie and quickly ducked into the empty dining room and out the door.

She had no intention of revealing her true

identity, but maybe if she kept her eyes and ears open she might learn something about the case from the sheriff. The trick was to ask the right questions without drawing suspicion. If she mentioned seeing a man in front of the Harvey House at night, she might be able to determine whether Ginger's beau was a suspect.

With a little luck she could conduct her business with the sheriff and return to the restaurant before anyone noticed her gone.

It was a warm spring day with not a cloud in the sky — too nice to be confined inside.

On the other side of the railroad tracks, purple, blue, and orange wildflowers mingled with tall prairie grass. Today, no cattle smell tainted the air. The door to the telegraph office was open and the tap-tap-tapping of the telegraph key floated to her ears.

Working in such close proximity to the telegraph office was a bonus. It made communicating with her St. Louis bosses a breeze. All telegrams to headquarters were to be addressed to "Aunt Hetty," every word carefully concealed behind a cryptic code. If the telegraph operator thought anything odd about the daily cables to her "aunt," he kept it to himself.

Holding the pie with both hands, she hurried down the alley and crossed the street to Main. The pastry was still warm to the touch, and the cinnamon smell made her mouth water. With a little luck maybe Chef Gassy wouldn't notice one of his newly baked pies missing.

She still wasn't sure how to handle the sheriff. They said that the way to a man's heart was through his stomach. She only hoped the pie did the trick — though she doubted it would make him any less hostile toward Pinkerton detectives.

Suddenly she saw something that stopped her in her tracks. The man who had so rudely knocked her down two nights earlier had just entered the Calico Bank. She'd recognize his ugly mug anywhere. The sheriff claimed he was a Pinkerton detective. If so, he was a master of disguise, because no one looking at him would ever guess his true profession.

She frowned. He better not be her "protector," that's all she had to say. Or assigned to her case. Not that she'd ever worked on a murder case before. Her specialty was tracking down embezzlers, larcenists, and other so-called *gentleman* criminals. The most lethal weapon any of the previous offenders used was ink and pen.

So the Harvey girl killer wielded a knife.

So what? She was ready for anything. More than ready. All she had to do was find the killer before the killer found her — or before she did something dumb like burning down the Harvey House restaurant.

Curiosity getting the best of her, she followed him inside.

Customers snaked up to the teller's cage, and the man was at the very end of the line. She took her place directly behind him.

First she had to be certain of his identity, and there was only one way to tell if he truly was a Pinkerton operative. "Would you mind holding this for me?" she asked.

He looked startled but nonetheless took the pie plate from her. "Smells good," he said, showing no signs of recognizing her as the woman he'd knocked off her feet. Hard to believe that with her blazing red hair, she could be so easily forgotten.

"Apple," she said. She pulled a lace handkerchief out of her sleeve and waved it like she had been taught to signal another operative in public.

She then tucked the handkerchief back into her sleeve and took the pie from him.

Right on cue, he pulled out his own handkerchief and flicked it across his hand. She couldn't tell if he was signaling her back or wiping away pie filling.

"Are you from St. Louis?" she whispered. He shook his head. "Kansas City."

Since they were working out of different offices, that meant he was probably working on a different case. That was a relief. Had Pinkerton sent another operative it would have meant a lack of faith in her abilities.

"My name is Miss Madison." Operatives never used their real names when working on a case, not even with each other. "What's your alias?" You never asked a working detective his real name.

"They call me Scarface," he said.

She could see why. Not only was his face pitted with pockmarks, his nose had been broken and he had a nasty scar over one eye. Either he'd been run over by a train or had dealt with some mighty tough thugs.

"What are you here for?" Since other bank customers had taken their place in line behind her she kept her voice low. "Counterfeiting or larceny?"

"Bank robbery," he replied, his voice hushed.

"I've worked a couple of those myself," she said.

He gave her an arched look. "Is that so?"

"A tough job. The last holdup nearly got me killed."

"Yeah, well, you gotta be careful. The

secret of success is good planning."

"I know what you mean." An undercover agent was required to invent a whole new history. She couldn't just say she hailed from Wisconsin and was the daughter of a cheese maker; she had to *be* that girl. She also had to know a lot about cheese.

"And of course, you have to have good timing," he added. "Today is Friday, and that's always the best day to rob a bank. That's when the railroad workers get paid."

"Good to know," she said. She'd never worked in such close proximity to the railroad and had no idea how or when the workers got paid. She glanced at the line in front of them and most were older folks. None looked like bank robbers, but one never could tell, and Scarface seemed to know his business. Maybe he knew something she didn't.

"The problem with some robbers is that they wait too late," he continued. "By noon, most all workers have cashed their checks, leaving the bank low on dough." He pulled out his watch. "Ten forty. Like I said, timing is everything."

"Do you need help?" she asked, keeping her voice low.

"Nah. I got it. I like working alone. Less chance of being noticed. But it's mighty nice of you to offer."

"That's what colleagues are for," she said. "Just watch out for the sheriff. He doesn't have much regard for the likes of us."

"They never do," he said.

"Next," the teller called.

Katie gestured with her head. "That's you."

He turned to face the bank clerk. "Watch and learn." He stepped toward the window and slid a piece of paper through the hole in the cage.

She furrowed her brow. Was that a note warning the teller that a robbery was about to take place? It seemed like a strange way to operate, but then she was no expert in bank holdups.

The thin male clerk suddenly got all jittery, and his eyebrows bounced up and down as if pulled by a puppeteer's strings.

Scarface glanced over his shoulder at her and winked. That's when she noticed the clerk stuffing money into a bag.

Gasping, she blinked in disbelief and almost dropped the pie. Scarface was robbing the bank!

After her initial surprise, she forced herself to think. She'd confronted her share of bank robbers, of course, but never during an actual holdup. It was always days or weeks afterward following a thorough investigation and with law backup in tow.

Now she was on her own.

Balancing the still-warm pastry in one hand, she walked up to him and tapped him on the shoulder. The instant he turned his head, she hit him square in the face with the pie.

Not only did this bring an uttered curse from her target but indignant protests from customers standing in line.

One woman clucked in disapproval. "Of all the rude things."

"The nerve!" muttered a man wearing a bowler.

By the time Scarface had recovered enough to wipe the buttery syrup out of his eyes Katie had already reached into her pocket for her weapon and held him at gunpoint.

A heavyset woman at the counting desk screamed and flung a handful of money in the air. "She's got a gun!"

Chaos followed the announcement. People ran out of the bank, crashing into those running inside to see what all the commotion was about.

Scarface looked about to bolt, but a click of her gun relieved him of that notion. "Wise decision," she said.

Globs of apples slid down the bank robber's face to his shirt and dripped to the floor. The messy syrup failed to hide his red-faced fury, but he did what he was told.

"If you had asked nicely, I would have split the money with you," he griped.

"A likely story," she said. "Move!" She gestured with her pointed gun. "If you try anything, I won't hesitate to shoot."

Before they reached the door, the sheriff ran inside. He slid to a screeching stop in front of them, revolver in hand, his stance as wide as his shoulders. He took one look at Scarface, still covered with pie, and directed an inquiring gaze her way.

"Caught him holding up the bank," she explained.

Astonishment crossed Whitman's face as he regarded the would-be thief dripping in syrup. "You're a bank robber?"

Scarface cursed. "Announce it to the world, why don't you?"

CHAPTER 12

Branch shoved Scarface into the empty jail cell next to Woody's and slammed the metal door shut with a bang.

He'd made the man wash before locking him up, but the cinnamon smell of apple pie still lingered. No complaints there. That was a whole lot better than how most of his prisoners smelled.

Woody wrinkled his nose. "What's he in for? Robbing a bakery?"

"Nope. Bank."

Woody pushed out his lips. "You don't say." He frowned. "With a mug like that he musta been sittin' in an outhouse when lightning struck."

Branch hung his hat and keys on wall hooks and turned to Miss Madison. She sat on a chair by his desk, feet together and hands folded on her lap. He'd told her to sit and not move, and surprisingly she'd obeyed without a word.

"He says you're a bank robber, too."

She sure didn't look like any criminal he'd ever dragged into his office. If anything, she looked as prim and proper in her black-and-white uniform as a schoolmarm — at least from the neck down. Above was a different story. The sun slanting through the windows turned her hair into red flames, an annoying reminder of how appealing those same copper locks looked in the moonlight.

Irritated by the thought and more than a little miffed that he'd misjudged not just one person but two, he slid a hip onto the edge of the desk and regarded her with narrowed eyes. Was that what she was doing the other night? Casing the bank?

Branch waited for her to either confirm or deny the accusation, but she remained silent. Was Scarface telling the truth? Hard to believe. Even so, he wasn't letting the lady out of his sight until he had some answers.

"Said you were riled that he got in line first to rob the bank."

Something flickered in the depths of her eyes, and he sensed an inner battle taking place. At last she leaned forward. "It's worse than that," she whispered.

He lowered his voice to match hers in volume. "Worse?" *Blast it all!* She was accused of bank robbing. How could it be worse?

She held a hand at the side of her mouth like a woman about to impart the most tantalizing gossip. "I'm a Pinkerton detective."

He reared back. Had she pulled out a knife and stabbed him, he wouldn't have been more surprised. Shocked, more like it. Stunned. "You?" he sputtered, forgetting to keep his voice low.

With a meaningful glance at the cells, she mutely reminded him that they weren't alone.

This time his voice was barely audible. "But you're a —"

She visually challenged him to continue, but he thought better of it. He couldn't believe it. All this time he'd been looking for the detective and he — she — had been right under his very nose.

She pulled a badge out of her pocket and held it in such a way that only he could see it. The polished metal shield said Pinkerton, all right. Clear as day.

He studied her in total disbelief. Hard to believe. She sure didn't look like any detective he'd ever encountered. He leaned forward, his voice barely a rumble in his chest.

"Harvey indicated they were sending a *male* detective."

She met his gaze with bold regard. "It's better for him not to know the details."

Branch doubted Harvey would agree. The man ran a tight ship and would control the moon and the stars if such a thing were possible. "And you think you're going to solve the Harvey girl killings?"

Her eyes flashed. "I caught the bank robber, didn't I?"

"Can't argue with you there, ma'am."

He drew back and rubbed his chin. What in the name of Sam Hill were the Pinkerton principals thinking? Two women were dead, so what did the detective agency do? It put another in harm's way. Now he felt obliged to look out for her welfare. As if he didn't have enough to worry about.

"I hope you don't take this the wrong way, but this is no job for a . . ."

She bristled with indignation, and her nostrils flared.

"Amateur," he said for want of another word.

Her eyes blazed with sparks of fire. "You're quite right. Which is why the office sent *me.*" Her whispered words lacked in volume but not in passion. "I always catch my man."

He folded his arms across his chest. "Do

you, now?"

"Yes," she said icily, "and I have a record to prove it."

"And how many of them were killers?"

Her hesitation was so brief that had he blinked he might have missed it. "What difference does it make?"

"Aha!" he said and then remembered to lower his voice. "This is your first murder case, isn't it?"

"I didn't say that."

"Isn't it?"

She glowered, and her lips thinned. "The same principle applies to all investigations regardless of the crime."

"Is that what your Pinkerton bosses led you to believe?"

"It's true. And if you weren't so arrogant, you'd be happy for my help."

"Is that so?" He now leaned so close to her that their noses were mere inches apart. So close that he could see the gold flecks in her eyes. So close he could smell the delicate fragrance of her perfume. "Why do I need your help?"

She showed no sign of backing down or even wavering. "We have resources. Mug shots. Criminal profiles. I've already sent headquarters descriptions of the Harvey House workers and regular customers." She sat back with a satisfied look on her face. "I even sent a description of you."

He pulled back. "Me?"

"Everyone in town is a suspect, and that includes you."

Staring at her from beneath raised eyebrows, he was momentarily at a loss for words. He didn't like being a suspect, but neither could he imagine anyone being so thorough.

"While you're on a wild-goose chase, I'm checking out *real* suspects," he said.

"A job that would be easier with Pinkerton help," she countered.

They glared at each other like two wild animals meeting over a slab of meat. "Is that so?"

She tossed her head. "Yes, that's so. Allan Pinkerton is an expert on the criminal mind, and he's trained his sons well." Her glance flicked over the messy stack of files on his desk. "You could learn a lot from them."

"Yeah, well I've seen some of their work and, lady, I'm not impressed."

"You should be. Their record for catching criminals can't be matched!"

Seeing no advantage to pursuing the argument, he changed the subject. "So were you ever going to tell me who you were?"

"I considered telling you the other night." She glared at him with reproachful eyes. "But you talked me out of it."

"How'd I do that?"

"I believe the snake did it. You know, the one you would rather work with. Or maybe it was the nefarious part."

He raked his fingers through his hair. "I guess I came on kinda strong, didn't I?"

She lifted her chin. "Not as strong as some."

He sucked in his breath. The woman posed more problems than a roomful of wild dogs. He tossed a nod at a sign on the wall.

"We have an ordinance in this town preventing anyone from carrying firearms." Not that she needed a gun. Those big baby blues of hers would weaken even the most hardened criminal.

Her gaze lit on the sign. The stubborn look on her face told him that if he had a mind to disarm her he'd have a battle on his hands. "It says all *men* are to turn in their guns. It says nothing about women."

Doggone it. She had him there. No matter. He wasn't about to confiscate her weapon. Not as long as she lived under the same roof as a possible killer.

"If I hear from anyone that you're carrying a gun, I'll be obliged to disarm you."

"I'll keep that in mind."

"See that you do." He lifted a finger in warning. "I don't know what kind of investigation you plan to conduct, but it better not interfere with mine."

She leaned forward, and her eyes blazed. "I plan a thorough and professional investigation, with or without your help."

"I don't work with Pinks."

She bopped her head. "And I don't work with mule-headed sheriffs!" She rose from her seat. "Would that be all?"

"For now." He slid off the desk, but for once his impressive height gave him no advantage. She didn't even give him the courtesy of looking cowed. Instead, she snapped her head and glared up at him — a force to be reckoned with.

"I'm due back at the house," she said. "I trust that you'll keep my identity secret."

He gave a curt nod. "As a professional courtesy, your secret's safe with me. But I must warn you that I'll expect the same consideration from you."

She tilted her head. "Meaning?"

"Meaning that anything relevant to the case must be shared with me."

"I report to my Pinkerton boss. No one else." She turned to leave.

He stopped her with a hand to her wrist before she reached the door. "Holding back information is an obstruction of justice," he hissed quietly.

Their gazes clashed like sparring swords. "I'll keep that in mind."

"See that you do."

She glanced down at his hand still on her arm, and he released her. Nothing in her stance or expression suggested compliance. Something told him his job just got a whole lot tougher.

"Good day, Sheriff." This time she made no effort to lower her voice or hide her disdain. With a glance at the bank robber, she walked out of the office, the door slamming in her wake.

Hands curled by his side, he stared at the door long after she'd left.

"That's some woman," Woody called from his cell. "I'd say she's got some snap in her garters. You should have just kissed her and been done with it."

Branch spun around, muscles tense. Kiss the Pink detective? Not in a million years. Wasn't going to happen. He had enough trouble as it was.

"The thought never occurred to me."

Woody shrugged and manually arranged his wooden leg onto the cot. "Sure did look like it to me."

Scarface concurred. "Looked like it to me, too."

CHAPTER 13

Katie was still shaking after she left the office. How dare the sheriff treat her like she was some — what did he call it? Amateur!

Not only was the man arrogant, he was stubborn as a bulldog's grip.

He had some nerve bossing her around like he had every right. Telling her what she could and could not do. Treating her like she was a child. Ha! Had it not been for her, Scarface would have robbed the bank and taken off before anyone knew what happened.

But did the sheriff give her credit? He did not. Oooooooh, he made her so mad! *Just wait, Sheriff Whitman. We'll see who solves the Harvey House murder case. Then we'll know who the* real *amateur is.*

The next morning, Katie was assigned to work behind the horseshoe counter in what was called the breakfast room, though lunch was also served there.

Abigail stood ready to train her. Most of the locals preferred eating in the less formal room as it didn't require men to wear coats. It was also less expensive than the dining room. Because of a shortage of personnel, the breakfast room was closed for supper.

Despite its informality the same care and attention to detail were given to the decor. Mr. Harvey collected Indian art, and intricately woven Navajo rugs graced the walls next to shelves holding a variety of Indian pottery. Tall vases decorated with eagles and geometric shapes shared space with round hand-painted bowls.

Still early, the restaurant was empty. The moment the train arrived, Abigail would move to the dining room, leaving Katie to fend for herself.

Abigail pointed out the location of plates, cups, and silverware. A slender woman with brown hair and hazel eyes, she spoke in such a way as to not call attention to herself. She also had a habit of looking over her shoulder. Even as she instructed Katie, she kept a watchful eye on the floor-to-ceiling windows overlooking the railroad tracks.

Katie set cups and saucers upon the polished wood counter as instructed, along with silverware and linen napkins. "How long have you worked here?" she asked.

"Almost two months," Abigail said with a wary glance. "I arrived just after Priscilla . . ." Her voice faded away.

"So you didn't know her."

"No."

"But you knew Ginger."

Abigail gave an audible sigh. "Yes, but only for a short time." She arranged salt, pepper, maple syrup, and sugar on the counter. "I didn't know about Priscilla till I got here. Now that two girls —" Her gaze circled the room as if making certain they were still alone.

Mary-Lou's and Tully's voices drifted in from the dining room. Outside, the omnibus boy paced back and forth. At the first sound of the approaching train he would strike the dish-shaped brass gong with a fabric-covered ball attached to the end of a wooden stick, thus signaling its imminent arrival to the staff.

"I'm not sure I want to stay," Abigail finished at last.

Abigail was older than the others, probably in her mid to late twenties. No white line appeared on her left hand, but her habit of rubbing the fourth digit with her thumb and forefinger indicated the recent removal of a wedding band.

The way she visually tensed with the arrival of each train implied she was running from someone or something. An abusive husband, perhaps? Either that or she was wanted by the law.

"Do you fear for your life?" Katie asked.

Abigail pursed her lips as if trying to decide how to answer. "Don't you?"

"Not really. Can't think of anyone who might want to see me dead except Chef Gassy."

The tension on Abigail's face morphed into a smile. "Don't let him hear you call him that."

Katie let the comfortable silence linger a moment before asking, "Did you know Ginger had a beau?"

Abigail nodded. "His name was Charley something. Seemed like a nice fellow."

"You don't suppose that he — ?" A fork stilled in Abigail's hand. "Charley? Oh no. He loved her."

Lots of men claimed to have loved the woman they killed. Thomas Horton, a man recently caught by Pinkerton detectives out of the Chicago office, was now serving a life sentence for killing not one, but two women he professed to love.

Katie examined her nails in an effort not to seem overly interested. Harvey rules required daily manicures, and she was already three days behind.

"Any ideas who might have wanted to see her dead?" Katie asked as if calmly inquiring about the weather.

"No, but —" Again Abigail glanced at the windows. "The day she died she acted rather . . . strange."

"In what way, strange?"

"She asked me to change stations with her. She seemed really upset."

Katie frowned. "Why would she do that? Change stations, I mean."

"I don't know. I thought at first that she and Charley had broken up. He usually sat at her table."

"Had they broken up?"

"Not that I know of. I mean . . . he took her death really hard."

Katie thought for a moment. "Do you remember who was at her station that day?"

"Not really. Most were travelers just passing through town."

Katie hesitated. She was pushing her luck with so many questions, but so seldom did anyone talk openly about the victims she couldn't resist asking one more. "I know Mary-Lou roomed with Ginger, but who did Priscilla room with?"

"She roomed with Ginger, too. That is

until —"

Two victims rooming together didn't necessarily mean much. No more than a half dozen or so girls worked at the restaurant at any one time, and that limited room combinations. Still, details that didn't seem important at first often turned out to be significant in the scheme of things.

Sensing that Abigail needed a friend, Katie chose her next words with care. "When I asked if you feared for your life, I was really asking about your husband."

Abigail froze, and the color drained from her face. "What — ?" She glanced around quickly and moved to Katie's side. "What do you know about him? Has he asked about me?"

"Whoa," Katie said. "I never met the man."

Abigail studied her as if trying to decide if she spoke the truth. She then slid her hand in the folds of her apron and moistened her lips. "Please don't say anything. Married women aren't supposed to work here."

"I won't say a word," Katie promised. "And I'll help in any way I can."

Abigail shook her head. "I . . . I don't need any help."

Katie had hoped to make a friend of her but felt something like a door closing in her face. "If you ever want to talk —"

Abigail's lips quivered with unspoken words, but before she said anything the omnibus boy sounded the gong. The morning madness was about to begin.

That night Katie stood in the shadows outside the restaurant and stifled a yawn. Shaking the weariness away, she pulled the shawl around her shoulders against the cool night air and forced her droopy eyelids to stay open.

If Charley planned on making his nightly vigil, he better come soon before she fell asleep on her feet. Tired as an old gold miner, she could hardly manage to stay awake, let alone remain alert.

Who would have guessed that restaurant work was such hard physical labor? Her feet hurt. Her back ached, and her eyes felt like two balls of lead.

Fortunately, she didn't have to wait long before spotting a shadowy figure making his way toward her.

She stayed hidden until the man took his usual place by the lamppost. She then stepped quietly out of the alley. He pulled his gaze away from the second-floor window as she approached.

Sun-bleached hair brushed against his collar. His deeply tanned skin was a testament to the hours spent working on the railroad. From a distance he looked older, more mature. Up close she could see he was only in his early twenties.

"Excuse me for intruding," she said, for the pain of grief was evident on his face as he gazed at the second-story window. "Are you Charley?" Working on the tracks had turned his muscles hard as stone, and the sleeves of his shirt bulged as if stuffed with paper.

"That's me," he said. "Who are you?"

"My name is Miss Katie Madison. I'm a new hire. I've noticed you standing here at night, and the other girls told me you were Ginger's friend."

He nodded. "We planned to marry."

"I'm sorry for your loss," she said and hesitated. People in grief generally jumped at the chance to talk about a loved one. She hoped the same was true for Charley, but she had to tread lightly so as not to make him suspicious. "The girls really miss her. Especially Mary-Lou."

His mustache quivered. "They roomed together."

"Mary-Lou said everyone loved her." When he made no response, she added, "She couldn't imagine anyone wanting to hurt Ginger."

His intake of breath told her she'd hit a nerve. "It was all my fault," he said, his voice thick as mud.

Momentarily surprised by the unexpected admission, she paused a moment before asking the next question. "Why do you say that?"

He glanced around as if to make certain they were alone. "We were supposed to meet that night after the lights went out. Right here in our usual spot . . ." He talked in a low, hesitant voice as if each word were hatched from a hard-shell egg.

"I was on a winning streak at faro. Time got away from me, and I showed up late. She wasn't here, so I figured she got tired of waiting and went inside. I hung around for a half hour or so in case she looked out the window. When she didn't, I left. I didn't know she was dead until the next day."

"I heard they found her in the alley," she said gently.

An anguished sob escaped him. "To think I stood in this very spot while she lay —" He blew out his breath. "Had I been here on time, Ginger might still be alive."

She patted him on the arm. "You don't know that."

"I know!" He thumped his chest with his

fist. Startled by his sudden movement, she jumped back. In a quieter voice he added, "I know."

He looked so anguished she felt sorry for him. "You mustn't blame yourself." She glanced up at the bright moonlit sky and thought about her own losses. Her own guilt. She'd left the family business to become a detective, leaving her father to run his tailor shop alone.

While she was away, he'd gone on a bender one snowy night and was thrown from his horse. Without anyone to help him, he died from exposure. Her sisters blamed her. She could still hear her oldest sister Belle's cruel words.

"It was your job to stay home and care for our father. But no, like a fool you insist upon running all over the country playing detective. No wonder Nathan chose me over you."

Maybe Belle was right. Maybe she had shirked her responsibilities. Had she been home, she would have known her father was missing and gone searching for him.

Charley's shoulders rose and fell in a shudder, bringing her back to the present.

"God wouldn't want you to blame yourself," she said as much for him as for herself.

"God? Why would He care? He didn't even care to help her."

"He cares," she whispered. "He cares."

He looked about to argue but instead lifted his gaze to the dark window above.

She studied his profile. His grief seemed real, but that alone didn't exonerate him. It wasn't unusual for killers to show remorse for a crime.

"You said you waited here for a half hour the night Ginger died. Did you see or hear anything in all that time?"

If her question struck him as more than just idle curiosity he didn't show it. He just kept staring up at that window. "No, nothing."

In the silence that followed she considered how to pose the next question and finally just came out with it. "Was there anything unusual about the crime scene? Something the sheriff might have overlooked?" This took her into murky waters; the average person wouldn't ask such an indelicate question.

If he thought her question inappropriate he gave no clue. Instead he said, "Other than the missing shoe, no."

"She was missing a shoe?" Mr. Harvey had provided the Pinkerton agency with a report, but there was nothing in it about a missing shoe.

"Yeah. Found it myself. On the corner of

Main and Sunflower. Lying in the mud. Recognized it soon as I saw it."

She glanced back at the alley. That was at least three blocks away from where her body was found. How did a woman lose a shoe? Two possibilities came to mind. One, she was killed elsewhere and dragged to the alley; two, she was running from someone or something.

"Do you know where she was killed?"

"The sheriff said she was killed right there." He pointed to the side of the building. His answer corresponded to the Pinkerton report.

She glanced up at the open window of the bedroom she shared with Mary-Lou. The night Ginger died the temperature had been in the forties. Sounds are louder after dark, and would have been especially loud on a cold night.

"And no one heard her cry for help?" she asked. Her roommate was a deep sleeper, but what about the others? Why had no one heard her scream?

"Far as I know, no one heard a thing."

"How do you suppose her shoe ended up somewhere else?"

"The only thing I can figure is that she came looking for me at the Silver Spur Saloon. She knew that's where I play faro."

It made sense. Ginger might have gotten tired of waiting for Charley and decided to meet him in town. But something must have happened, something that made her run back to the Harvey House so fast as to lose a shoe.

He blinked and turned his gaze on her. "Why are you so interested in this?"

"It's just . . . I've heard so many nice things about her, I feel like I know her."

He nodded. "You would have liked her," he said. He pulled his watch out of his pocket and held it to the light. "It's late. I better go."

She nodded. "Nice meeting you."

"Nice meeting you, too." With that he shoved his watch into his pocket and walked away. She watched him cross the street and sighed. Guilt was a heavy load to bear.

Did he kill his fiancée? Her instincts told her no, but she wasn't ready to completely absolve him. At least not before checking out his story.

She was still contemplating the conversation when a male voice broke the silence. "Are you out of your mind?"

CHAPTER 14

Jumping as if she'd been shot, Katie whirled about just as the sheriff stepped out from the shadows with Midnight behind him. The swish of her skirt matched the rush of blood to her face.

Hand on her chest, she gasped. "You startled me."

"Yeah, well you're lucky that's all I did." He tethered his horse and turned to face her. "I should have thrown you in jail when I had the chance. Looks like that's about the only way you're gonna stay out of trouble."

She glared at him. "You have no right —"

"I have every right. If you insist upon meeting strange men in the dead of night, I not only have a right, I have an obligation. I sure don't aim to have another dead body on my watch."

Seething, she knotted her hands. "I don't need your protection. I'm quite capable of taking care of myself. I've been trained —"

"If this is how Pinkerton trains its employees, then its methods are worse than I thought."

"I don't have to listen to this." She spun around.

"So what's the verdict? Is Charley Reynolds guilty or not?"

The question stopped her in her tracks, and she turned back to face him. If he thought he could mine her for information, he better think again. "Why should I tell you?" Even the shadows of night couldn't hide his disapproving frown. Nor could it hide his handsome square face or the challenge in his eyes.

"Ah, so you don't know." He practically crowed as he said it.

"He's not guilty," she snapped, not willing to be found remiss in his eyes.

He lifted an eyebrow and pushed his hat back a notch with the tip of his finger. "And you decided this how?"

"With deductive reasoning." Oddly, her earlier fatigue had lifted, and she suddenly felt wide awake. "How did *you* decide his innocence?"

He stiffened as if surprised by the question. "What makes you think I did?"

She managed to keep a triumphant smile

from touching her lips. "For one, he's not in jail."

"And for good reason," he said. "He has an ironclad alibi."

"Such alibis are so rare I seldom take them seriously — unless the alibi is death and there's a gravestone to prove it."

"You don't need a gravestone for this one."

She studied him. "Would you care to elaborate?"

"Not really, but since you insist. Witnesses say that Charley didn't leave the Silver Spur until almost eleven. Ginger's watch stopped at 10:26. That tells me the time of death was at least a half hour before Charley left."

"Witnesses aren't always reliable," she said. There were many reasons for this, poor eyesight and nervous tension being the top two. Most people, however, simply didn't pay close enough attention to what went on around them.

"Normally, I would agree with you, but not this time," he said.

"Why not?"

"I happened to be one of the witnesses. I saw Charley leave at eleven."

She arched her eyebrows. "And there's no chance you might be mistaken?"

"Mistaken? Me?" he asked. "Never."

The indignant look on his face made her laugh, and a suspicious softening of his mouth told her that somewhere in that thick head of his a sense of humor could be found. If she was willing to look for it, which she wasn't.

She mentally ticked off Charley's name from the list of suspects. "Does this mean you're going to work with me?"

"Oh, I'll work with you all right, ma'am." The tension eased from his stiff frame but not from his face. "But not by choice."

"What is that supposed to mean?"

"I'm trying to save your pretty neck."

For some reason the word *pretty* quickened her pulse, though she doubted he meant it in the conventional sense. "Like I said, I don't need your protection."

"A killer is on the loose and here you are meeting strangers in the middle of the night."

"I thought we established that Charley was innocent."

"Yes, but you didn't know that when you met him."

Resentment welled up inside, and she fought to keep her temper. As a female detective she was used to others doubting her abilities, but somehow she resented it more coming from him.

"I don't need your protection," she snapped. With that she started for the alley. She could outride, outshoot, and outsmart most if not all of her male colleagues. She didn't need the sheriff watching out for her.

He grabbed her by the arm and swung her around. He was so close his warm breath fanned her face — so close she feared he could hear the wild beating of her heart. . . .

"Maybe you do and maybe you don't." Voice low in her ear, he pulled her a tad closer. "Right now I'm of no mind to find out. So whether you like it or not, I'm watching out for you."

His gaze dropped to her lips before releasing her. No doubt he meant to intimidate her, but she had no intention of letting him.

She glared up at him. "Don't do me any favors," she snapped. Turning, she walked away as quickly as her legs could carry her.

"Wouldn't think of it," he called, his voice bouncing off the brick walls.

Just as she reached the end of the alley she spotted a movement in the shadows and gasped. Something . . . She opened her mouth to call to the sheriff, but a soft mew made her hold her tongue. Hand on her chest, she watched the cat streak away.

She snapped her mouth shut. Appalled

that her first thought in the face of possible danger had been to summon the sheriff's help, she gave herself a mental kick and hurried away.

Branch watched her move alongside the building, the moon turning her hair into bright orange flames. For some reason he even sensed her glancing back at him before vanishing around the corner, though he couldn't see her face.

A female detective. He shook his head. Still hard to believe. What would be next? A female sheriff? What would possess a woman to take on such a difficult and thankless job?

Now that he knew her true identity she seemed even smaller in stature. Even more vulnerable. Crime solving was a tough business even for a man. He'd been shot at more times than he cared to remember and once took a bullet to the shoulder.

The fool woman had no idea what she'd gotten herself into. He'd seen the bodies. The two victims never even had a chance to defend themselves.

Miss Madison packed a small pocket gun, which, in his opinion, was just this side of a suicide special. It was suicide to depend on one, and suicide was about all they were good for.

Find the killer. That's what he had to do. He also better keep his eye on the intriguing lady detective. A *very* close eye.

The following morning, Katie slipped the silk hairnet over the twisted knot in back. The room she shared with Mary-Lou was located directly over the kitchen, which was why Chef Gassy's shrill voice could be heard coming through the open window.

Hardly a day went by when he didn't have a conniption about one thing or another.

Mary-Lou worked a black lisle stocking up her leg and attached it to her garter. "Wonder what got him riled up this time."

Katie glanced out the window just in time to see the iceman racing to his horse and wagon. The poor man practically flew into the driver's seat. He took off lickety-split, his wagon swaying from side to side as it swung around the corner and raced up Main.

Things quieted down with the iceman's departure only to start up again as Katie and Mary-Lou reached the ground floor. As far as Katie could make out from the thick-accented rants, someone had either trampled on his pies or crumbled his ties. Hard to tell which.

Just as Katie entered the kitchen a gray-striped cat shot past her. She recognized it as the same cat that had startled her the night before.

For some reason her presence only fueled the chef's anger. "Look, look," he yelled, pointing to the row of pies on the cooling shelf. The rest he said in French, but Katie didn't need an interpreter to know that the whipped cream paw prints were the source of his fury.

"I ask you," he said, switching back to English. "I ask you. How did cat get in? Doors locked. Windows locked. Still cat get in. Spook Cat!"

The mystery of Spook Cat still hadn't been resolved by that afternoon. After a thorough search, Katie finally found the cat hiding in back of the cleaning supply closet.

Dropping down on her haunches, Katie held out her hand and talked softly. "Well hello, there, Spook Cat. I wish you could tell me how you got inside."

She hadn't let the cat in, that was for sure. That meant someone had either entered or left the house after her. The question was who and why?

Gazing at her with amber eyes, the cat flipped its tail.

"If only you could talk."

Her voice seemed to have a calming effect

on him. At least he inched forward enough to allow her to stroke him on the head. But it took considerably longer before Spook Cat allowed her to pick him up and carry him outside.

The moment she set him down he sauntered away and disappeared around the side of the house, taking the answers to her questions with him.

CHAPTER 15

Katie's favorite part of the day was the early-morning hour when the locals came for breakfast. The rail workers were the first to arrive, along with the local cattlemen. While everyone else paid seventy-five cents for meals, train personnel only had to pay a quarter. This didn't sit well with the cattlemen, and the two sides seldom socialized.

Most of the trainmen were in their twenties and early thirties. They were a rowdy bunch who openly flirted with the Harvey girls and joked with the restaurant manager.

Ginger's beau, Charley, was never among the group, though Katie always looked for him.

"Why can't a locomotive sit down?" one of the men yelled out.

"I give up," Pickens said with better humor than he ever showed his staff.

"Because he has a tender behind!" This

124

brought gales of laughter from his companions.

Tully rolled her eyes. "If I hear that joke one more time I'll scream." She picked up a tray and walked toward the merry group with a full Harvey girl smile.

No sooner did the railroad workers and cattlemen leave than the local businessmen arrived. This was a more somber group who preferred reading newspapers to telling jokes.

Katie was quick to learn their names and had sent descriptions to headquarters. So far none had a known criminal record. James Wilcox ran the local hardware store and Harry Foxx owned the hotel. Both were family men with churchgoing wives and a bunch of children.

The postmaster, Carl Swenson, was a widower. Newlywed Evan Hopkins owned the bookstore.

Her favorite diner was the man known as Okie-Sam who always sat at the counter next to the cigar case. He, too, had red hair, though nowhere near as brash as hers. Teasing her about being a long lost relative separated at birth, he called her sis.

His friendly manner didn't get him off the hook. She still sent his description to headquarters, and according to the telegram back, no one matching his description had a criminal record. Of course, that didn't clear him completely. The Pinkerton criminal files were impressive but far from complete. At least they gave her a place to start.

Today Okie-Sam slid onto the stool and greeted her with a nod. "How's my favorite sis?"

"If you don't stop calling me that, I'll have to start calling you brother."

He laughed. "Brother, huh? People will think I'm a monk or something."

"Not with your hair," she said. If the brassy red color wasn't bad enough, he made it even more noticeable by wearing it long and pulled back into a ponytail. His bushy red mustache and beard didn't help, either.

She slid a cup of coffee on the counter in front of him and tossed a nod at his newly bandaged hand. "What happened to you?"

He discounted her concern with a shrug. "Cut it on some glass. The doc had to sew me up."

"That's too bad." She glanced at the clock. The train was due to arrive in a few minutes, which meant she had less time to devote to locals. "Don't you have to work or something?"

"Not me," he said. "I'm what you might

call independently wealthy, thanks to my royal family."

She eyed him with curiosity. His cheap trousers, stained shirt, unkempt hair, and shabby boots pegged him at the low end of the economic scale — the very low end. "You have royal blood?"

"You could say that. My father is the king of spades and my mother the queen of hearts."

She laughed. "You had me going there for a while. So you're a gambler." Judging by the poor condition of his clothes, not a very good one.

"Yes, but I only bet on a sure thing." He tossed a coin on the counter and winked. "Right now I'm betting on your fine cackle-berries and bacon."

"I'll have the same," Sheriff Whitman said, slipping onto the stool next to Okie-Sam.

The unexpected appearance of the sheriff put her in a state of confusion, and it took her a moment to recall what Okie-Sam had ordered. Fortunately, a whiff of bacon reminded her.

She called the orders to the kitchen and reached for a clean cup and saucer. Bracing herself with a deep breath, she placed it on the counter in front of the sheriff.

Whitman tossed a nod at Okie-Sam's right

hand. "What happened there?"

Katie answered for him. "He cut it on some glass."

The sheriff shrugged. "Guess that messes up your game."

Elbow on the counter, Okie-Sam held up his bandaged hand and regarded it with a rueful stare. "For a while."

Katie filled the empty cup. "Anything ever mess up your game, Sheriff?"

Whitman stared straight at her. "Not for long."

He'd promised to keep her identity as an undercover detective secret, and she had no reason to doubt him. If only he didn't look at her with such disapproval. So was it the woman he disapproved of? Or the detective?

"I didn't know you were a gambler, Sheriff," Okie-Sam said.

Whitman's gaze held hers. "Depends on the stakes."

Okie-Sam's gaze swung from the sheriff to her and back again as if he sensed the tension between them.

"One thing you'll never see me gambling on and that's marriage." Okie-Sam paused for a moment and chuckled. "Nope. Ain't never gonna happen. Too dangerous."

The sheriff dropped a sugar cube into his

cup and stirred. "I can think of a whole lot of things more dangerous. Can't you, Miss Madison?"

"More dangerous than marriage?" she asked with an innocent air. "Nope. Can't think of a thing."

That night Katie waited until Mary-Lou was asleep before tiptoeing out of the room.

She closed the door softly and stood in the hallway straining her ears. It was only a little after eleven, and the gaslights lining the walls hissed and sputtered. When no other sounds broke the silence she made her way down the stairs, careful to walk on the side where the boards were less likely to creak. She had carefully mapped out the hall and stairs for loose boards.

A thin strip of light glowed beneath the kitchen door. Someone was still working. She opened the door to find the assistant cook, Howie Howard. He claimed the reduplicated name traced back to his Welsh roots and was not the result of parents lacking in imagination.

Tonight she found him chopping onions, tears rolling down his cheeks.

"You're working late," she said.

Howie looked up as she entered and saluted her with a raised knife. "Always work late on Thursdays. Got to get things ready for the weekend." He was a thin, hatchet-nosed man with droopy eyes, crooked teeth, and high forehead. Like the other kitchen staff, he had small pea-size marks on the back of his hands and arms from the spattering of hot oil. He also had calluses on his right hand on the base of his fingers.

He certainly knew how to wield a knife. Chop, chop, chop and just that quickly an onion was reduced to tiny pieces.

Watching the flash of the blade, Katie couldn't help but think of the way the two Harvey girls met their demise. Luckily she'd thought to attach her gun holster to her leg. She thrust her hand in her false pocket ready to draw if necessary.

"What are you doing up at this hour?" He scooted the chopped pieces to the side with the blade of his knife and reached for another onion.

"Couldn't sleep." She waited for him to finish chopping. "How do you like working with Chef Gassée?" she asked, taking care to pronounce the name in a suitable French way.

Howie shrugged. "He's all right. It gets pretty hectic in here at times and tempers flare."

He apparently had no intention of bad-mouthing his boss, and that was okay with her. It wasn't the chef she wanted to talk about.

"One of the other girls told me that Ginger used to sneak out at night to meet her beau. Did you know anything about that?"

"I knew." His knife stilled midair. "Sometimes I lent her my key to get back in. Now I wish I hadn't."

"Oh? Why is that?"

"She might still be alive had I not helped her leave the house." He pointed the tip of his knife at her. "So don't go getting any ideas. No more giving out my key. Anyone wanting to leave the house after curfew won't get any help from me."

So Charley wasn't the only one feeling guilt over Ginger's death. "Has anyone else asked for help in leaving the house?"

He resumed chopping. "Not recently. After what happened, even I don't like leaving the house after dark."

She bit her lower lip. No sense asking for his key. "The alley cat got inside and into the pies. Do you know how that could have happened? Did you let him in?"

"Not me." He paused with narrowed eyes. "Everything was locked up good and tight when I left. So don't go blaming me, you hear?"

"I wasn't," she said. *Touchy, aren't we?* Mary-Lou told her that Howie rented a room at the boardinghouse on Fifth. "What time did you leave last night?" she asked.

She hadn't seen him when she left the house, nor when she returned, but he could have been in the cellar.

He chopped for a moment before answering. "I finished the prep work around . . . I don't know. Nine or ten, maybe."

If what he said was true, then he left the house before she did.

He lifted his knife off the chopping board. "How come you're asking all these questions? Did the chef put you up to this?"

"The chef?" she asked and frowned.

"Did he ask you to spy for him?"

"No, of course not," she said. "I'm just . . . curious about the cat."

He grunted and began chopping again. Did he believe her? Hard to know. She wanted to ask more questions, but since that would only make him more suspicious she decided against it.

"Good night." She left the kitchen and headed back to her room. If what he said was true, then someone else had opened the door last night after she had returned to the house. Either that or the cat had let himself in, and somehow she doubted that.

CHAPTER 16

Katie woke the next morning to the sound of the howling wind. It growled and snorted and scratched at the windows like an angry cat demanding entrance.

The wind lasted for the next two torturous days, making it hard to leave the premises. Dust filled the nose, the eyes, and mouth until even the food tasted like grit. But no one complained more than the bookkeeper, Mr. Culpepper, whose watery eyes looked like two red marbles.

"Can't see a blasted thing," he growled as he sat by the front door collecting money from diners. "Can't tell my mother from a jackrabbit."

Each time someone entered or left the restaurant, sand crept over the floor like an army of tiny ants. The wind kept blowing, and the omnibus boy wielded his broom. His name was Ken Montgomery, but everyone called him Buzz because he darted around like a bee. Of all the workers, he was the hardest to interview, mainly because he was always on the move.

In his mid to late twenties, he was in charge of the heavy cleaning. He complained about the railroad workers and local cowboys messing up his floors with their dirty boots or leaving grimy fingerprints on the brass doorknobs.

"I think this is it," Okie-Sam added between mouthfuls. "Kansas is finally about to blow away."

The wind kept Katie inside but not the locals. The citizens of Calico struck Katie as a hardy bunch. They took a sort of civil pride in saying that Calico's summers blazed the hottest, the winters the coldest, the locusts the hungriest, and the wind the most torturous. Living with the whims of nature made them hold on to life with one hand and God with the other.

By the second day of relentless wind, Katie's patience was spent. She decided to embrace a Kansan's tough skin and venture outside. She was anxious to check the corner where Ginger's shoe was found. Not that she expected to find anything at this late date, but no stone must be left unturned during an investigation.

Head bent against the wind, she protected

her face with an upraised arm. The hem of her skirt flapped against her ankles, and strands of flame-colored hair escaped from beneath her bonnet. The town windmill spun and squealed like a pig caught in a trap.

Reaching her destination, she glanced around, shielding her eyes from the wind the best she could. The Calico Bank commanded one corner and a general store the other. Across the street was a lawyer's office and land assayer.

At ten thirty at night, all businesses would be shuttered and most of the residents in upstairs apartments already asleep. That meant if Ginger was in trouble she had two choices: run toward Saloon Row or return to the Harvey House. The restaurant was closer, but not by much. Why not run to the closest saloon where people were awake and more likely to help?

She was still pondering this as a gust of wind slammed into her. It lifted her bonnet clear off her head and carried it away. It would have blown her off her feet had it not been for two strong arms that materialized seemingly out of nowhere.

A male voice shouted in her ear, but the gushing wind muted the words. Blinded by dust, she had no idea who he was or what he had said.

With a sturdy arm around her waist, her rescuer guided her into the bank, protecting her from the wind with his tall, straight form. Inside, he released her.

"Whew." She blinked her eyes and pushed the stray hair away from her face. "Thank you —" She looked up and caught her breath. "Sheriff!"

Her watery eyes did nothing to mute his powerful presence, and her knees threatened to buckle.

He inclined his head. "We meet again." He hung his thumbs from his belt. "What are you doing out in this weather?"

Before answering she glanced around, but the only person present was the teller behind a cage counting money.

She and the sheriff faced each other. Standing close, they were like two bookends holding up a single slim volume. Nevertheless she kept her voice low. "Pinkertons never sleep, nor do they let a little thing like the wind stop them."

For a split second she imagined seeing what looked like admiration in the dark depths of his eyes.

"So the shoe bothers you, does it?"

She tilted her head back in surprise. "How do you know?"

"It bothers me, too."

She moistened her lips. "Any theories?" she asked.

"None that make sense. You?"

She hesitated. Was he really asking her opinion? "Maybe Ginger saw someone or something that frightened her, and ran."

"Perhaps. Or maybe the killer dropped the shoe to get us off track."

"Possibly. Or accidently dropped the shoe he meant to keep." A serial killer in Chicago kept a trophy of each of his victims — a piece of jewelry. An article of clothing. "Were any of Priscilla's personal belongings missing?"

"Not that anyone noticed."

They tossed theories back and forth, their low voices creating an intimate bond that all but cut them off from the rest of the world.

But not from the wind; outside it continued to howl. The building creaked and groaned like the bones of an old man. But while nature rampaged beyond the walls, inside hearts began to thaw.

Surprisingly, she enjoyed his company. She had no idea how much she needed that, needed to talk without watching her every word. Working undercover was like being mentally and emotionally chained. Seldom did she have the luxury of talking openly about a case, except to her Pinkerton colleagues. One had to always be on guard. One misstep — one misspoken word — and her cover could be compromised.

Oddly enough, she sensed a loneliness in him that matched her own. She also shared his frustration at the stalled investigation.

"Two women are dead and I haven't got a clue how to find the killer," he admitted, and she sensed his difficulty in doing so.

She commiserated with a shake of her head. "Whenever I hit a wall my bosses tell me to go back to the beginning and start over as if it were a new case."

"Does it work?" he asked with none of his usual condescension.

"Hasn't so far." She laughed, and he did, too.

She didn't think about the time or the restaurant until a sound from outside caught her attention. Not the wind. Something else. She perked up her ears. Was that church bells? It couldn't be. Not already.

"What time is it?" she asked.

He reached into his vest pocket for his watch. "Noon."

She gasped. "Oh no!" Where had the time gone? "The train —" She had less than a half hour to get ready for the lunch crowd.

She whirled about and headed for the door.

"Wait," he called after her.

But she didn't wait; no time. The door practically ripped from her hand as she dashed outside, skirt swirling. The wind at her back, she ran all the way to the Harvey House on winged feet and a prayer. *Please, please, please don't let Pickens catch me!*

CHAPTER 17

Branch headed straight for the bank first thing that Monday morning. The bank president had been out of town, so Branch had yet to talk to him about Mrs. Bracegirdle's complaint.

Crossing the street, he sidestepped a pile of horse manure. The wind had finally stopped except for an occasional gust, but the sky was still murky gray from dust. Clay shingles, broken signs, and other debris littered the ground.

He waved to shopkeepers sweeping doorsteps and businessmen surveying the damage to roofs. Mrs. Bracegirdle's son was boarding up his shop's broken window.

Miss Katie Madison was very much on his mind. He could still envision her standing in the middle of the street in the wind. Fool woman. Stubborn as a sore tooth. Slight as she was in frame, she was lucky she hadn't been blown away. Still, the memory of her bravely fighting the wind brought an unbidden smile to his face.

Much as he hated to admit it, her capabilities as a detective were impressive. Not only had she captured a bank robber, she'd given the case much thought and her theories and observation skills were equal to his own, if not better.

The woman might look fragile, but she knew how to handle herself in a pinch.

That didn't make him feel any better about her safety. If anything, it worried him more as she was likely to take chances. Until the killer was behind bars, every woman in town was at risk, and that went double for the Harvey girls — real and make-believe.

Pushing his thoughts aside, he ducked beneath the loose wooden sign that swung back and forth on a broken chain, and strode into the bank. With only a quick glance at the line in front of the teller cage, he walked to the president's office and rapped on the oak door.

Miles McPherson rose from his desk as Branch entered his office. A portly man with face-hugging sideburns, he made a funny hissing sound when he breathed.

As they shook hands, McPherson indicated a chair with a nod of his head. "Have a seat." He waited for Branch to sit before lowering his bulky body behind his desk again.

"Glad you stopped by. Gives me a chance to thank you for your speedy action in nabbing that bank robber. Heard all about it."

"I didn't do anything," Branch said. "You should be thanking Miss Madison."

"Miss Madison? Oh, you mean the waitress?"

"Harvey girl," Branch said. "She's the one who stopped the man." Her pie-in-the-face method was unconventional, but it did the trick. "I just happened to arrive in time to finish the job."

The bank president waved his protests away. "You're far too modest." He opened a wooden box and picked out a cigar. "I'd offer you one, but I know you don't smoke. What a shame. Harvey stocks only the best. All the way from Cuba." He lowered the lid of the box. "So tell me about this latest robber."

"Not much to tell. All I can say is that he won't be causing you any more trouble."

McPherson shook his head. "I'm telling you, these bank robbers are getting more brazen every year. Ever since we changed over to a tamper-proof vault, the thieves simply walk up to the tellers and demand money like it's their God-given right." He rolled his cigar in his finger and sniffed. "I don't know what the world is coming to."

Branch nodded. "Crime fighting is like trying to stop a sinking ship. No sooner do you plug up one hole than another one springs up."

McPherson clipped off the end of his cigar. "Any suspects in the killings?"

"Not yet."

"Hmm. Nasty business, that."

"Yes, it is."

The banker stuck the cigar in his mouth and lit it with a match, rotating the tip into the flame. "So what brings you here today?"

"Mrs. Bracegirdle."

Grimacing, the banker shook the match until the flame went out. "Not her again. What is it this time? Tommy knockers?"

"Not exactly. She claims she hears noises coming from the bank at night. They keep her awake."

McPherson removed his cigar from his mouth and blew out a ring of gray smoke. "There's no one here at night."

"No one working late?"

"Nope. The bank's locked up tighter than a spinster's virtue."

"What about the upstairs apartment? Who lives up there now?"

"Nobody. I rented it out to a young couple

144

a few weeks ago. They changed their mind before they even got the furniture moved in. Claimed the place was haunted."

"Haunted, huh? Mind if I have a look?"

"Don't mind at all, but you're wasting your time. You won't find anything there."

"Regardless, I'm obliged to check out all complaints."

McPherson opened a drawer and tossed a brass key across the desk. "Return it when you're done."

The only way to reach the upstairs apartment was from the outside stairwell. Branch took the stairs two at a time. He paused in front of Mrs. Bracegirdle's door before turning to the empty apartment next to hers and inserting the key in the lock.

A stale, musty smell greeted him as he walked into the dwelling. Translucent cloth window shades were half-drawn, and sun filtered through the grimy windowpanes.

The place was empty except for a rumpled carpet on the parlor floor and a lantern on the kitchen counter next to a box of matches. He checked all the cabinets and drawers and found only mouse droppings and a thin layer of dust. The kitchen sink contained a single tin cup.

A banging from the direction of the bedroom alerted him, and he spun around. He checked the room and again found nothing. He turned to leave, but a thud from the window stopped him in his tracks.

He moved across the room, unlocked the window, and threw open the sash. Sticking his head outside, he immediately spotted the problem. One of the shutters had worked loose. The wooden flap creaked and rattled and slapped the building with every gust of wind.

He leaned over the sill and drew the shutters in place, hooking the latch.

Satisfied that at least one problem had been solved, he locked the apartment and tapped on Mrs. Bracegirdle's door to tell her the news.

A bloodcurdling scream snapped Katie out of a sound sleep. Instantly alert, she grabbed her gun from under the pillow and jumped out of bed. Racing across the room on bare feet, she reached the door before Mary-Lou.

The dorm matron rushed out of her room at the end of the hall, her flimsy white nightgown trailing behind her like the wings of an enormous moth. "Who screamed?"

"I think it came from Tully's room," Katie called over her shoulder. The pantry girl, Cissy, opened her door and stuck out her head. Seeing Katie and the others advance toward her, she quickly pulled back and slammed the door shut. The girl was as skittish as a newborn colt.

Katie burst through Tully's bedroom door without knocking. "What's wrong? What happened?"

Miss Thatcher and Mary-Lou crowded in the doorway behind her.

A match flared in the dark, and the lamp lit up. "It's just Tully," Abigail said. She blew out the match. "She had a bad dream."

All eyes turned to the bed against the far wall where Tully sat looking pale and disoriented.

Lacking a pocket, Katie hid her gun in the cotton folds of her nightgown.

"Is that all?" Miss Thatcher said, looking both annoyed and relieved. "You practically scared us to death. We thought —"

Katie waited for her to finish. The dorm matron looked different tonight with her dark hair flowing down her back. Sleep had wiped away years of bitterness normally engraved on her face, leaving behind a glimpse of the young and carefree girl she once was.

Miss Thatcher gave her head a good shake as if to remind herself of her duties. "Go back to bed, all of you." With that she turned and stomped from the room.

Mary-Lou lowered herself onto the edge of Tully's mattress. "Are you all right?"

Tully blew her nose in a handkerchief. "I think so."

Tonight, her dark hair fell to her shoulders making her look younger than her twenty-two years. She glanced in turn at each of them. "I'm sorry. I didn't mean to wake you all. It's just . . . I keep seeing Ginger. It's like she's trying to tell me something." Without her usual cynical countenance, Tully looked surprisingly vulnerable.

Katie moved closer to the bed. "Maybe we should talk about it." The women had been reluctant to say much about either Ginger or Priscilla except on general terms.

"I don't think we should," Abigail said, rubbing her naked ring finger. "I mean —" She looked at each of them in turn. "I'm afraid that talking might make things worse. Sometimes it's best not to think of sad things."

"I disagree," Katie said. "I think talking helps."

"Maybe she's right," Mary-Lou said, though she sounded dubious.

Tully frowned. "What's there to talk about? I had a bad dream. Haven't you ever had a nightmare?"

Katie nodded. "Yes, and I found it really does help to talk." When no more protests were voiced, she continued. "What do you most remember about the first girl who died?" If she could just get them talking about Priscilla, she might learn something of value. Sometimes people knew more than they realized.

Tully was the first to speak. "Priscilla played the piano." She spoke slowly as if each word was an effort. "But she had to sell her piano to help pay her father's debts. She was saving her money to purchase another one. The night she was killed . . ."

"Go on," Katie said gently.

Tully inhaled and cleared her throat. "One of our customers was entertaining out-of-town guests and asked Priscilla to play for them. After curfew, I snuck downstairs and unlocked the dining room door so she could get in, but she never came home." Tully dabbed at her eyes with her handkerchief. "I didn't know what to do. I didn't want to tell anyone she was missing for fear of getting her in trouble."

Tully's voice faded away, and Mary-Lou continued in her soft Southern lilt. "They found her body the next morning out front by the railroad tracks."

Katie listened intently, but neither Tully

nor Mary-Lou told her anything that wasn't already in the Pinkerton file.

The conversation had a sobering effect on the four of them and a long silence followed.

"We're never going to know who killed her," Tully said at last. "Ginger, either."

"Yes, we will," Katie said with more confidence than she felt. The other three girls looked at her all funny-like, and she quickly added, "The sheriff is doing everything he can."

Tully made a face. "He hasn't done anything yet."

"And probably won't," Abigail added.

"Why do you say that?" Katie asked. She and the sheriff didn't always see eye to eye, but he seemed to take his job seriously and she had no reason to doubt his intent.

Abigail folded her arms across her middle and tossed her head. "Years ago in St. Louis, a good-time gal was found strangled. And you know what? They never found who did it. Far as I could tell no one even bothered looking. No one cared what happened to the likes of her. A man can do anything he wants to a woman and no one gives a fig!"

With a slight gasp she covered her mouth with her hand as if she'd given away too much. Katie felt sorry for her. Abigail had left an unhappy marriage, but the fear, and maybe even the guilt remained, and that was taking a toll.

Mary-Lou was the first to break the awkward silence that followed Abigail's outburst. "This isn't the same," she said gently. "We're not one of those . . . women."

"There're those in town who think we are," Abigail argued. "You know yourself how we've been shunned from certain social activities. We even get strange looks in church." A note of bitterness crept into her voice.

Katie glanced at her roommate. "Is that true?"

"I'm afraid it is," Mary-Lou said. "But they're wrong. We're good girls. Mr. Harvey would never hire anyone who wasn't."

Tully threw up her hands. "I just wish we had time to do all the things we're accused of doing."

Abigail gave her a playful punch in the arm. "No you don't."

Mary-Lou shrugged. "My mother said that the only people who live on the second floor are soiled doves. If she knew that's where I lived, she'd turn over in her grave."

Abigail laughed. "Does that mean that old lady Bracegirdle is a prostitute?"

"And what about Reverend Bushwell?"

Tully asked.

The four of them burst out laughing, and the tension left the room. They chatted more, a lot more. Mary-Lou talked about living in Georgia. Tully opened up about her bitter childhood.

"My mother couldn't take care of me, so she gave me away to a New York foundling home. I was only eight when I was shipped to Kansas City on an orphan train. They dressed us up with silly ruffles and bows and made us sing so we would look more appealing."

Mary-Lou frowned. "Oh, Tully, that's awful. Were you adopted?"

"Yes, but the woman didn't like my New York accent." She shrugged in her usual sardonic way. "So she whipped me and made me sleep in the barn with the animals."

Abigail's eyes widened in horror. "Didn't you tell anyone?"

"What? And get whipped again?" Tully laughed, but this time her laughter rang hollow.

Katie leaned across the bed and squeezed her hand. "I'm so sorry."

A look of surprise crossed Tully's face but only for the instant it took for the usual devil-may-care mask to fall in place. But

Katie had seen the hurt, and she knew.

Tully withdrew her hand. "Now it's your turn."

Katie frowned. "What?"

"You know all about us, but we know nothing about you," Tully said. "What's your story?"

Katie had a story all right — a simple one about growing up on a Wisconsin cheese farm. Not one word of it was true, of course, but part of a carefully designed disguise.

While the others were open and honest with her, she couldn't return the favor. She hated lying, but the truth could jeopardize her investigation and maybe even put her life in danger. It was a reality she'd more or less learned to live with through the years, though not without guilt.

Still, she couldn't bring herself to lie to Tully and the others. Not tonight. Not after Tully had bared heart and soul to the small group.

"Another time." Yawning, Katie stood and stretched. "Right now we need to go back to bed. Morning will be here before we know it."

CHAPTER 18

During her afternoon break, Katie left the restaurant and walked the three blocks to the office of the *Calico Gazette.* Though the wind had stopped two days prior, a slight breeze kept dust in the air, and the sun looked like a big copper button that had popped off someone's coat.

The editor looked up from his desk and gazed at her from beneath his green celluloid visor. He was a short man with a stubby mustache and ink-stained hands. A small sign on his desk read MR. CLOVIS READ.

Katie introduced herself as the new Harvey House employee. "Would it be all right if I go through the back issues of the paper?" she asked. Most big-city newspapers kept back issues on hand, and she hoped the same was true for this town.

"It's about time someone did," he said, rising. "Been keeping files for years, and you're the first to ask to see them. Any special month or year?"

"Not really." She didn't want to reveal her real interest in looking through old newspapers. "Since I'm new, I thought it would be a good way to get to know the town better."

"You came to the right place. Won't find better information anywhere than what you'll find here. That's because I won't print anything that's not accurate." Barely taking a breath, he continued.

"Got one of those fancy writing machines for the office, and you know what happened? Made my reporters too wordy. Would you believe that one reporter turned in five column inches just to describe a dogfight? Now I ask you — who wants to muddle through a block that size to read such nonsense? The entire story of the creation can fit on a single front page. Anything short of that needs only two or three inches. Four, at the most."

The man kept up a constant stream of chatter as he led her to the back room. How such a talkative man could confine his written narrative to mere inches was a puzzle.

He waved his hand at the oak file cabinet. "These are all the newspapers for the last five years. If you want to go back any further, you can look in the second drawer there. That includes papers that go all the way back to the great tornado of '72." He gave his head a rueful shake. "That one took eleven column inches to report, but that was before my time."

"I heard something about that," she said. "It must have been awful."

"Yes, it was. It's almost the eight-year anniversary, and I'm planning a special commemorative issue. It's part of the town's history." He pulled out the top drawer of a wooden cabinet. "You probably should skip the articles about the Harvey girl killings. No sense getting yourself all worked up."

Resisting the urge to inquire as to how many inches Ginger and Priscilla had commanded, she asked, "Do you think they'll ever solve the murders?"

"Beats me." He shook his head. "But I'll tell you somethin'. Putting a bunch of pretty girls under the same roof is just askin' for trouble."

"I imagine a man of your intelligence would have an idea or two as to who the killer might be," she said. Flattery — deserved or otherwise — was often a detective's best tool for encouraging confidential information.

"If you ask me, it's that French chef."

"Gassy? Uh . . . I mean Gassée?"

"That's the one. I heard him yelling at that girl Ginger the day before she died."

"The chef yells at everyone."

"Yeah, but not everyone is found dead the next day."

He had a point there. She glanced at the cabinet, and taking the hint, he backed away.

"If you need me, I'll be at my desk," he said.

"Thank you." After he left, she began flipping through newspapers, stopping now and again to read a headline or peruse an article.

The editor was right about one thing: the *Calico Gazette* wasn't much for verbiage. The death of both Harvey girls totaled no more than five column inches. The information was accurate but offered nothing in the way of new information.

Another dead end.

As much as she wanted to solve the case, Katie wasn't anxious to end her stay at the Harvey House. A hotel was the closest she'd ever been to living under the same roof as a suspect, but it wasn't just the convenience that such an arrangement offered. Not since her sisters married and left home had she lived in such close proximity with other women.

Since the Harvey girls shared so many of the same day-to-day experiences, she couldn't help but get involved in their lives. Whispering with Abigail, Mary-Lou, and even Tully behind Pickens's and even Miss Thatcher's backs was a temptation too delicious to pass up.

"Did you see that woman sneak the food left over at her table into her bag?"

"And what about that cute peddler who couldn't take his eyes off Mary-Lou?"

Though she engaged in girlish chatter, she remained constantly on guard, and this took an emotional toll on her.

Sometimes she lay awake at night and wondered how it was possible to be surrounded by so many people and feel so completely and utterly lonely.

Today, as the four of them stood ironing aprons, Tully told them about a man who popped the question. She made a face. "Can you imagine me marrying a traveling salesman?"

Katie listened but didn't say a word. Tully garnered proposals like a gunfighter collected notches.

"You know what they say about us Harvey girls," Tully said, exchanging a cool iron for a hot one. "Marriage proposals for the pretty ones take but a day. The less attractive ones have to wait three days." She looked straight at Katie. "How many marriage proposals have you received?"

"Me?" Katie felt her face grow warm. She shook her head. "None."

Mary-Lou as usual jumped to her defense. "Give it time. She's new."

Abigail lifted an apron off the ironing board and hung it on a wooden peg. Whenever talk turned to marriage, she normally remained silent or left the room. Such talk seemed to bring back unwanted memories of the life she had escaped.

But today she surprised Katie by saying, "I think she's already spoken for."

"I am?" Katie tightened her grip on the wooden handle of the sadiron. "I don't know what you mean."

Abigail lowered her voice. "I'm talking about the sheriff, of course. I saw the way he looked at you this morning at breakfast."

"I didn't notice." Katie had been so busy juggling orders she'd hardly had time to give the sheriff more than a cursory glance. She lowered the iron to the bib of the apron, hoping for a change of topic.

Much to her dismay, Mary-Lou persisted. "Maybe you should. He's nice to look at and always treats us with respect."

Katie managed to pretend disinterest, but

the apron she was ironing sure did take a beating. If it wasn't already flat it would have been. "I guess he's okay."

Mary-Lou laughed. "But only if you like handsome, tall men with dark dreamy eyes — right?"

Katie's mind was still on the handsome part when suddenly Abigail cried out, "Your apron!"

"What?" Katie lifted the iron and stared in horror at the brown scorch mark on the starched white bib. There was no help for the apron. Nor for her blazing cheeks.

By the start of the third week, Katie had the restaurant routine down pat. The cup code? Now that was a different story. So was taking orders. Whose bright idea was it to make Harvey girls work without benefit of pen and paper?

She had better luck remembering the names of the locals. Some of her favorites included Bert the blacksmith, a large dark-skinned man with a robust smile and a ready joke. Reverend Bushwell had breakfast every day except Sundays and always spread good cheer along with a Bible quote or two.

She also knew all the cowboys by name. The names all corresponded with physical features, so memorizing them was a cinch.

Tall Texas Joe and Big Foot Pete were her favorites and always good for a laugh. But as a whole the cattlemen were more close-mouthed than the AT&SF trainmen, which probably meant they had more to hide.

Not only were rail workers more verbal, they dealt out marriage proposals like faro dealers dealt out cards. Katie was taken aback the first time one proposed to her. She soon learned it was done in jest. In no time at all she found herself promised to a dozen or more men. For once she felt like the belle of the ball rather than a wallflower.

The unaccustomed attention amused her to no end. Her sisters should see her now. They wouldn't recognize their dull, red-headed, freckle-faced sister.

Long-Shot was another favorite local. He'd run for every possible office in the county, including sheriff, and lost. Whenever he walked into the restaurant someone would invariably call out, "Hey, Long-Shot. What are you running for next?"

Long-Shot never seemed to take offense. Instead, he'd throw out an answer such as dogcatcher or grave digger, and the place would explode with laughter.

Katie envied his ability to laugh at himself. That was something she had never been able to do, but she was learning. Oh, yes, indeed she was. When the railroad workers teased her about her hair and freckles she gave back as good as she got.

They called her Red and Carrot-Top, and her freckles earned her the name Sprinkles. In return she called the workers such names as Ironman, Rails, and Groundhog.

Her banter never failed to bring a roar of laughter from the men and an approving nod from Long-Shot. "That's the way to do it," he'd always say. "Don't let them get to you!"

Not only was she having fun, but joking around with the men gave her ample opportunity to interrogate them.

"Hey, Ironman, did you know Ginger?"

Ironman was burly with a squinty face. The anchor tattooed on his arm and his sea leg swagger marked him as a former sailor. "Charley's girl? Yeah, I knew her." He shook his head. "Terrible thing."

"Charley said he was playing faro when she died," she said. "He feels guilty."

"Yeah, well he should feel guilty. He cleared us all out that night. Left me with nothing more than a plugged nickel."

Little by little she learned the whereabouts of most of the regulars on the night Ginger died. Those with no alibi remained on her suspect list and their descriptions sent to

Pinkerton headquarters.

Her duties didn't allow for much free time. In between meals, the girls were expected to keep busy. That meant polishing silverware, a chore no one liked. It seemed like everything was silver: vases, coffee urns, pitchers, and cutlery.

"If you come to my wedding," Tully announced during a silver-cleaning ordeal, "don't anyone give me silver."

Katie didn't mind the cleaning and polishing as much as the others, for it gave her a chance to listen, observe, and think.

Setting the tables was her big bugaboo. You couldn't just set a plate any old way. Oh, no. Each plate had to be placed an equal distance from the table's edge. The water glasses had to be a certain length away from the knives, and the starched napkins folded just so.

Currently, the restaurant employed only the four Harvey girls, including Katie, and was understaffed by half as four girls had quit after Ginger's death. At least three more women were due to arrive at the end of the month after completing a thirty-day training course. Katie avoided the month-long training by using falsified references stating she was an experienced waitress.

Aside from the manager, bookkeeper, and

omnibus boy, Chef Gassy had three cooks and a baker working under him. Two of the cooks were Mexican and could speak no English. Between the chef and his fractured English and the Spanish-speaking cooks, it was a wonder that the kitchen ran as smoothly as it did.

The ebony-skinned pantry girl attracted Katie's curiosity. Cissy never spoke, ate by herself, and quietly retired to her room at day's end. Katie's every attempt to be friendly had been rebuffed.

The only ones who lived on the premises were the Harvey girls, Cissy, and Miss Thatcher. Even local girls were required to stay in the dormitory. The other employees roomed at the nearby boardinghouse or in town.

Pretending she was looking for salt, Katie was finally able to corner Cissy in the kitchen making salad. She guessed the girl was in her early twenties. She wore her hair parted in the middle and pulled back like the Harvey girls, but her frizzy locks defied any effort on her part to be smoothed into a neat and tidy bun.

"How long have you worked here, Cissy?" she asked.

Deerlike eyes regarded her with suspicion. "Six months."

"So you knew Priscilla and Ginger."

"Kind of."

"What do you mean, kind of?"

"I never talked to them, and they never talked to me." With an air of dismissal she continued tearing lettuce leaves apart and tossing them into a bowl.

Refusing to take the hint, Katie persisted. "But you lived under the same roof. How could you not talk to each other?"

Cissy cast a glance her way. "Don'tcha know? I'm just the pantry girl."

"I'm sure it won't be long until you become a Harvey girl." Though the girl would have to improve her demeanor before that happened. Grammar, too. Mr. Harvey was a stickler for proper English.

Cissy shook her head and gave Katie a wistful look. "Blackies like me ain't allowed to be Harvey girls. Them's the rules."

CHAPTER 19

Later that same day Katie stood at her station behind the counter, scanning the room. Had she not been so alert she might have missed Tully slipping a piece of paper to Buzz.

A pretty girl, a handsome young man. It didn't take a genius to figure out what was going on, but at this point in the game Katie couldn't afford to overlook anything or anyone.

She waited for Buzz to take his place by the gong outside and quietly followed.

As rigid in countenance as he was in dress, he wore an immaculate white shirt and razor-creased trousers. His brown hair was neatly trimmed and nails perfectly manicured. Had he fallen into a tub of starch he couldn't have carried himself more rigid. He hardly seemed the type to resort to anything as messy as murder, but of course the possibility couldn't be discounted.

Pretending she had stepped outside for air, she leaned against a post and fanned herself with her hand. On the other side of the railroad tracks the prairie stretched out for as far as the eye could see. A gentle breeze turned the tall grass into a sea of waves but offered no relief from the heat.

A sign on a wheelbarrow offered free rides to the hotel. It was meant as a joke, but one matronly traveler took it seriously and actually climbed into the handcart, much to the amusement of restaurant employees.

"It sure is hot," she said. Though May had only begun, the wooden thermometer outside read nearly eighty degrees.

He agreed with a nod. "Looks like we're in for an early summer."

"Sure does." A strand of hair had escaped from her bun, and she brushed it away from her face. "How long have you worked for Harvey?"

"Since the restaurant opened nearly two years ago."

"So you knew both Priscilla and Ginger?"

"Yeah, I knew them." He paused for a moment before adding, "Prissy and I started working here about the same time. Mr. Harvey wanted an experienced waitress, so he transferred her from Florence."

"Sure is a shame what happened," she

said. His expression remained neutral, and he made no attempt to comment. "Any idea who might have wanted to harm them?"

He let the question hang for a moment before answering. "No, but —" He lowered his voice. "There're some in town who would like nothing better than to see the restaurant fail."

"But why?" Harvey had practically put the town on the map with his innovative approach to dining.

"It put Ma Gibson's restaurant out of business, and there are those who think the Harvey girls are setting a bad example for the community. Some even say they're serving more than just food and beverage here. Even my own pa thinks that and hasn't forgiven me for working here rather than the family business."

Katie felt her spirits sink. If what he said was true, then the suspect pool just got a whole lot larger. "I noticed that you and Tully seem close."

"Shh." He glanced around again as if to check for eavesdroppers. "We plan on getting married."

That was a surprise, especially since Tully openly flirted with anyone in trousers, including the railroad workers.

"I thought it was against the rules for a

Harvey girl to wed."

"Only for the length of a contract. After that, they're free to wed but can't work at the restaurant anymore. Don't tell anyone. Employees aren't allowed to get involved with one another, and we could both be fired."

"If you don't mind my asking, why are you working here?" He couldn't be making that much money. Certainly not enough to support a wife.

"Mr. Harvey promised to make me the manager of one of his restaurants. He's opening a new one in Arkansas City, and he says it's mine if I keep my nose to the grindstone. That's why I'm here. I'm learning the ropes."

That made sense. He certainly seemed ambitious enough.

"Once I'm made manager," he continued, "there'll be no need for Tully to work and we can get married." He frowned. "You won't tell anyone, will you?"

"I won't breathe a word," she said.

From the far distance came the high-pitched wail of a train whistle. True to form, Buzz turned like a wooden soldier and struck the gong with his stick. The job might not require much in the way of skill, but he gave it all he had.

The dish-shaped gong was still vibrating when she turned and hurried back inside.

Katie was given a promotion of sorts, much to her surprise. Instead of working behind the counter, she was now allowed to work the tables. That meant having to deal with a more involved and complicated menu.

The gong had announced the arrival of the twelve-twenty-five, and Katie sighed with irritation at spotting the sheriff walk through the door. Since the day he rescued her from the wind, they had called a truce of sorts and were no longer at loggerheads.

Still, she had a hard enough time serving a bunch of strangers under Pickens's critical eye without the sheriff's distracting presence. All he had to do was walk into the room and suddenly she couldn't think of anything else. Today was no different. She was so busy staring at him she almost poured the coffee in a diner's lap.

He paid his money and headed straight for her station. Lunch was served in the breakfast room, so no jackets were required. He greeted her with a crooked smile and touched the brim of his hat with his finger.

Heat rose up her neck. "These seats are taken," she said, her voice thick with swirling emotions.

She hoped he would take the hint and sit at another station, but no such luck. Instead, his gaze circled the table.

"Nine are taken," he said pulling out a chair. "That leaves one chair empty."

She sidled up to him. "Wouldn't you rather be served by one of the more experienced girls?" she whispered in his ear.

"I'll take my chances with you," he said, and the tone of his voice made her draw in her breath. He glanced at the blackboard. "I'll have the roast beef."

Wiping her damp hands on the side of her skirt, she backed away and took the other orders.

The kitchen was a beehive of activity. Everyone was shouting orders, and Chef Gassy and Howie Howard shoved plates of steaming food onto trays faster than you could say Abe Lincoln.

Katie grabbed a tray marked number three and walked up to Mary-Lou. "Tell me again where the blue mussels are from?" She raised her voice to be heard above the noise. Why people cared one way or the other where food originated she couldn't imagine.

"You mean Blue Point oysters, and they come from Long Island," Mary-Lou shouted back. She reached for her own tray and started toward the breakfast room. Katie followed.

"And don't forget to say that the quail is sage fed, the turtles are from the Gulf of Mexico, and the whitefish came straight from the Great Lakes," Mary-Lou called over her shoulder.

Katie sighed as the two parted company. And she thought the cup code was complicated.

She set the tray on a small tray table at her station and lifted a steaming plate. She purposely ignored the sheriff, but she could sense his gaze on her, and warmth crept up her neck.

"Wonderful choice," she said, setting the plate of oysters in front of a middle-aged woman who stared at the shellfish through a jeweled lorgnette like she was reading their fortunes.

"All the way from the Great Lakes," Katie added.

"But I thought Blue Points lived in salt water," the woman said.

"You must be thinking of their cousins," Katie said. A detective had to think quickly and so apparently did Harvey girls. She chanced a glance at the sheriff. He kept his head lowered but not enough to hide the upward curve of his mouth.

Train passengers were served first, and most locals knew not to drop in during certain hours. For that reason she purposely kept him waiting until everyone else had been served before placing the plate of roast beef before him. He should know better than to arrive during her busiest time.

Though the other patrons were now on dessert, Katie's table was still working on the main dish. That's because the unpleasant man with the bald head and yellow teeth insisted he'd ordered chicken. His checkered coat pegged him as a traveling salesman. She couldn't imagine what wares he hawked. Probably coffins or something equally as dour.

"Eat the blasted fish," she muttered under her breath after unsuccessfully trying to reason with him. The only way he would get his right order was if she grabbed the chicken away from the woman who kept declaring her "fish" delicious.

Remembering the number one rule of the house, however, she did smile, for all the good it did her. The unhappy diner scowled back. By the time the travelers rose from their seats to board the train, Katie was ready to call it a day.

The sheriff was the last to leave the table. He stood lazily, tugged on his hat, and leaned closer. "It seems you're a better detective than you are a waitress," he said, his voice low in her ear. Reaching into his vest, he produced a manila folder. "Thought you might like to see this."

He held it so she could read the name *Harvey* written on it. She stared at him with narrowed eyes, not knowing what to think. "Does this mean we're partners?"

"Depends," he said, his voice as noncommittal as his expression.

"On what?"

"Whether you agree to do things my way."

"Over my dead —"

He stopped her with a shake of his finger. "My town. My rules."

"You can take your rules and —"

Pickens called out. "Meeting in the kitchen."

She glanced over her shoulder. "I'll be right there." She turned back to the sheriff.

He arched an eyebrow. "You were saying?" He dangled the folder in front of her and made no effort to hide his look of triumph. He knew how badly she wanted that folder. What he didn't know was how far she would go to get it.

Without warning she snatched the folder out of his hands and ran. Racing out of the breakfast room, across the hall, and through the formal dining room, she ducked into the kitchen and peered through the open pass-through. He didn't see her, but she could see him. He hadn't moved from where she'd left him. Only his profile was visible, but it sure did look like a smile on his face. Now, wasn't that the oddest thing?

During the afternoon lull Katie slipped outside. She found a shady spot next to the building where she couldn't be seen and opened the file.

Handwritten notes contained details about the crime scene, the bodies, and timeline. Whitman's masculine writing was large and bold and easy to read. A list of people interviewed was included, along with notations of significant information. All restaurant workers had been questioned, even some who no longer worked there. Local diners had also been queried. So had the guests who attended the party where Priscilla played the piano.

Missing from the information was his personal relationship with Ginger. Mary-Lou told her the two were on friendly terms and that Ginger often took supper to his office. Was there more to it than that?

His records were precise but contained nothing she didn't already know, and that worried her. Providing pointless, useless, or false information was an old spy tactic and one she'd used herself on occasion in an effort to earn someone's trust. Was that what Whitman had done?

She didn't want to think it, but he'd made it clear from the start that he had no intention of working with a Pinkerton operative. Then all of a sudden he handed her his file. She had every right to be suspicious.

The smile spotted on his face earlier might have had a more sinister meaning. Perhaps she'd been too hasty in disregarding him as a suspect.

She tucked the file behind her apron and returned to the restaurant. Sometimes she hated her job. . . .

CHAPTER 20

As Katie got ready for bed that night, she found a note pinned to her pillow. The note read simply *I no who did it.*

Katie glanced across the room. Luckily Mary-Lou was so intent on counting brush-strokes, she didn't notice the note. Not a day went by that her roommate didn't give her hair the recommended hundred strokes. "Forty-five, forty-six . . ."

Katie focused her attention back on the note. Someone had gone to a lot of trouble to cut words out of a newspaper. That meant that same someone hadn't wanted to take a chance on being identified through handwriting.

That took the Harvey girls off the hook. They weren't allowed to write down orders, so the likeliness of her recognizing any of their handwriting was remote.

Chef Gassy jotted down everything in French, but his chicken scrawl would be recognizable even in English. The loud-mouthed man hardly seemed like the type to sneak around. Even in her room she could track his every move by the banging of pots and pans or his raised voice from the floor below. Still, she couldn't discount him.

Nor could she discount Culpepper, who signed checks in block letters rather than Spencerian script, the standard writing style taught in schools.

The misspelled word suggested he or she had little education, but then that was true for almost everyone who worked there. Or possibly the note writer hadn't been able to find the word *know*. On the other hand, maybe the misspelled word was a deliberate attempt to confuse matters.

Who could have left such a note? And why? Had someone seen through her disguise? But how? And more important, who?

Still pondering these questions an hour later, she stared out the window of the dark room. She envied Mary-Lou's ability to fall asleep the minute her head hit the pillow. Katie couldn't have asked for a more accommodating roommate.

She was so deep in thought she almost missed the movement below her window.

Someone was sneaking around the building.

The white ghostlike image wasn't Charley, that was for sure.

She pulled off her nightgown and quickly dressed in a skirt and shirtwaist kept handy for just such an emergency.

The door squeaked as she opened it, but Mary-Lou didn't move. Closing the door softly, Katie hurried along the hall and down the stairs. The kitchen was quiet, but not wanting to take a chance that someone might see her, she walked through the breakfast room and grabbed a spoon off one of the tables.

After unlocking the main entrance, she stepped outside. Spook Cat greeted her with a mew and rubbed against her skirt as she stooped to insert the spoon in the threshold.

Earlier she'd set out a bowl of milk, and the tom had lapped it up hungrily. Now, seeing that she had no such treat, he soon lost interest and strutted away with what seemed to Katie a disgusted grunt.

"Ha. So that's how you are?" she muttered. "Ingrate!"

Straightening, she glanced up and down the platform. The steel tracks gleamed in the moonlight like two knife blades coming to a point in the distance. The thought made her shudder. She pulled the door shut, and just as she'd hoped, the spoon kept it from closing all the way.

She pulled out her gun before walking the distance to the side of the building. The lingering smell of food grew stronger as she made her way along the alley. The yellow glow of a full moon poured down the side of the Harvey House like melted butter.

Since working at the restaurant, everything seemed to have taken on a food-like quality.

The night air felt cool. Tugging the shawl tight around her shoulders with one hand, she held her gun with the other. Just as she reached the corner of the building an iron-like clamp encased her arm.

Startled, she cried out.

"Shh. Do you want to wake the dead?"

She recognized the hushed masculine voice at once. "Sheriff!" She yanked her hand away from his. "You near scared the life out of me."

"Yeah, well try being on the business end of a gun." He pushed the barrel of her derringer sideways.

She pocketed her weapon but was reluctant to release her hold. Better keep up her guard until she knew the name of his game.

The brim of his hat shaded all but his

mouth, which he held in a straight line. He looked dangerous, all right, in a masculine sort of way. He was, in fact, the most attractive man she'd ever met, which did nothing for her peace of mind and even less for her investigation.

"What do I have to do to convince you to stay inside at night?" His voice sounded like gravel in her ear. "You're putting your life on the line."

"What are *you* doing here?"

"I asked first, but if you must know, there was some trouble in town. I was on my way home when I saw someone sneaking around. Thought I'd better check it out. I should have known it was you."

"It wasn't me. I saw someone, too." She released her gun and pulled her hand out of her pocket. "From the bedroom window."

The heat of his body warded off the chill, and she loosened her wrap.

"It's kind of late to be window watching, isn't it?" he asked.

"I was going over some things. Like the file you gave me."

"You mean the file you *stole* from me." He pushed his hat to the back of his head. "Does that mean you agree to my terms?"

She gave him an arched look. "What terms are those?"

"I don't want you running around at night by yourself."

"Is that a command or request, Sheriff?"

"It's an order," he said, and before she could object he added, "And we can drop the formalities. From now on you can call me Branch."

"Branch, huh? Never knew anyone by that name." Oddly enough it suited him. He was certainly sturdy as a tree, and his presence every bit as commanding.

"I guess that makes me one of a kind. What do I call you?"

"Katie," she said.

"Is that your real name?"

Still not 100 percent certain she could trust him, she hesitated. "My real name is Katherine Jones."

"Madison suits you better. Jones is too ordinary." Was that a compliment? She couldn't begin to guess, and she wasn't about to ask.

"So what have you found out so far?" He had dropped his harsh tone, and his low voice was a pleasant rumble in her ear. A whiff of bay rum hair tonic tickled her nose — a vast improvement over the stale cooking odors still lingering in the night air.

Considering that she'd only been in town a short while, the question was a bit premature. "Not much," she said softly. She decided to keep the mysterious note found on her pillow to herself, at least for now.

"I'm not even certain that the killer is an insider." She paused for a moment, waiting for a reaction, and when none came, continued. "One of the workers told me that some people object to the restaurant. It's possible that someone is trying to put the Harvey House out of business." According to a brief sentence in the *Gazette,* business at the restaurant had declined following both deaths.

"Anything's possible," he said. "But I've pretty much reached a dead end in that regard."

He sounded discouraged and frustrated, but it could be an act to find out if she was holding anything back.

"Abigail told me that Ginger behaved in an odd manner on the day of her death."

She felt him stiffen. "In what way?"

"She asked to change stations and seemed worried. Maybe even scared."

"Hmm. Haven't heard that before."

"See? There is an advantage to working with a female detective." She expected him to object, but instead he surprised her with a chuckle.

"I'm sure you feel the same about working with me," he said.

"It has its good points," she admitted. Especially since she liked to keep her suspects where she could keep an eye on them. "Anything I should know about the murder weapon?"

"Only that the same knife was used on both women, and it didn't match the knives in the kitchen."

That would have been her next question.

He started to say something more but instead grabbed her by the arms. "Shh."

Startled, she fought to keep her composure. He was so close that if either of them moved she feared an even more intimate touch. Holding herself perfectly still was the only sane solution.

His fingers pressed into her flesh, and his warm, sweet breath fanned her face. Her nose edged higher as did the proximity of her lips to his. She could feel the power and strength of him, and that seemed to present more of a problem for her than the intruder. A gun would handle any outside danger, but she didn't know what to do about her wildly beating heart.

"Can you see who it is?" he whispered.

Who what is?

The jingling of keys snapped her back to reality. Someone was heading their way. The moon was practically overhead, leaving only a small dark spot in which to hide.

He pressed closer, and for a split second she imagined his lips in her hair. Her breath caught, and she didn't dare exhale for fear of bridging what little space remained between them.

The footsteps grew louder, and a white, shadowy figure emerged. At first Katie thought she saw a ghost but then recognized the dorm matron. Oddly enough, Miss Thatcher was wearing — of all things — her nightgown.

The woman paused in front of the kitchen door that opened from the alley. Could she see them? For a moment Katie feared that their presence was known, but then Miss Thatcher pushed against the door and vanished inside. The door shut with a soft clicking sound, but not before Spook Cat slithered inside. Aha! So that's how the tom gained entrance. At least one mystery had been solved.

"That was close," Branch whispered into her hair. He released her arms but made no effort to move away.

His nearness was doing strange things to her. Never could she remember standing next to a man without wishing she were someone else — someone smarter, prettier, and less clumsy. Crazy as it seemed, tonight she imagined she was all those things and so much more.

"What do you suppose Miss Thatcher was doing out this late?" she whispered.

"Maybe she has a lover."

The thought of the pinched-face spinster having a beau was hard to imagine, but in the silvery moonlight, anything seemed possible.

"What do you know about her?" she asked.

"Only that she started work about a year ago," he said. He backed up just far enough that his head was now out of the shadows.

She stared up at him. Had she only imagined his lips brushing against her hair? Just the thought made her knees threaten to buckle. "I'll see if I can find out anything more," she said, her voice hoarse.

He studied her a moment but she couldn't read his expression. "You better get some shut-eye," he said. "We both should."

Nodding, she said good night. Anxious to make her escape, she ran up the alley and around the corner of the building. The gaslight in front of the railroad station lit the way. Reaching the main entrance, she removed the spoon and slipped inside.

It took a moment for her eyes to adjust to

the dark and even longer for her to catch her breath. She couldn't decide what disconcerted her more: seeing Miss Thatcher outside in her nightgown or the thought of working with Branch.

At last she made her way to the dining room exit. Reaching the stairs, she paused at the bottom to listen. The only sound she could hear was the thump-thump-thumping of her still-pounding heart.

CHAPTER 21

The note was very much on Katie's mind the next morning as she prepared her station for the breakfast rush. That and the unexpected encounter with Branch the night before.

Irritated by the way he kept intruding upon her thoughts, she forced herself to focus on Miss Thatcher. What was she doing out that late at night? In her nightgown, no less.

None of the other girls knew much about her or her background. According to Mary-Lou, Miss Thatcher took over the job from a Miss Jenkins who left the house to wed.

"She takes her responsibilities seriously and seldom leaves the premises," Mary-Lou said as they stood waiting for the gong to sound that morning. "She only leaves to go to church Sunday mornings."

"Does she have family in town?" Katie asked.

"None that I know of." Mary-Lou gave her a questioning look. "Why so interested in Miss Thatcher all of a sudden?"

"No particular reason."

She studied her roommate. Did Mary-Lou leave the puzzling message on her pillow? She didn't think so, but she couldn't afford to trust anyone. Not at this stage of the investigation. She couldn't even trust Branch, which is why she didn't tell him about the note. Pinkerton policy — trust no one until verification — had proven to be worthy advice in the past, and she wasn't taking any chances.

After the breakfast locals left, Katie ran upstairs to put on a fresh apron for the train crowd. The door to the dorm matron's room was ajar, and she paused in front of it.

Just as she reached for the knob, the door suddenly flew open and Miss Thatcher stared at her like one might regard an unwelcome salesman.

"Do you want something?"

"No, I . . . uh . . . saw your door ajar and was just about to close it."

"As you can see, I'm quite capable of closing my own door." She stepped into the hall and shut the door after her to illustrate.

"Run along now." She waved her hand like a harried parent chasing off a demanding child. "I'm sure you have work to do."

Katie nodded and scurried down the hall. Before entering her own room she glanced over her shoulder. The dorm matron hadn't moved and was watching her like a hawk spying a mouse.

That night Katie sat quietly in the dark breakfast room and waited.

Her seat gave her ample cover while still allowing a full view of the hall and stairs. She couldn't see the clock but guessed it was close to midnight. A single gaslight in the kitchen was still lit, but the employees had left for the day.

Maybe Miss Thatcher wouldn't leave the house tonight. Katie decided to give her another half hour or so to make an appearance — no more. Waitressing was hard work, and if she didn't get some sleep she'd be dead on her feet in the morning during the breakfast rush. Pickens was already on her case for yawning during lunch.

The minutes passed slowly. Shadowing was a big part of her job, and the chore she least liked. On rare occasions it paid off handsomely, like the time a suspect led her to a warehouse of stolen art. But mostly surveillance resulted in hours of boredom and little else.

She'd just about given up the wait when a creak of a floorboard alerted her. Someone was coming down the stairs.

The soft jingle of keys told her it was Miss Thatcher, though she couldn't see more than a shadowy form pass by the breakfast room entrance. A flash of filmy white indicated the dorm matron had entered the dining room and was probably heading for the kitchen.

Katie draped her blue knitted shawl over her head. Her blue skirt and shirtwaist provided the perfect combination for shadowing. Black was not a natural color in nature and stood out in the dark of night. Blue was much more suited for her purposes.

Opening the glass door leading outside, she placed a spoon in the frame. There was no sign of Spook Cat tonight, but a still-full moon bathed the landscape in silvery light and glinted off the railroad tracks.

Earlier she thought she heard gunshots in town, but now all was quiet.

The bright light was both a blessing and a curse. She could see everything, but then so could anyone else who might happen to be lurking around. *Just don't let me bump into the sheriff again.* Tonight she needed to keep her wits about her — impossible to do whenever he was around.

Peering around the corner into the alley, she waited until Miss Thatcher had reached the front of the house.

Walking between the two brick buildings, Katie was careful to stay in the shadow of the baggage room. She paused briefly in the same exact spot that she and Branch stood the previous night. She could almost feel his breath in her hair and the pressure of his hands on her arms. A shiver ran through her. Not good. Not good at all.

Shaking away the memory, she continued along the length of the alley and spotted Miss Thatcher walking down the middle of the road.

Pulling back, Katie dropped on her haunches to peer around the corner — one of the tricks taught at the Pinkerton detective school. People looked up, not down, and she was less likely to be seen close to the ground.

The lone figure was easy to spot. Miss Thatcher walked slowly but with purposeful steps, as if this particular path had been taken many times before. Again, it appeared she was wearing her nightgown. Filmy fabric flowed from her like spilled milk.

Katie shook her head in disbelief. What was the woman thinking?

Earlier the wind had kicked up and the dust made it hard to breathe, but tonight the air was still. Even nature seemed to hold its breath.

Lifting the corner of her shawl to her nose, Katie followed at a discreet distance. Some detectives covered their faces in mud so as not to be seen. She found a shawl just as effective, though nothing would adequately hide her in this bright moonlight. Her goose would be cooked should Miss Thatcher turn around, but she would just have to deal with that problem should the need arise.

The road came to a dead end ahead, but Miss Thatcher turned and crossed over the railroad tracks. Katie took cover beneath the shadow of the only tree in the area — a large cottonwood.

What was the woman doing? There was nothing here but empty fields. Could the dorm matron be meeting someone? In her nightgown?

Presently, Miss Thatcher did something completely unexpected. She raised her arms over her head and swayed back and forth like a sapling in the wind. Katie shook her head and blinked. It soon became clear that the dorm matron was dancing. Her face floated over the ruffled neck of her night-gown like a second moon — a plainer, less brilliant moon. Her eyes gleamed like polished stones. Her feet moved in a slow, dreamlike waltz. She held her arms in such a way as if dancing with a partner that only she could see. Her slender body seemed to move to the rhythm of some inner music.

Katie's brain clicked. Of course. She should have known. Miss Thatcher was sleepwalking! That would certainly explain her attire. The thought was followed by another. If she danced in her sleep, what else was she capable of doing while in slumber?

Katie tried to think of everything she'd heard or read about somnambulism, but it wasn't much. She did know that it had been blamed for many crimes, including violent ones. From Allan Pinkerton she'd learned about the strange case of French detective Robert Ledru. While investigating a crime, he'd discovered, much to his horror, that he had done the deadly deed himself while sound asleep.

Did Miss Thatcher kill Priscilla and Ginger and not even know it? Hard as it was to believe, Katie couldn't discount the possibility. Proving such a thing would be difficult if not altogether impossible.

As suddenly as Miss Thatcher had started dancing she stopped. She then cut across the field toward the Harvey House. Instead of her usual military march, tonight her movements were slow, dreamlike, as if she were being pulled by an invisible rope.

Katie followed a distance behind. She waited for Miss Thatcher to enter the house before running up the alley and around back.

She pushed against the dining room door, but it held tight. *No, no, no! Please don't let it be true. Please don't let the door be locked.*

Dropping down on hands and knees, she frantically felt on the ground and found the spoon. Someone had moved it from the doorframe. But who?

A movement made her look up. Spook Cat peered at her from behind the glass door. She groaned. Dumb cat. "Now look what you've done. See if I give you any more milk!"

Jumping to her feet, she grabbed the handle and gave it a good shake. The cat took off, but the door remained firm.

Running around the house like a dog with a bone to bury, she checked every window and door. Never before had she encountered such a fortress. During her five years as a detective, she had broken into hotel rooms, offices, private homes, and even an insane asylum, but the restaurant was locked up tighter than a miser's purse. Every window was barred. Every lock burglar proof. Fred Harvey had spared no expense in installing the most up-to-date security measures.

She had no choice but to try and wake her roommate. She searched around for something to throw and carried a handful of gravel to the street side of the house. The first stone hit the bedroom window with a ping. She waited. When Mary-Lou failed to appear, Katie tossed another stone and then another. A whole handful of pebbles later, she gave up.

Just her luck to have a roommate who slept like a rock in a well.

Pulling her shawl tight around her shoulders, she followed the narrow path between the two buildings. Her back against the brick wall, she slid to the ground.

She couldn't see the moon, but its silvery sheen made the narrow strip of sky overhead shine like satin ribbon.

Okay, God, what am I supposed to do now?

Sighing, she hugged her knees to her chest and yawned. She was tired, so tired. Her lids drifted downward. She forced her eyes open with a shake of her head.

Got to think. That's the only way she could

stay awake. Go over the facts of the case, the clues. Soon enough her thoughts turned to the note on her pillow. Who would leave such a message?

Coming up with no plausible answer, her thoughts drifted and her eyelids felt heavy as lead. She shook her head, yawned, and patted herself on the cheeks, but none of it did any good. She tried humming, but that only helped for a while.

Tired . . . she was so utterly bone-weary tired. . . .

A shadowy form appeared at the end of the alley. Heart pounding, Katie reached for her gun. Much to her horror, the holster was empty. God, no. This can't be happening. *She frantically checked her pockets, her waistband, the ground. Where was it?*

A glimpse of a moonlike face hovered over her followed by the glint of a knife. The blade flashed through the air, and Katie screamed.

CHAPTER 22

"Katie, it's me!"

Katie battled her way through the sleep-induced fog. A dark form slowly came into focus. "Sheriff? Branch? Is that you?"

"It's me, all right." Kneeling next to her, he held her by the arms and shook her gently as if to bring her to full consciousness.

"W—what happened?" she stammered.

"That's what I want to know. You sure know how to scare a fellow." He sounded both angry and relieved, like a parent whose child had narrowly escaped injury after running in front of a racing horse. "When I saw you here I thought —"

She drew in her breath.

His fingers pressed into her flesh. "Are you okay?" The concern in his voice added to her dismay. Controlling her emotions when they were at loggerheads was hard enough, but this new, gentler side of him

198

made it altogether impossible.

"Yes," she said. "I — I must have fallen asleep." What an utterly foolish thing to do. She'd spent many a night shadowing suspects and had managed to stay awake and alert without any difficulty. But never before had her job required such physically demanding work. Anyone who made a living working in a restaurant deserved the deepest respect.

He released her. "Well, you sure picked a funny place to get some shut-eye." The edge had returned to his voice, and that made it easier to control her emotions. "What are you doing here, anyway?"

"I got locked out."

"Locked out, eh? Well, you better figure out a way back inside before Miss Thatcher catches you."

"What time is it?"

"A little after one."

She groaned. Howie Howard wouldn't report to work for at least another four or five hours. Branch must really think she was an amateur now.

He lifted his gaze to the dark building behind her and shook his head. "You can't stay here." He shifted his weight. "You better come back to the house with me."

She glanced at him askew. "I — I don't

think that's a good idea."

"Why not? It's just up the road a piece. You'll be safe there."

"If my boss finds out I spent the night at a man's house, I'll lose my job."

"Oh?" His eyebrows arched. "And what boss is that? Pinkerton, Harvey, or me?"

"You're not my boss."

"No, but I'm doing a better job of watching out for you than the others."

She didn't want him watching out for her. Yet the very thought sent warm currents rushing through her. In an effort to calm her confused emotions she blew a strand of hair away from her face. "I was referring to Mr. Harvey."

He sat back on his heels. "I'm sure a proper Englishman like him would insist you spend the night at the hotel."

As tempting as a hotel sounded, the better choice was to stay where she was and pray someone let her in before Pickens or Thatcher found her. "I better wait for Howie. Maybe I can bribe him not to say anything."

Branch moved to her side and leaned his back against the building, his shoulders brushing against hers.

"W—what are you doing?"

He stretched his legs along the length of

hers and removed his hat. "Settling down for the night. Can't let my partner in crime stay here by herself." He folded his arms in front and rested his head against the brick wall.

"Oh, now we're partners."

"For the time being."

"I never agreed to your conditions."

"You will tonight if you know what's good for you."

She eyed his profile. "You should go. There's no sense us both losing sleep."

"Do you think I'll get any sleep knowing you're out here alone?"

"I'm awake now and have my gun with me." Recalling her dream, she patted her pocket, the bulky feel giving her a measure of comfort.

"That makes two of us."

She blew out her cheeks. "Are you serious? About staying?"

"Yep."

"W–would . . . would you stay if I were a man?"

"Absolutely not." After a beat he added, "Wouldn't be as much fun."

"Fun? You call this fun?" She sighed and tugged her shawl tighter.

"It's not often I get to spend the night with a pretty woman."

Heat rose up her neck, and she was grateful for the cover of night. No one had ever called her pretty. But then, he probably didn't mean it in the conventional sense. He was just being polite.

"Don't you have a wife waiting for you at home?" she asked. He never mentioned one. Nor did he wear a wedding band, but neither did he have the needy or hastily put-together look of a bachelor.

"Not married," he said.

Her heart gave a little lurch, though she had no idea why. So he wasn't married. It made no difference to her, either way.

Still, it was hard to believe that such an attractive man hadn't been snatched up by some pretty miss.

"You still haven't told me what you're doing out here," he said, breaking the silence.

"Miss Thatcher left the house again tonight, and I followed her."

"Why so interested in her? Surely you don't think that she — ?"

"I don't know what to think. But I do know one thing — she's a sleepwalker."

"A sleepwalker?" He shifted his weight, and his shoulder rubbed against hers. "Is that what she was doing last night?"

"I'm pretty sure it was."

"Well, I'll be. So what does she do when

she sleepwalks?"

"She dances."

"What?"

She described Miss Thatcher dancing beneath the silvery moon.

He shook his head. "Never knew anyone who walked in their sleep. Let alone danced."

"It's not all that rare." Recalling her nightmare, she shivered. "Some people have even committed crimes in their sleep."

"You don't say."

"It's true." She then told him about a well-known case where a man got off on a murder charge because he claimed he was sleepwalking at the time. "You don't suppose Miss Thatcher is the killer, do you?"

He rubbed his chin. "Based on the crime scene, I'm fairly convinced our killer is a man."

Momentarily distracted by the pronoun *our,* she cleared her voice. "There's more." If he was going to sit up all night with her, the least she could do to show her appreciation was to share information. She reached into her pocket for the small square of paper. "I found this pinned to my pillow."

He took the paper from her and held it up. The moonlight had grown dimmer, the shadows darker. "What does it say?"

"It says, 'I know who did it.' "

"Hmm. Why would anyone pin this to your pillow unless —"

"He or she knows I'm an operative." The thought had occurred to her, of course, and it worried her. "Far as I know, you're the only one who knows my reason for being here. Harvey doesn't even know. He thinks the detective he hired is a male working on the outside."

"Then how do you explain the note?"

"I can't."

He folded the paper. "Do you mind if I keep this?"

"I'm required to send everything to head-quarters."

"I'll give it back. I just want a chance to study it in the light."

"It won't help much. The words were cut out of a newspaper. What I don't understand is why someone went to all the trouble to write it. It doesn't really say anything."

"If we knew the answer to that, we'd know who wrote it." He tucked the paper into his vest pocket.

She moistened her lips. "The other girls told me that you and Ginger were friends."

"Guess you could say that." He fell silent for a moment. "She knew how I hated wear-ing a dinner coat, so she'd bring supper to me whenever she knew I was working late. Her invalid mother lives in Iowa, so I'd give her a little extra to send home." He blew out a ragged breath. "No one should die that young." His harsh tone grated on her ears. "I won't rest till I bring the killer to justice."

The passion in his voice sent chills down her spine. She knew that kind of passion. Understood it. He meant every word, and a feeling of profound relief washed over her. Branch Whitman wasn't guilty of anything, except perhaps in his own mind.

"We'll find him," she said, surprised that her earlier doubts had disappeared. Somehow he made her believe that anything was possible, even cracking a puzzling case.

The darkness hid all but the soft glow of his eyes, and she sensed something like a silent pledge pass between them.

For the longest while neither spoke. No spoken words were needed.

She rested her head against the brick wall. "It's so peaceful," she said, breaking the silence. It was hard to believe that two violent crimes had been committed in this very alley. She remembered thinking something similar upon visiting a battlefield years after the war had ended.

"Don't let the quiet fool you," he said, his

voice soft as velvet in her ears. "I had to break up a card game earlier when one of the men starting shooting. Even now, trouble's brewing somewhere in town. You can bet on it."

"How do you know?" she asked.

"I have faith in human nature. That's how."

Her laughter solicited a chuckle from him.

"Do you mind if I ask why you became a detective?" He gazed into her eyes. "Doesn't seem like a job a woman would cotton to."

"Actually, there's not much to tell. When I was in grade school, a friend gave me a book titled *The Revelations of a Lady Detective.* The name of the protagonist was Mrs. Pascal, and she was a widow left in financial ruin by her husband. She earned a living by solving crimes, and I was absolutely intrigued. I'd never heard of a lady detective, and I decided I wanted to be just like her. Without the widow part, of course."

She never thought she'd have the nerve to follow such a dream. Never really even took it seriously until Nathan Cole broke her heart by running off with her sister. But then she decided she had nothing to lose.

"Do you think me strange?" she asked. Lord knows, her family certainly did, even after proving successful at her job.

"Strange, no," he said. "Unusual maybe."

"My father had a fit when I told him what I wanted to do."

"I can imagine."

Actually that was an understatement. The truth was that her father threw her out of the house and told her not to come back until she had gained some sense. It wasn't long after that final argument that he had his accident and was found dead by the side of the road. Now, as always, the thought brought pangs of guilt.

"Not sure I'd want a daughter of mine chasing after criminals," he said.

"Would you feel the same if you had a son?"

"I have a son and, yes, I feel exactly the same."

His having a son surprised her. "How old is he?" she asked. "Your son."

"He'll soon be eight. His name is Andy."

"Shouldn't you be home with him?"

"I had some out-of-town business to attend to. I knew I'd be late, so I asked my housekeeper to take Andy home with her. She treats him like family."

"You're lucky to have someone you can depend on," she said.

"No argument there. After my wife died, I prayed for someone to help me care for my son, and God sent an angel."

Never had she known a man to talk so frankly about his faith, and her opinion of him went up another notch. "Your wife . . . How did she die?"

"Tornado," he said simply. "In '72."

"I'm sorry." When he offered no other details, she changed the subject. "Why did you become a lawman?"

"Not much to tell. I actually ran a freight company. Was pretty good at it, too. But that was before the tornado. The town as we knew it no longer existed, and I took whatever work I could find. When we learned the train was coming to town, Reverend Bushwell talked me into running for sheriff."

"Any regrets?" she asked.

"About being a lawman? Nope." He tilted his head to the side as he gazed at her. "You? Any regrets about becoming an operative?"

Regrets? Some, but if given the same choice she would do it all over again. "If I hadn't become a detective I don't know what I would have done."

"That's easy," he said. "You'd be married with a passel of kids tugging on your apron strings."

The picture he drew in her mind was no

different from what she had once envisioned for herself. She had been so certain that was God's plan for her, especially after falling in love with Nathan, but that turned out not to be true.

"I like my job," she said, "but since the train has reached most major towns, it's getting harder."

"Harder how?"

"Outlaws know we can move around quicker, and they're getting better at hiding their tracks."

He shifted his weight and crossed his ankles. "I guess we just have to get better at what we do."

She sighed. Given the rudimentary tools of her trade, it appeared at times that criminals had the upper hand. "What if we don't find the killer?" It was the first time she expressed that worry out loud.

He covered her hand with his own, and a slow but steady warmth inched up her arm. "If he's still in town, we'll find him," he said.

His confidence stoked her own. "I just hope we do it before he kills again."

"We will," he whispered with a squeeze of her hand. "We will."

That did a lot for her peace of mind but nothing for her heavy eyelids. She stifled a yawn.

"Hope it's not the company," he said in a low, soothing voice.

Yes, it was the company. For oddly, she felt safe and secure with him, like a baby in a cradle. Never had she felt like that with anyone. Not even Nathan.

He released her hand and drew her close, his embrace warm and inviting. The battle to stay awake was lost the moment her head landed on his strong, broad shoulder.

Chapter 23

Branch reached the cemetery early that morning and reined in his horse. "Whoa, boy."

A slight breeze blew across the prairie, and fluffy white clouds played hide-and-seek with a dazzlingly bright sun. He dismounted and tethered his horse to the weathered fence.

Recent talk about Andy's birthday brought him here today. At least that's what he wanted to believe. He didn't want to think that spending the night with Katie — holding her in his arms while she slept — had anything to do with his sudden urge to visit his wife's grave.

Reaching Hannah's burial place, he dropped down on one knee and laid a single rose against the headstone. A white rose . . . her favorite.

Eight years she'd been gone. Sometimes it seemed like only yesterday. Today, it seemed like a lifetime ago.

In years past, he had only to kneel by Hannah's grave for a vision of her to come to mind. Lately, though, the vision had grown dimmer.

Today, another image took her place, an image of pretty red hair, deep, expressive eyes, and a freckled, pert nose.

He shook his head in dismay. It wasn't right to stand at the grave of his wife while thinking of another woman. Not right at all. But he couldn't seem to help himself. Nor could he help recalling the feel of Katie's head on his shoulder. Or forget her sweet, delicate fragrance — a cross between lilacs and freshly mowed grass — and both tantalized his senses like springtime.

He rubbed his forehead. He was tired, and his body ached from sitting on the ground all night. The Harvey cook hadn't arrived at the house to bake the bread for breakfast until after 5:00 a.m.

The poor man practically had heart failure when Branch approached him in the wee hours of the morn.

After Katie was safely inside, he'd ridden the short distance home but was only able to get three hours of shut-eye before his son woke him and the smell of freshly brewed coffee coaxed him out of bed.

No wonder he wasn't thinking straight. In his youth he could stay up all night and still put in a good day's work, but those days were long gone.

A rabbit hopped past, bringing him out of his reverie. With a guilty start, he forced himself to focus on his wife's headstone.

Our boy's doing good, Hannah. Real good. Such a handsome fella and smart as a whip. You'd be right proud of him.

He remained on his knee for several minutes before pushing to his feet. Hannah no longer felt close. Worse, he couldn't bring her face to mind. The loss of a loved one was never about one death, but many.

Today, he had yet another loss to mourn.

He turned to leave, but something made him stop. Though it was still early, he wasn't the only one visiting the cemetery that day. Normally, he wouldn't have paid any heed to the stranger. Today he paid close attention to the man who stood in front of the grave of Andy's real mother.

Normally, he wouldn't think of disturbing another mourner. People came here to grieve, not socialize, but he was tempted to ask the man what he was doing there. Why so much interest in the grave of a woman who died nearly eight years ago?

Still curious about the stranger, he peered

across the grave-studded grass from beneath the lowered brim of his hat. Minutes passed. The man remained in front of Dorothy Clayborn's grave site, so this was no passing interest.

But who?

The stranger finally donned his hat and stepped back. After a moment he walked away.

"Excuse me, sir!"

The man turned and waited for Branch to catch up to him, an inquisitive expression on his face. He had a full-grown beard that made him look older from a distance than he actually was. In reality, he was probably closer to Branch's thirty-three years.

He looked vaguely familiar, mostly around the eyes, but Branch couldn't think where they might have met, if indeed, they had.

"I noticed you at that grave. I hope you don't mind my asking, but did you know her? Did you know Dorothy Clayborn?"

The man took so long to answer that at first it appeared he wouldn't. Finally he gave a slight nod. "I knew her," he said. "She was my wife."

Shock shot through Branch like a bullet, and his jaw slackened. Hackles rose at the back of his neck, and suddenly he couldn't breathe. *God, no! Don't let it be true.*

■ ■ ■ ■

"Gable?" he asked hoarsely when at last he found his voice. It couldn't be. He was seeing things. Had to be. "Gable Clayborn?"

The man looked momentarily startled before recognition crossed his face. "Branch? Is that you behind that sheriff's badge?" As if to answer his own question, he broke out in a smile. Grabbing Branch's hand, he shook it like he was priming water from a pump. "Well, what do you know? Guess you never thought to see me again."

Withdrawing his hand, Branch's initial shock gave way to disbelief. "No, never did," he managed between wooden lips. "Dorothy said you were . . . dead."

The smile vanished. "Dottie said that?"

Branch nodded. "Said you died in an accident." Heard it with his own ears.

Gable sucked in his breath. "You know what they say about a woman's fury."

Branch felt his skin crawl. For eight years he'd thought this man — Andy's true father — dead. Never once in all that time had he imagined that Dorothy had lied. Why would she say he was dead when clearly he wasn't?

"Why'd you come back?" Why now, after all this time?

"Didn't know about Dottie or the tornado. Had I known I would have come back sooner. Didn't know any of that until I arrived in town yesterday." He rubbed his hand across his bearded chin. "Calico sure does look different. Hardly recognized it. Thought I came to the wrong place by mistake."

"We pretty much had to rebuild after the tornado," Branch said, his voice hollow.

Gable shook his head. "Terrible thing."

"Yes, it was." Little did he know just how terrible.

"What are *you* doing here?" Gable asked. He then glanced at the distant grave with the single white rose. "Hannah?"

Branch's jaw tightened. "She died, too. Eleven people died that day."

"Sorry to hear that," Gable said.

Branch didn't want his sympathy. Didn't want anything from him. Hannah would still be alive had she not left the house that stormy night to deliver this man's baby.

"Where you been all these years?" Branch asked.

"Here and there," Gable said with a shrug. "Done some mining. Montana, Utah. Got me some religion." He gave a self-conscious laugh. "My preacher said I needed to come back and mend fences. That's why I'm here.

Wanted to tell Dottie I was sorry for taking off on her like that."

"You deserted her?" Is that why Dorothy said her husband was dead? Because she was too ashamed to admit that he'd simply walked off?

Gable shrugged as if it was of little consequence. "I was young and didn't know any better. Guess I was just doing what my pappy did to me."

Gable's cavalier attitude infuriated Branch. He walked out on his expectant wife and then came back years later as if nothing had happened. What kind of man would do such a thing?

"Guess you won't be staying long now that you know about Dorothy."

"Haven't made any definite plans yet, but I've got some business to attend to before I leave town."

"What kind of business?" Branch asked sharply. Any business of Gable's was suspect. The man didn't know the meaning of earning an honest living, and his get-rich schemes always led to stay-poor results.

"Some legal stuff." Gable scratched the side of his neck. "Maybe you can help me. Do you know what happened to the infant?"

Branch stared at him. He wanted Gable gone. The sooner, the better. The blood pumping through his veins felt like ice water one moment and wildfire the next. "What do you think happened?"

"Yeah, well here's the thing. Before he died, Dottie's father set aside a substantial sum of money in trust for the child. If something happened to his grandchild, the money reverts to the living parent, which" — he cleared his voice — "is me. The problem is, I need proof of the child's death before I can claim the money."

Branch felt his temper rise. The man just found out his wife was dead, and his first thought was for his own gain. No surprise there.

"Don't see how I can help," Branch said, hiding his contempt behind a neutral tone.

"I was hoping you'd know how I can get hold of proof of death."

Branch frowned. "Proof of death?"

"Dottie was carrying our child, and I need something that says the infant died with her."

Branch tightened his hands into fists by his side. Gable didn't know the baby arrived before the tornado hit, and Branch had no intention of setting him straight.

"Far as I know no official record exists," he said. Marriages and deaths were some-times recorded at the county office, but not always. Following the chaos left by the tornado, he doubted any vital statistics made it into official records.

A look of annoyance crossed Gable's face. "Yeah, I'm sure you're right. But I was hoping I could get a doctor or someone to sign a statement. You know, saying what happened and all."

" 'Fraid you're out of luck there. Dr. Harris died five years ago."

"Really? That's a shame." He cleared his throat. "Maybe you can sign."

"What?"

"It's got to be someone in authority. You're the sheriff. You knew Dottie. You knew she was carrying a child when she died. Who better than you to sign?"

Branch stiffened. Shock quickly gave way to fury. Suddenly it seemed like there wasn't enough air to breathe in the whole of Kansas. Sign a statement that Andy was dead? He could no sooner do that than deny God's existence.

"I can't talk about this right now." He nodded at his wife's grave. "Gotta go. Got work to do." He turned and stalked away but not quick enough.

"Are you saying you won't help me?" Gable called after him.

Branch stopped midstep, his back ramrod

straight and throat dry as kindling wood. Before him lay Dorothy's grave. Dorothy, Andy's real mother. Behind was the resting place of his wife, Hannah, who had in her own special way given Andy life, too.

He turned to the one man in the world he didn't want to face. Out of respect for the two deceased women, he kept his voice low but made no effort to hide his contempt. "You left her. You left your wife." Not trusting himself to say more, he walked away with quick, angry steps.

This time Gable let him go without comment.

Mounting his horse, Branch gripped the reins until his fingers turned white. From atop his saddle he could still see Gable watching him, their gazes colliding like sabers over the graves of their wives.

What a nightmare! One moment everything was fine and the next . . . It was like living through the tornado all over again.

Pressing his legs against his horse's side, Branch rode away. *God, why did You let this happen? Why now, God, why now?*

Where money was concerned Gable was like a hound dog. He wouldn't give up until he got what he came for. The only way to get rid of him was to sign the statement he asked for claiming Andy was dead. That meant the money would go to Andy's ne'er-do-well father. Dorothy would no doubt turn over in her grave.

Still, he was tempted to do what Gable asked of him. Once the man had the money in hand, he would no doubt leave and never come back. Oh, yes, he was tempted.

But how in good conscience could he do such a thing? How in the name of Sam Hill could he not?

CHAPTER 24

Katie was assigned to work the counter that morning, and the first customer of the day was an old woman with a cane. She was a regular, but this was the first Katie had served her. The woman seemed to have difficulty seating herself on a stool.

"Would you be more comfortable at a table?" Katie asked.

"That's all right, dearie. I like sitting here at the counter. If my Harry was alive today, this is where he would sit. And he'd want what I want."

"Starting with a cup of hot coffee, the stronger, the better. Am I right?"

The woman laughed. She wore her age like a shawl, hugging her years to her with a frown and throwing them off with a smile. "Indeed you are. How did you know?"

"Only serious coffee drinkers sit at the counter." Katie hadn't been on the job long, but already she'd observed certain behavior patterns among some of the customers.

The widow stretched her hand across the counter. "You can call me Mrs. Bracegirdle."

Katie took the small, parched hand in her own and gave it a gentle shake before releasing it. "My name is Katie."

"Nice meeting you, Katie."

"You, too. You're all dressed up. It must be a special occasion."

Mrs. Bracegirdle's bright purple dress was an eye-opener, as was her matching boat-shaped hat. The feathers bowed with each nod of her head like actors on a stage.

The worn face caved in with a near toothless smile. "Dearie, when you're my age, every day is special."

Katie laughed as she turned to the coffee urn. After filling a cup, she placed it on the counter. "You're here early."

Mrs. Bracegirdle laid her cane on the empty stool next to her. "Well, who can sleep with all that racket?"

"Racket?"

Mrs. Bracegirdle leaned over the counter and lowered her voice. "There's this cat who sings opera. *Rigoletto,* I think, though I'm no expert. My husband and I traveled abroad before the war, and we saw several operas, but it's been years. All I can tell you is that the cat is a soprano."

"It's probably not a *tom*cat, then," Katie said.

Mrs. Bracegirdle laughed. "Probably not."

The woman might be off her rocker, but Katie couldn't help but like her. "We have a cat problem, too. His name is Spook Cat, and he sneaks in at night and eats pie. He also locked me out."

"Is that so? Hmm. Maybe we should get your cat and mine together."

"Only if your cat promises not to teach ours opera."

Mrs. Bracegirdle's thin shoulders shook with girlish giggles and the feathers curtsied. She picked up the bill of fare and perused it. "I told Branch about the cat, but I don't think he believes me."

At mention of Branch's name Katie's heart took an unexpected leap. *Oh no you don't. You're not going to read more into last night than was there.* Branch stayed with her simply because he didn't want another murder to solve. That was the reason. The *only* reason.

The thought did little to relieve her mind. Twice she'd fallen in love with men who didn't seem to know she was alive. One ended up with her best friend and the other married her more attractive sister. Not only did that bring her more heartache than she thought possible, it made her question her own worth. At least as a Pinkerton detective she was judged on merit and not appearances.

Mrs. Bracegirdle closed the menu. "I think I'll have my usual flapjacks with sausage," she said.

Katie called the order to the kitchen and turned back to her customer.

Mrs. Bracegirdle took a sip of her coffee, her rheumy eyes studying Katie. "I've known him all his life, you know."

"I'm sorry. Who have you known?"

"Why, Branch, of course."

"Oh." This time Katie's heart stayed in place, but her breath caught in her throat.

"Darling boy, he was. Always had a big smile. And so polite. Terrible thing what happened."

"What happened?" Katie hated herself for asking, but her detective instincts wouldn't let a statement like that go unchallenged. Nor would her womanly curiosity.

"The tornado. Ripped this town in two and killed almost a dozen people, including Branch's wife."

"How awful," Katie murmured, not letting on that she knew about his wife. Better to let the old woman talk. Branch had seemed reluctant to go into details. Apparently, it still hurt.

"Awful doesn't begin to describe it. It happened in '70 or '71." She thought a moment. "No, it has to be '72. Come to think of it, Friday will be the eight-year anniversary."

She shook her head. "My, where does the time go? I swear, when you get to be my age the days go by in twos and threes."

"What was his wife like?" Katie asked, the question seeming to pop out of her.

"Hannah Whitman?" The woman thought a moment. "She was a real beauty, that one, and always had a kind word for everyone."

Katie felt her spirits drop. Of course his wife had been a beauty. Would a man like Branch Whitman marry a woman who wasn't? She doubted it.

"Patches and logs," Chef Gassy yelled out from the window behind her, his accent turning the simple phrase into an unappetizing *ashes and loo*.

Katie turned and lifted the plate of flapjacks and sausages from the pass-through. "Here you go," she said, setting it in front of Mrs. Bracegirdle.

The woman reached for the syrup and continued the conversation without pause. "He hasn't even looked at another woman since his wife died. If you ask me, it's a crying shame. A handsome man like that going to waste."

"He must have loved her very much," Katie said.

"Yes, he did. We all did."

Katie wanted to hear more. A lot more. But the train rumbled into the station early, rattling dishes and windows and causing a flurry of activity around her.

Branch had planned to go straight to his office following his visit to the cemetery. Instead he rode his horse to the Calico Community Church.

Never before had he felt it necessary to seek the Reverend Bushwell's counsel. Normally, he worked things out for himself, seeking God's help through prayer. That's how he'd gotten through Hannah's death. That's how he'd gotten through a lot of problems. But today God seemed far away, leaving him to feel like a drowning man about to go under for the third time.

Reverend Bushwell greeted him with outstretched hand. "What brings you here today?" An older man with long white sideburns, he peered through pince-nez eyeglasses with an inquiring look. "Something serious, I see."

Branch nodded as he shook the minister's hand. "I'm afraid it is serious. Is this a good time?"

"It's always a good time to see you. Come in, come in." He motioned Branch inside with a wave of his hand.

Branch followed him into the cool interior of the church. They entered a small office and library located to the left of the narthex.

"Have a seat."

Branch lowered his frame onto the indicated chair, and the leather cushion whooshed beneath his weight. Instead of taking his place behind the desk, Bushwell drew a chair next to Branch's and sat.

"So what's put that frown on your face? Andy okay?"

"Andy's fine. At least for now."

The reverend's bushy eyebrows rose. "What does that mean?"

"Gable Clayborn is alive."

Bushwell sat back in his chair. "What?"

Branch quickly told him about his early-morning encounter at the cemetery.

The reverend was momentarily speechless. Shaking his head, he finally spoke. "But his wife said he'd been in an accident and died. Sat in that very chair you're sitting in and told me as much."

"She told me the same thing. Far as I

know it's what she told everyone. She even donned widow's weeds." Branch felt a throbbing in his temple. Elbows on his lap, he rubbed his forehead with his fingers. "The truth was, he ran out on her."

The preacher clucked his tongue. "So what did he say when you told him about his son?"

Branch pulled his hands away from his face. "That's just it. I didn't tell him. I can't."

The reverend's eyebrows inched upward. "He'll find out soon enough."

"Only two people know the truth." He pinched his forehead with two fingers. It *was* only two people, wasn't it? So much confusion existed following the tornado, it still seemed like a blur. "Far as I know you and Mrs. Bracegirdle are the only two who know. I trust you to keep a confidence. Not so sure about her. She hasn't been acting herself lately. Has all kinds of illusions. I don't know if she even remembers what happened back then. You've talked to her. What do you think?"

Bushwell studied him. "I think the bigger question is whether you can live with the secret knowing what you now know."

"It's not about me. It's about what's best for Andy."

A skeptical look crossed the older man's face. "The boy will be living a lie, too. Whether or not he knows it."

"The man doesn't deserve a son." He and Hannah had tried for three years to have a child, and no amount of praying had helped. Yet God saw fit to bless a scoundrel like Clayborn. It didn't seem right. "He certainly doesn't deserve a son like Andy."

The reverend rubbed his hands together. "What about the boy? Do you ever intend to tell him about his real parents?"

"I planned on telling him when he was older. Now I'm not so sure that's a good idea."

"The truth always comes out in the end, and not always the way we want or expect."

"That's the chance I'll have to take." Branch blew out his breath. "There's more." He explained about the trust. "He wants me to sign a document that states the infant died with his mother. If I sign it, he'll get his hands on the money that rightfully belongs to Andy."

"And if you don't sign it?"

"He'll probably ask for your signature. I'm afraid that will put you in an awkward position."

"I see."

"The only way out is for me to do what

he wants and sign the blasted thing."

"Can you live with that?" the reverend asked.

"I don't see that I have a choice. With a little luck, Clayborn will leave and we'll never see him again."

"I can't tell you what to do," Bushwell said. "But I can tell you what the Bible says about living in darkness. And that darkness almost always begins with a lie."

"I didn't know Clayborn was alive." Would he have done things any differently had he known? Probably not.

"You know now," Bushwell said. "Signing that document would be signing your name to a falsehood. No one can have a relationship with God while living a lie."

"What you're asking me to do is choose between God and my son."

The reverend adjusted his glasses. "Your situation reminds me of Abraham. Remember him? As proof of his faith, God asked him to sacrifice his son, Isaac."

"If God is testing me, then I'm afraid I'm no Abraham."

"We don't always know how deep our faith is until we're put to the test."

"So you're saying I need to tell Clayborn the truth."

"What I'm saying, Branch, is the only way

231

out of this mess is to put your trust in the Lord."

Branch left the church feeling more unsettled than ever. He wasn't sure he could trust anyone with the fate of his son. God included.

CHAPTER 25

The breakfast rush over, Katie yawned as she finished cleaning her station. Culpepper sat at the end of the counter, tallying up the receipts from breakfast. Though the wind had stopped, his eyes were still watery and his nose cherry red. He couldn't have looked worse had he rolled in an onion patch, and she couldn't help but feel sorry for him.

Her body still aching from the night spent in the alley, she drained the last of the coffee from the urn into a coffeepot. Fred Harvey insisted the coffee be made fresh before each meal.

Catching a glimpse of herself in the silver urn, she held her breath. She was paler than usual from lack of sleep. Her pallor made her hair look more red, but her eyes were bright as two shiny gems.

How incredulous to think that Branch had stayed with her through the night. No one had ever done such a thing, not even when she was a child.

At age seven she became deathly ill with pneumonia. Her fever spiked, and if it hadn't been for her sisters forcing liquids down her throat, she might not have survived. She was stunned to learn later that though she was in danger of not making it through the night, her pa had gone as usual to his favorite saloon.

No wonder Branch's kind gesture had touched her like no other. But that's all it was: just a kind deed, and thinking it anything more was a waste of time.

Her thoughts scattered at the sound of Culpepper's voice.

"Fifty-eight meals in thirty minutes," he announced with a thick, frog-like voice. He sounded a bit disappointed, but that was normal for him. The record was seventy-six meals, and he lived for the day that record was broken.

Knowing the hard work involved, Katie hoped that day wouldn't come to pass until after she was long gone.

"More coffee?" she asked. "There's just a little bit left." She needed to empty the pot and make fresh.

For answer he held up his cup.

As she poured the coffee she couldn't help

but notice his fingernails. Harvey rules demanded waitresses keep fingernails clean and trimmed. Apparently, the same rules didn't apply to male employees for his nails were black with . . . what? Ink, grease, dirt? Since he lived at the boardinghouse that seemed odd.

"Are you a gardener?" she asked.

He set his cup down and reached for the sugar. "What?"

"I just asked if you like to garden."

"Not with my hay fever."

She considered other possibilities and finally decided it was probably shoe polish from dyeing his hair.

A movement outside drew her attention to the window. A distinguished-looking man stood outside talking to the train master.

Her mouth dropped open. *Oh no!* Setting the coffeepot down, she whirled about and ran all the way to the kitchen yelling, "The British are coming!"

No sooner was the code for Mr. Harvey out of her mouth than the kitchen staff sprang into action.

Chef Gassy pulled a pitcher of orange juice out of the icebox and shoved it into her hands. "Hide it!"

Katie turned quickly, and the beverage

spilled all over her apron. Mr. Harvey insisted that orange juice be freshly squeezed as needed. Any found in the icebox was a clear violation of the rules, and heads would surely roll.

Before she had time to hide the evidence, Mr. Harvey strolled into the kitchen dressed to the nines in a dark suit and top hat. He walked with the elegance of the British, but his sharp gaze was as bold and alert as any detective on the scene of a crime.

Katie froze in place. Dumping the juice into the sink was no longer an option. Fortunately, she stood behind a counter, allowing her to hold the pitcher out of sight, at least temporarily.

Harvey doffed his hat. "Good morning," he said in his clipped English accent and immediately set to work.

He wrapped a clean white handkerchief around his fingers and ran them along the cupboard doors and counters. He checked the icebox, oven, and smoker. As he worked, Katie moved clockwise around the kitchen counter, keeping herself hidden from the waist down.

Katie had heard horror stories about past inspections. Tully said he once pulled a tablecloth off a table, sending dishes flying, simply because the silverware wasn't correctly aligned.

Mr. Harvey stepped past Cissy and walked into the pantry. In addition to her duties of making salad and sandwiches for the porter, engineer, and other train crew, Cissy was required to keep the pantry in order. Now as she stood twisting the corner of her apron she looked about to burst into tears. Hoping to ease the girl's mind, Katie smiled at her, but the girl failed to respond.

Meanwhile, Katie was still stuck with the pitcher. The pantry offered a full view of the sink, so dumping the juice down the drain was out of the question.

Her gaze lit on the large kettle of pea soup simmering on the stove. With no time to spare, she lifted the lid and poured the juice into the kettle. Ignoring the look of horror on Gassy's face, she quickly hid the empty pitcher in the oven, which Harvey had already inspected, and joined the other girls.

Mr. Harvey stepped out of the pantry. "Well done," he said. Cissy, who looked like she'd been holding her breath, immediately burst into tears.

With a startled look, he handed her a clean linen handkerchief and moved away, his attention now on the line of employees.

Katie's stomach knotted. She didn't have a chance to don a clean apron like the others, and the wet orange spot now seemed the size of Texas.

Harvey spoke in a friendly tone as he stopped to talk to Tully. Mary-Lou would be next to undergo inspection and then Katie.

Just as Harvey moved away from Mary-Lou, Chef Gassy stepped directly in front of Katie, hiding her spotted apron from view. "Vould you care for some refreshment, Monsieur Harvey?" he asked.

Harvey sniffed the air. "How about some of that English pea soup? It smells especially good today."

Katie held her breath. *Dear God, not the soup. Anything but the soup . . .*

In his usual animated way, Chef Gassy tried his best to steer Harvey toward another choice, but Harvey's mind was made up. No one could talk him out of his favorite soup.

Gassy muttered something under his breath in his native tongue, but out loud he said, "Very vell. Tully, escort Monsieur Harvey to the dining room."

"No need to bother," Mr. Harvey said. "I'll eat right there." He moved to the table normally reserved for staff and pulled out a chair.

The chef's ploy worked inasmuch as Harvey seemed to have forgotten the inspection. But that offered small comfort to Katie. The owner was particular about the food, and she dreaded what he would do upon discovering his prize pea soup had been tampered with.

Meanwhile, Katie pulled off her apron and donned a clean one while the other girls scampered to make him comfortable. Tully supplied him with silverware while Mary-Lou laid a neatly folded napkin by his side.

Looking almost as green as the soup he spooned into a bowl, Chef Gassy glared at Katie.

The chef's demeanor caught Mary-Lou's attention, and she shot a questioning look at Katie.

Katie held up her dirty apron and motioned to the soup pot.

Mary-Lou's mouth dropped open, and a look of horror crossed her face.

Chef Gassy set the bowl in front of Mr. Harvey and stepped back as if expecting the soup to explode.

"Ah, my favorite," Harvey said.

The Englishman picked up his spoon, and Katie's stomach clenched. Everyone watched as Mr. Harvey dipped the spoon into the soup, blew on it gently, and lifted it to his mouth.

He closed his eyes and smacked his lips. An eternity passed, or so it seemed, before his eyes opened and a puzzled expression fleeted across his face. He slanted his head, scooped up another spoonful, and again brought it to his mouth.

Finally, he set his spoon down and drew the napkin to his lips. "This is the best soup I ever tasted."

Air rushed from Katie's lungs, and Chef Gassy broke into a grin that practically reached his ears. Winking at Katie, he wrung his hands together like a mad scientist conducting an experiment.

"It's a special recipe all the vay from France."

"Is that so?" Mr. Harvey looked impressed. "I never thought to say this, but the French certainly know how to make English pea soup."

CHAPTER 26

Branch didn't see hide nor hair of Gable for three days. Where he was staying Branch had no idea. He certainly wasn't at the hotel or boardinghouse. Maybe he'd left town. Now wouldn't *that* be an answer to his prayers?

Still, it was with grave concern that he walked to the Harvey House dining room late that Friday afternoon with his young son by his side.

They were early, and he planned it that way. The train wasn't due in for another hour or more. He hoped that would work in his favor and the staff would allow him to celebrate his son's birthday without having to don a straitjacket.

A quick glance around relieved his mind. No sign of Gable. The restaurant was empty except for employees still putting the finishing touches on tables already set with spotless white cloths and vases of fresh flowers.

241

His gaze immediately lit on Katie, talking to the others in back of the room.

Oddly enough, the mere sight of her made him forget his worries about Gable, and he relaxed for the first time in days. She looked every bit as soft and desirable today as she had the night he held her in his arms. He had a hard time taking his gaze off her.

Spotting him, she broke away from the small group and hurried over to where he and Andy stood. She greeted him warmly, but her pretty smile was so intriguing he could only nod in response.

"And this must be Andy," she continued. Taking Andy's hand in hers, she gave it a gentle shake. "How do you do? My name is Miss Katie." She released his son's hand and straightened. "So what's the occasion?"

Normally shy in front of strangers, Andy looked almost as intrigued by the redheaded woman as Branch was. Like father, like son.

"It's my birthday," Andy said, grinning.

"Your birthday!" Katie made it sound like the day should be declared a national holiday. "Well, you've come to the right place to celebrate. How old are you, Andy?"

"I'm eight."

"Oh my." She pressed her hands together. "Such a big boy for eight."

Actually, Andy was small for his age,

mainly because he was such a picky eater. He practically drove Miss Chloe up the wall with his poor eating habits.

Katie tapped her finger on her chin as she studied him. "An important occasion like this requires a certain dress. But not to worry. I have the perfect coat for you."

Branch opened his mouth to protest when he realized she was addressing his son.

She led the boy over to the coatrack and pulled out the shortest coat there. "It might be a tad big, but I think it will do."

The coat practically buried Andy. It reached his knees, and the sleeves were way too long, but he didn't seem to notice as he gazed into the mirror. Instead, a slow grin inched across his face.

The smile did Branch's heart good. Not only did the boy tend to be shy around strangers, he was serious minded with a lot of unfounded fears. Yet, here he was all smiles for a woman he'd only just met.

"Here, let me fix your sleeves." She rolled the cuffs to his elbows and straightened his collar. Branch was so busy watching his son's delighted face he failed to notice that her attention was now on him.

"It's your turn," she said, pulling another coat off a wooden peg.

"I'm not wearing —"

"But you have to, Pa," Andy said. "It's my birthday."

Something flickered in the depths of Katie's eyes. "You were saying?"

Branch hesitated. His choice was to stand up for male emancipation or give in like a lassoed calf.

She had him over a barrel, and he couldn't do a thing about it — except to disappoint his son. That he would never do, especially on his birthday. Feigning good humor, Branch turned and slipped his arms through the sleeves of the coat she held up for him.

The coat was ridiculously small, and he stood like a scarecrow with his arms spread out.

Andy giggled in delight. "Mine's too big and yours is too little," he said. "Isn't that funny?"

"Hilarious," Branch muttered.

Katie looked like she was trying to keep a straight face. "I think you both look like codfish." As an aside to Andy she said, "That's restaurant talk for a well-dressed diner."

"I feel more like a sardine packed in a can," Branch grumbled.

This time Andy laughed so loud the other three Harvey girls stopped what they were doing to stare.

"Come along and I'll show you to your table," Katie said, acting all businesslike for her coworkers' benefit. In a softer voice for Branch's ears only, she asked, "Would you rather another waitress serve you?"

"I think Andy would object to that."

"And you? Would you object?"

His gaze met hers, and something snapped between — a spark of lightning. "Should I?"

"Most definitely." She pulled out a chair and held it for Andy. She then handed out bills of fare, one for him and one for Andy.

"I'll have coffee," Branch said.

"One cup of joe coming up. And what about you, young man? Would you like some of our splendiferous moo juice?"

Andy frowned. "What's moo juice?"

"Why, it's milk, of course."

Andy giggled, his shoulders shaking with delight. He was obviously having the time of his life.

"Tonight's special is twelve alive in a shell." She lowered her voice to a conspirator's whisper. "Those are oysters, and they're not the friendly type." Louder she said, "But I recommend Bossy in the bowl. . . ." Covering her mouth with her hand as if telling a secret, she interpreted. "That's beef stew." She cited several other

245

options.

Andy hung on to her every word as she explained the meaning of the strange lingo.

At one point his eyes almost popped out of his head. "Are those real bullets?"

She laughed. "Bullets are what we call baked beans."

"Sounds good to me," Branch said.

Andy's head bobbed up and down. "I want some bullets, too."

"Two orders of beef on the hoof and bullets coming up," she said as she headed for the kitchen.

"And don't forget my moo juice," Andy called after her.

Branch was so busy watching his son's bright face he failed to notice that someone else had entered the dining room.

"Fancy meeting you here."

Gable's voice sent chills down Branch's spine. Through sheer determination he was able to manage a polite nod. The man had shaved off his beard, and his hair was now neatly trimmed. His appearance was greatly improved, but then, so was his resemblance to Andy. They had the same color hair and similar brown eyes.

Icy fingers clutched Branch's heart, and his muscles tightened. "I thought you'd left town."

"Nope. Just checking out the old home-stead. Nothing left of the place. The current owners have rebuilt. Dottie would have loved the new house."

Branch clenched his hands tight. He had no patience with men who deserted their families. In his book, that meant Gable had no right talking about his wife's likes and dislikes. He had no right mentioning her name at all.

Gable's gaze fell on Andy. "And who do we have here?"

"This is my son, Andy." A knifelike pain shot through his middle as Gable leaned forward to shake Andy's hand.

"Your son, eh?"

"It's my birthday," Andy said with a bright smile.

"Is that so? How old are you?"

"I'm eight."

"Eight, huh? Well, happy birthday."

If Gable thought there was anything significant about Andy's age it didn't show. Instead he turned back to Branch. "Didn't know you had a son."

Branch masked his inner turmoil behind a cool, calm voice. "I guess you didn't stick around long enough to find out."

"Guess not." Gable rubbed his chin. "Do you mind if I join you?"

Branch clamped down on his jaw. He didn't want Gable anywhere near Andy. Didn't want him in the same town as Andy. But there really was no way to turn down his request without making a scene.

He gave a curt nod, but before Gable took a seat, Katie suddenly appeared and stopped him with a hand to his arm. "I'm sorry, sir. These seats are reserved." Her smile satisfied Harvey's requirements but was far from the smile Branch had come to know.

Gable frowned. "Reserved?"

She nodded. "The train will be in shortly. If you like, I can show you to another table."

"That's all right. I'll get something to eat at the hotel." He glanced at Branch. "See you around." And just like that he left.

Branch's body sagged against the back of his chair. Crazy as it sounded, he had a mind to hug Katie for sending Gable away. She couldn't possibly know what she'd done. Or how grateful he was. Still, he decided it best to say nothing. It would only make that curious mind of hers go to work, and that's the last thing he needed.

Katie lifted a glass of milk from her tray and set it on the table in front of Andy. "Moo juice for you," she said. "And our very special beef on the hoof and bullets." She then set two plates on the table.

248

"Smells good," Branch said.

Andy waited for Branch to give a quick blessing before picking up his glass. He took a big gulp then set to work on his meal.

Branch was surprised to see Andy diving into his food with such enthusiasm. Miss Chloe should see him now. On second thought, maybe not. She would only take the boy's sudden interest in food as an affront to her cooking.

Katie moved to Branch's side, and he caught a faint smell of perfume. It wasn't as strong as when he held her in his arms, but still pleasant. "And a joe for you," she said. As she poured his coffee, she whispered, "Getting rid of your unwanted guest was my way of thanking you for the other night."

He sat back to look at her. "How did you know?" he mouthed.

But already she had moved away and was fussing over Andy.

CHAPTER 27

That night like clockwork Miss Thatcher left the house. It was after eleven. Watching from the dark shadows of the breakfast room, Katie counted to ten before racing up the stairs to the dorm matron's room.

The curtains fluttered in the soft breeze, allowing just enough gas streetlight into the room to locate the box of safety matches on the nightstand. After lighting the kerosene lamp, she glanced around.

The room was almost identical to the one she shared with Mary-Lou with one exception: it had only a single bed. Other than the rumpled blankets, the room seemed strangely vacant. Whereas the other bedrooms were decorated with photographs, vases of flowers, books, and other keepsakes, this room was as devoid of personality as its occupant.

She started her search with the large oak bureau, checking each drawer one by one.

The expected corsets, bloomers, and stockings were folded and neatly stacked. She found nothing of a personal nature except clothes.

Next she flung open the paneled wardrobe doors. Plain black and gray dresses hung from wooden pegs. A pair of high-button shoes stood side by side at the foot of the bureau, the pointed toes dating them back to the War between the States. On top, band boxes held an assortment of hats, most of them sadly out of style. The room's main purpose seemed to be storing articles from the past, much like a museum.

She closed the doors and crossed to the steamer trunk beneath the windowsill. The flat-top traveling chest was unlocked. She raised the lid, releasing the faint smell of cedar. Folded neatly inside was a wedding gown.

The unexpected find made her pause for a moment before reaching inside to touch the beautiful satin bodice. The top was embroidered with imitation pearls and edged in delicate lace. The skirt was full and meant to be worn over a hoopskirt. That dated the gown back to the war years.

A vision of Miss Thatcher dancing beneath the moonlight flashed through her mind. Only this time it was a younger, happier bride she pictured, waltzing in the arms of a handsome groom.

So what happened? Why the dress and no husband? Why did Miss Thatcher's wedding never take place? Had her fiancé died in the war like so many other young men? Possibly.

Katie sighed. It seemed she had more in common with the strange dorm matron than she would have guessed. Dreams of her own wedding had never materialized, though she'd not been so close as to order a dress. God had made it clear that He had other plans for her life, and none involved husband and children, no matter how much she'd wished otherwise.

Why, oh why, did she always fall in love with men who could never love her back? Matthew Spacey had been the first. Then Nathan and now Branch . . .

Alarmed by the unexpected thought, she gulped. She didn't mean Branch. She'd learned her lesson in the past and wouldn't make the same mistake again. He was still in love with his wife. Even if he wasn't, he would never fall for a graceless redheaded woman — a Pinkerton detective, no less. No, falling in love with Branch was strictly out of the question.

The lamplight hissed and flickered, bringing her out of her reverie. She would have to hurry to finish her search before the lamp ran out of fuel or the room's inhabitant returned.

She reached into the trunk. Hidden among the satiny folds was what looked like a diary. She lifted the leather-bound book and examined it by the lamp's dim light. A tiny gold lock prevented her from skimming the pages.

Returning the diary to the chest, she lowered the lid and stood. Hands at her waist, she glanced around the room before checking under the bed. Finding nothing of interest, she turned off the light and quickly left the room.

One day later, Branch walked into the breakfast room, and Katie's heart soared. It was early, and the railroad workers had yet to arrive.

He paused at the entrance, a newspaper tucked under his arm. His gaze swept the room before zeroing in on her and bringing a flush to her face.

He then made a beeline for the counter. No smiles today. Instead he looked serious as a signpost. He appeared not only disgruntled but tired. The fine lines in his forehead and around his eyes suggested he'd had little or no sleep.

He straddled a stool, and she pulled a clean cup and saucer out from under the counter. "You're up and about early."

He laid the newspaper on the counter and reached into his vest pocket. "You know what they say about the early bird." He slid something across the counter. It was the note found on her pillow. The note reminded her that she had yet to return the Harvey file to him.

She filled his cup and set it in front of him, puzzled by both his appearance and remote eyes. Instead of his usual open stance he sat hunched over as if to keep everything in — or maybe everything out.

"Getting up early didn't do much for the worm," she said, hoping to tease a smile out of him. When none came, she picked up the note and slipped it into her pocket.

"In that case, I'll settle for the usual," he said. "Apple pie."

Thinking he was kidding, she placed her hand at her waist. "For breakfast?" She was putting on a good show, and anyone watching would never guess how fast her heart was beating beneath her bibbed apron.

He shrugged. "I believe in starting my day with dessert." His congenial voice hardly seemed to go with his guarded expression.

"And you owe me two pieces, remember?"

"I remember," she said, and she filled his cup. Instead of pie, she'd served him and his son cake, complete with a candle.

She set the coffeepot down. "Anything?" she whispered, patting her pocket.

He shook his head. It was no more than she expected. Still, she couldn't help but feel disappointed.

He sipped his coffee as he watched her. "The other night . . . How did you know to get rid of my unwanted company?"

"Are you talking about Mr. Gable Jacob Clayborn?"

Branch set his cup down. "Now looka there. The lady makes it her business to find out the man's full name." His eyes narrowed. "How did you know he wasn't welcome at my table? Don't tell me your Pinkerton bosses taught you to read minds."

"A woman knows these things." She'd have to be blind not to have seen the look on Branch's face as the two men talked.

"Is that so?" He took another sip of coffee, but his gaze remained on Katie. Oddly enough, it was as if only the two of them were in the restaurant. Every word and look they exchanged held multiple meanings.

"What else do you know about him?"

It pleased her that he thought she knew

more, and she accepted it as a compliment to her investigative skills. "Mr. Gable is a widower and served time in prison for embezzlement."

Branch jerked his hand away from his cup. "Embezzlement?"

She nodded. The Pinkerton agency collected newspaper articles from around the country for the sole purpose of keeping track of criminals. Names were then cross-referenced with crimes and filed away for easy retrieval. It wasn't a perfect system by any means as it depended on lawmen to send in relevant clippings, but it was better than nothing.

"Stole from a mine owner in Colorado." Since she had received a telegram from headquarters in answer to her query, she was able to cite the date and place of his birth, past employers, and last-known address, all retrieved from the newspaper files. The Pinkerton logo *We never sleep* proved to be true in more ways than one.

She doubted she told Branch any more than he already knew or suspected, but it gave her great pleasure to watch his eyebrows inch up in astonishment as she cited facts.

His surprised expression soon gave way to suspicion. "Why would you bother checking

256

up on him?"

"The way you were acting, I thought perhaps he was a suspect in the Harvey case."

He shook his head. "Nope. Not a suspect."

He pretty much confirmed what she'd already found out. Clayborn wasn't even in town when the killings took place. She waited for him to say more, and when he didn't, she asked, "Anything else you wish to know about him?"

"No, that will do," he said. No sooner were the words out of his mouth than he corrected himself. "Well, maybe one thing. Do you know anything that might make him unsuitable for certain activities? Marriage, for example?"

She lifted an eyebrow. What an odd question. "Only that he was working in Montana at the time of his wife's death. It's my guess he walked out on her."

He seemed to consider her answer a moment before asking his next question. "What about children? Anything that would indicate he'd make an unsuitable parent?"

She slanted her head. Far as she knew, Mr. Clayborn didn't have any children. So what was Branch really asking? And why? "You don't think spending time in jail and desertion makes him unfit for parenthood?"

"Maybe," he said. "But given that criteria, half the men in the West would be rendered unfit."

"Only half?"

He answered her question with a shrug. Something definitely didn't sit right with him.

She picked up a knife and sliced the pie. Fred Harvey insisted that pies be cut in fourths and not eighths like other restaurants. The piece filled the plate, oozing a buttery syrup along with a sweet cinnamon smell.

Hoping the pie would put him in a better mood, she pushed the plate toward him, and he reached for his fork.

"Looks good."

"I stayed up all night baking it," she replied.

"Did you now?" He looked at her for a moment. Recalling the warmth of his arms and the strength of his shoulder, she averted her gaze.

"Sounds like you've been busy," he said. "Anything else you can tell me?"

She chanced another look at him. "About Mr. Clayborn?"

"About anything."

"That's all I can tell you, but I do have a question," she said. "What's with you and

Clayborn?"

"Just some old business." His voice was curt, his look dark, his meaning clear. He was done talking about Clayborn and intent upon pushing her away.

"That covers a lot of territory," she said, refusing to take the hint.

He took a bite of pie, his manner as precise as a watchmaker. The barrier between them seemed formidable as a chasm too wide to cross.

She moistened her lips. "Thank you," she said, thinking a change of subject might help.

He lowered his fork. "For what?"

"For staying with me the other night."

His tight expression relaxed but only for an instant. "I hope you learned your lesson."

"What lesson would that be?" she asked.

He dabbed his mouth with a napkin. "If you persist in meeting strange men at night, and sleeping in alleys, you're just asking for trouble."

"Trouble is what I came here to find."

Before he could respond, Okie-Sam walked up and slapped him on the back. "Morning, Sheriff."

"Morning."

Greeting Katie with a tip of his floppy hat,

Okie-Sam sat on a stool next to Branch and rested his injured hand on the counter. Today he wore his hair loose, and it fell to his shoulders like a stringy red curtain. "Always good to see our local lawman hard at work. So how you doing?"

Branch tossed a nod at Okie-Sam's bandaged hand. "Better than you."

Okie-Sam shrugged and turned his attention to Katie. "I'll have what the sheriff's having."

No sooner did she serve Okie-Sam his pie than the rest of the local regulars arrived, including Long-Shot.

But even as Katie served the others she couldn't shake the feeling that Branch was sitting on a keg of dynamite about ready to explode. Maybe they both were.

Chapter 28

Branch felt bad for pushing Katie away emotionally if not physically, but it was for her own good as well as his. Holding her in his arms — watching her sleep — made him realize how easily he could fall in love with her. He wouldn't allow himself to go that route. It would be disastrous.

She was used to excitement and adventure. A town like this would bore her to tears. Just like it had bored Hannah.

That's why his wife kept working even though he'd begged her to quit. How he'd hated her leaving the house at night, but she'd refused to let him accompany her. *"No sense us both staying up all night,"* she'd say.

He'd had good reason to worry. Predatory Indian bands still roamed Kansas back in the early seventies. The town had not been attacked, but that didn't stop him from worrying.

Once she'd been robbed. Another time

she'd been chased in horse and buggy by a gang of hoodlums, and still she refused to quit. It was the one thing they'd argued about. Her job had been a thorn that pricked holes into an otherwise perfect marriage.

He was no less worried about Katie's habit of leaving the Harvey House at night, but that was the least of it. Hannah had dealt mainly with expectant mothers and nervous fathers. Katie's job required her to rub noses with murderers, robbers, and other social misfits.

If anything happened to her . . .

Nope. Wasn't traveling down that road again. Not with Katie. Not with any woman.

Still, there was no denying that Katie was a distraction, and that was the last thing he needed. Not with Clayborn watching him like a vulture.

Did Clayborn suspect something? Hard to know. For certain he couldn't be put off much longer. Nor, apparently, did he intend to leave town without getting what he came for. Branch had already warned his housekeeper to keep Andy away from Clayborn, though he didn't explain why.

He considered all his options and always came back to the same thing: Clayborn understood money. That's about all he understood.

Branch did a mental check of his assets and grimaced. He couldn't afford to pay off a church mouse, let alone a money-hungry mongrel like Clayborn.

The tornado had wiped him out business-wise, and it had taken years to get back on his feet. Not till the last year could the town afford to pay him a decent wage.

A bank loan? He discounted the idea as soon as he thought it. His house was already mortgaged to the hilt. It was the money he'd lived on while the town was being rebuilt.

It would have been easier had he left like the others, but that would have meant leaving Hannah, and that he could never do. Her grave held him to the town like the roots of a tree.

But staying to rebuild Calico had been a mistake. Not only had it taken a toll physically, emotionally, and financially, but had he moved elsewhere he might never have come face-to-face with Clayborn.

He grimaced. No sense thinking about what he should and shouldn't have done. Concentrate on the present. That's what he had to do. Figure out how to handle Clayborn.

One thing was certain; he was quickly running out of time. How he knew that he couldn't say. It was just something he felt in his bones, as if some inner clock were ticking.

As for Katie, he best stay away from her while he still could.

Pen and paper in hand, Katie slipped outside through the main restaurant entrance. She left the other girls eating lunch in the employee dining area off the kitchen. Employees had only a thirty-minute lunch break, and she meant to make the most of hers.

The weather had taken a dramatic turn for the worse. Earlier the air had seemed almost too heavy to breathe. Now a brisk wind tugged at her skirt and cut through her shirtwaist, bringing with it the smell of rain. Clouds gathered on the distant horizon dark as thick smoke. Flashes of lightning zigzagged downward followed by the mutter of thunder.

Tornado weather, Mary-Lou had announced over breakfast. Katie had never experienced an actual tornado, but recalling the aftermath of a twister that hit a Nebraska town days before she'd arrived on assignment, a shiver coursed through her.

Mrs. Bracegirdle's words echoed in her head: *"Ripped this town in two and killed almost a dozen people, including Branch's wife."*

Now, as always, whenever Branch came to mind she lingered over the thought like a mother over a newborn. What an awful thing to lose a wife in such a horrible way. He was lucky his son survived, but it couldn't be easy raising a youngster alone.

Maybe that's why he had been so protective of Andy. He certainly looked ready to fight off an army when Clayborn asked to join his table. Not that she could blame him, of course, knowing what she now knew of the man. Still, she couldn't shake the feeling there was more to the story. A whole lot more.

The memory of Branch's expression when she told him what she knew about Clayborn puzzled her. Even as he sought information from her it felt like he was slamming a door in her face.

Not that it mattered. Okay, maybe a little, but that was all she was willing to concede. Actually, he'd done her a favor by forcing a distance between them. His efforts had served as a reminder that her real purpose was to find a killer. Losing her heart along the way was not an option.

With a determined nod, she glanced around for a place to sit. She should have brought a wrap, but not wanting to waste time going to her room, she headed for the bench outside the railroad baggage room. The building at her back helped shield her from the wind.

Ignoring both the clouds on the horizon and the ones in her heart, she pulled her notebook out of her purse along with a nib pen and bottle of ink. She set her writing supplies on the bench by her side.

Finding the time to write the daily reports required by the Pinkerton agency was always a challenge, but this particular assignment made the task even more difficult. Just being seen with pen and paper brought Pickens flying to her side to demand the reason.

Pinkerton procedures required all communications be sent in cipher. Timelines had to be accurate and dialogue written exactly as spoken.

It worried her that she didn't have a tangible new lead or clue to add to today's report. No matter how many times she went over the facts in the case, she always came up empty.

There were many reasons that someone might resort to murder. Unless they were dealing with an insane killer or in this case, sleepwalker, one of them would surely apply. Greed and money topped the list, but neither victim had anything of value. Murder was often a crime of passion, but nothing suggested love or obsession was involved.

Protecting something or someone was another motive for murder. Did Ginger and Priscilla know something that put them in harm's way? A secret of some sort?

The wind suddenly grew stronger, rustling the pages of her notebook and lifting her skirt above her ankles. Just as she closed the writing tablet, a gust of wind ripped it out of her hands. *Oh no!*

Jumping to her feet, she chased after it. Her notes were written in code, but still, she couldn't take the chance on someone finding them.

Hopping off the platform, she ran along the train tracks, the wind at her back. The notebook blew against the water tower where she was able to retrieve it, but by then most of the pages had been ripped away.

Just as she turned toward the Harvey House, she noticed a young boy chasing his hat. Something was vaguely familiar about him. She brushed her hair away from her face and narrowed her eyes.

"Andy?" she called, the wind carrying her voice away. "Andy! Is that you?" This time she waved her arms to attract his attention.

The boy stopped running and waved back. By now the wind was blowing so hard he was having a hard time remaining on his feet.

The clouds had taken on a greenish tint, and without warning, hailstones fell, hitting the ground like locusts.

"Come!" she yelled, gesturing wildly. "Come with me."

The boy turned away, presumably to look for his hat, but it was gone. He started toward her, but the stinging wind knocked him to the ground.

A gale-force rush of air roared in her ears and pushed her forward. "Hold on!" The words were snatched out of her mouth. Blinded by dust and debris and battered by hail, she was lucky to find the small, huddled body.

She lifted him into her arms and held him close. Fortunately, he was slightly built, but even so, she struggled to walk with the added weight. Arms around her neck, he buried his head against her chest, his slight frame shaking. His hair blew in her face, mingling with her own.

Body bent, she moved forward, using the railroad tracks as her guide. Her eyes watered, blurring what little vision was left.

A thunderous sound filled the air and shook the ground. No train was due, so what could it be? She stared at the dark wall ahead and froze. Much to her horror a herd of stampeding cattle headed their way.

Branch tethered his horse to the railing in front of the deserted cabin. It used to be the Connor place, but old man Connor died two years ago and it had been deserted ever since.

Or maybe not. That's what he was here to find out. One of the local farmers stopped by his office that morning to report seeing lights in the old place. He'd asked Branch to check it out.

The wind had picked up quite a bit in the last few minutes, beating against him like angry fists. A gust blew so hard that the prairie grass lay flat as a carpet and the nearby cottonwoods threatened to break in two. A storm was definitely brewing. He just hoped it wouldn't turn into a tornado. This was the time of year for them.

Anxious to get back to town, he took the steps leading up to the porch two at a time and pounded on the weathered wood door. Nothing.

The door sprang open with only a slight turn of the knob, thanks to the wind.

"Hello! Anyone here?"

He stepped inside. The windows were covered with oil cloth, and it took a moment for his eyes to adjust to the dim light. The cabin smelled of chimney smoke and dust and, strangely enough, something else: danger.

A quick glance around soon convinced him that the latter was merely a figment of his imagination. Or maybe it was simply the brewing storm that kept him on edge.

The cabin was lightly furnished with a scarred wooden table, chairs, sagging sofa, and woodstove.

A bedroll was spread out on the wood plank floor next to a lantern and box of safety matches. He checked the kitchen. The counters were empty except for a rotting apple and ashtray full of cigar butts. In the sink was a tin cup.

Someone had been here, all right. Since the arrival of the train, it wasn't all that unusual for vagrants to make themselves at home in vacant cabins. Only last year Jeff Parker arrived home following a trip out of town only to find his house had been taken over by a family of drifters.

A distant roar made him stiffen. No train was due at this hour, and it was too loud for thunder. *God, no!* He reached for the door, and it almost ripped out of his hands as he opened it. Squinting against the wind and the dust, his worst fears were confirmed: a dark spiral had touched the ground in the distance and was heading straight for town.

Fear twisted inside him like the blade of a knife, and the blood in his veins turned to ice. *Andy!*

Bending his body against the wind and fighting off the pelting hail, he ran for his horse.

CHAPTER 29

Katie miraculously reached the safety of the restaurant before the panicked cattle overtook them. She huddled next to the building, protecting Andy with her body, and waited for the frenzied herd to pass. Even the wind couldn't drown out the sound of clashing horns and pounding hooves.

The moment she thought it safe, she hustled Andy to the restaurant door.

The door flew open with only a slight twist of the handle, and she almost tripped as the wind pushed her inside.

Heavy gusts blew through the open door, lifting napkins off the table and knocking over vases of flowers. Overhead, the chandelier swung back and forth, the prisms dancing like hollow bones.

Andy clutched at her arm, his fingers white with pressure. "Help me close the door," she shouted over the wind.

Reluctantly, he released his hold but

stayed glued to her side. Together they battled the door shut.

It had grown noticeably darker, and the windows rattled with pounding hail and unrelenting wind.

Her breath escaped in short pants, and it took a great deal of effort to find her voice. "What were you doing out there? Where's your pa?"

"I don't know." Andy looked close to tears. "I couldn't find him. He's not in his office. I think he's at home."

"Why aren't you in school?" Surely the schoolhouse had a storm shelter.

"Our teacher t–told us to go into the c–cellar, but I was worried about Pa."

The boy was visibly shaken. They both were. Hand on his shoulder, she forced a smile. "Your pa will be fine." *Dear God, make it so.*

Something banged against the outside of the building, and Andy flew into her arms. "Let's get away from old Dragon Breath." Hugging him tight, she moved as far away from the windows as possible.

"That's not a dragon," he said. "That's the wind."

"Shh. Don't let the dragon hear you say that. He gets very upset if people don't give him his due."

Pickens popped his head into the dining room. "Quick!" he called, motioning frantically with his arm. "In the cellar!"

She grabbed Andy by the hand, and together they raced out of the dining room.

A musty smell greeted Katie's nose as she tried coaxing Andy down the stairs. Standing on the top tread, she held out her hand, but he refused to take it.

"I'm scared of the dark."

"What?" She feigned surprise. Reasoning with him hadn't worked. It was time for a little make-believe. "Afraid of muddy air?"

An uncertain look crossed his face. "And spiders, too."

"You're afraid of eight legs on the hoof?"

His eyes widened, and a ghost of a smile touched his mouth. "Spiders don't have hooves."

"They most certainly do. And I'll tell you something else. They don't like muddy air."

Andy glanced down the cellar stairs. "They don't?"

"Nope. Can't see to spin their webs. So hurry before the dragon catches us." This time Andy took her offered hand. Casting a worried glance over his shoulder, he followed her down the stairs.

A single candle provided the only light in

the cellar, but it was enough to illuminate the pale faces of the other employees.

"Praise the Lord," Mary-Lou said. "I was so worried. No one knew where you were."

Katie sat Andy on a food crate and drew a wooden barrel next to him.

"And who is this?" Tully asked.

"This is Andy. He's the sheriff's son."

Tully exchanged a meaningful glance with Abigail but said nothing.

Mary-Lou smiled. "I remember now. You just celebrated your birthday, right?"

Andy nodded. "I'm eight."

Chef Gassy leaned toward him, holding out a paper bag. "Have some bonbons. All the vey from France."

Andy stuck his hand in the bag and pulled out a foil-covered confection. Since the pea soup episode, Chef Gassy had gone out of his way to be pleasant to Katie. After offering her one as well, he turned to Miss Thatcher, who sat opposite him.

"Vould you care for one?"

"No, thank you," Miss Thatcher said, clutching a book in her hands. Katie recognized the leather cover as the diary she'd found in the trunk with the wedding gown. Even in the dim light it looked like the spinster's face had turned a shade darker. Maybe she wasn't as oblivious to Chef Gassy's admiring glances as she led everyone to believe.

Gassy's interest in Miss Thatcher obviously didn't escape Tully's notice, either, and she whispered something in Abigail's ear. The two giggled, drawing a disapproving look from the dorm matron.

The air was rife with meaningful glances and stilted conversation. Buzz and Tully made an effort not to look at each other, but anyone with half a brain knew that something of an amorous nature passed between the two of them.

Off to the side sat Culpepper, wheezing like a cat with a hair ball.

Pickens told about a tornado back in his home state of Nebraska. "Plucked the feathers clear off the chickens," he said.

Behind him the two cooks sat on either side of a whiskey barrel, playing cards while Howie Howard looked on.

After Pickens finished telling his story, he climbed the stairs, cautiously opened the door leading to the kitchen, and vanished. A moment later he called the all clear sign and, one by one, they left the cellar.

Something fell out of Miss Thatcher's book, and Katie stooped to pick it up. It was a daguerreotype of a young man in an army uniform. He had a full, round face, dark hair, and sideburns. The seriousness of his dark sack coat and forage hat provided a striking contrast to the impish gaze he afforded the camera.

By the time Katie and Andy reached the top of the stairs, Miss Thatcher was nowhere in sight.

"Gid-up!" Branch shouted to his horse. He covered his mouth with a kerchief to keep from breathing in dust. His hat blew off, but the stampede string kept it from flying away. Instead it bobbed against his back like a loose shutter, the leather cord tugging at his neck.

Wind usually didn't bother Midnight, but then, the horse had never confronted a storm quite like this.

Sensing danger, Midnight crow-hopped. "Come on, boy. Come on!" Branch forced the horse in the direction of town. But even then his gait was choppy. A wooden crate blew across the road, pieces of wood flying in every direction. The horse bucked, and Branch held on with sheer willpower, but he was badly jolted.

He tugged hard on the reins, pulling Midnight's nose to his leg. The gelding moved around in a tight circle until Branch loosened his hold.

"That's it," he shouted over the wind. "You can do it." He had to repeat the procedure several times before Midnight got the message and stopped trying to buck.

The closer they got to town the more dust and debris filled the air. Even with the kerchief covering his nose and mouth, he struggled to breathe. Pieces of a wooden fence flew by, along with roof shingles and someone's wash still attached to the clothesline.

Horses ran by along with several steer and a goat. Rounding up escaped animals would be a big job.

By some quirk of nature, the twister changed course before reaching town, and the immediate danger appeared to be over. The funnel was still visible, but at least it was moving away, leaving behind pieces of broken fences, scattered farm equipment, and, inexplicably, an upright piano turned on its side.

Reaching the brick schoolhouse, he swung from his saddle and tethered his horse to the fence, tail end facing the wind. A tree had toppled, and its white roots crawled along the ground like thick fingers. The yard was littered with debris, but the school building remained intact. *Praise the Lord.*

He found the wooden door that led down

to the storm shelter and banged on it. "Miss Appleton! It's Sheriff Whitman. Everything all right down there?"

The door lifted slightly, and he opened it the rest of the way. Miss Appleton stood on the ladder looking up at him, face pale as a wintry moon.

He never thought to see a more welcome sight. "Everything okay?" he asked again.

"Yes." She hesitated. "Did Andy find you all right?"

His heart thudded. "Andy? Isn't he here?"

Alarm crossed her face. "No. He took off. Said he had to find his pa. I tried to stop him but —"

The rest of her sentence fell behind as he raced for his horse.

CHAPTER 30

Moments later, Branch ran into the house shouting Andy's name. He found his housekeeper in the kitchen.

"He's not here," Miss Chloe said, her dark face creased like old parchment. "Isn't he at school?"

"No, I checked."

Her eyes widened in alarm, and she grabbed hold of the counter as if to steady herself.

He frowned. "What are you doing here? Your house —"

"My house is fine. Just making sure yours was, too."

"Go home. Andy could show up there."

She nodded and grabbed her purse.

Spinning around, he left the house on the run. He leaped astride his horse and rode like a madman through town.

People milled in a daze, hugging each other and assessing the damage to properties. The ground was covered with shards of broken glass and missing shingles. A wagon was upside down and part of a windmill had toppled. So far there was no report of injuries or deaths, but neither had anyone seen Andy.

He rode up one street and down the other, calling Andy's name. *Where are you, Son? Was* this God's punishment for failing to tell Clayborn the truth? *God, surely not. You wouldn't be that cruel, would You? I'm the one to blame. Not Andy.*

He raced his horse across the railroad tracks. Midnight's hooves pounded the ground as Branch's heart pounded his ribs. He rode full circle, and now the Harvey House restaurant loomed ahead of him. Maybe someone there had seen his son.

Katie.

A previously unnoticed woodshed had collapsed by the side of the road. What if Andy had sought shelter there? He slid out of his saddle and frantically pawed through the debris. The memory of digging through another pile of rubble and finding his wife draped over a stove filled him with unspeakable horror. *Not again, Lord. Not again.*

"Andy!" he yelled. "Do you hear me?"

"Pa!"

His heart stilled along with his hands. It

281

took a moment to realize Andy's voice came from behind and not from under the collapsed structure.

He whirled about just as Andy flew into his arms, practically knocking him over. Hugging his son close, his vision blurred. *Thank You, Lord. Thank You . . .*

"I was scared," Andy said, head pressed against Branch's middle.

"I was scared, too, Son." Was that Andy trembling or him? "But you're safe now. We all are."

He blinked away the burning sensation in his eyes and noticed Katie standing a short distance away.

She pushed a wayward strand of red hair behind her ear. "I made him come inside with me until the danger passed." Her apron, normally spotless, was now smeared with dirt, and her bun had worked free, allowing red tendrils to curl around her face.

"Thank you." His voice hoarse, he cleared his throat and thanked her again. If words existed that could convey his gratitude, he had no idea what they were.

Gazing down at his son's upturned face, he said, "Come on. Let's get you home." There was cleanup work to be done in the town, but judging by the way Andy clung to him, he needed his pa; they needed each other. The rest would have to wait.

He looked up to say something to Katie, but already she was heading back to the restaurant. "Wait!" he called.

She stopped and turned.

"Care to join us?" For some reason he couldn't explain, he needed her every bit as much as Andy needed him. "My house is just up the road a ways." When she hesitated he added, "I have it on good authority I make a pretty good pot of coffee." It was a humble offering, but it was all he had to give at the moment.

Andy looked up. "Joe, Pa. Coffee is called joe."

Katie pursed her lips, and Branch felt something stir inside. "I make a good pot of *joe.*" When she still hesitated, he persisted, "So how about it? I'm sure your boss will make allowances given the circumstances."

"The restaurant is closed for the rest of the day," she said.

He frowned. "Did you have much damage?"

She shook her head. "Just some broken windows. I heard there's debris on the tracks, so trains have stopped running."

"Well, then?" He arched his eyebrow. "The invitation still holds."

"Pleeeeeease," his son said.

Andy's plea brought a smile to her face, and Branch was surprised to find himself wishing the smile was for him.

"Very well," she said, and this time the smile *was* for him. His heart leaped with joy. "Count me in for a cup of joe."

CHAPTER 31

Branch lived in a brick house about a half mile up the road from the restaurant. The house had a small yard surrounded by a white picket fence, parts of which had blown away.

Recalling his cool demeanor the last time they'd met, Katie was reluctant to accept his invitation. But this time he seemed genuinely grateful to her for protecting Andy, genuinely warm.

Branch handed the reins of his horse to Andy. "Take care of him, Son."

Andy took the reins but hesitated with a glance at the sky.

Branch placed a hand on the lad's shoulder. "It's gone," he said. "We're safe now."

The trust in Andy's eyes as he gazed up at his father made Katie's heart ache. It had been a long time since she'd had that much trust in anyone — if ever.

The boy took the reins from his father and

started for the barn. The horse was skittish but followed Andy with little resistance.

She followed Branch up to the porch, and he held the front door open for her.

The parlor was tastefully furnished with a walnut-framed horsehair settee, flanked by two wing chairs. A colorful rag rug graced the wood plank floor in front of the stone fireplace. A polished maple side table held a kerosene lamp.

Next to a small writing desk, a shelf of books caught her eye, and she longed to run her fingers across the leather spines. Her current assignment didn't allow for much free time, and she barely had time to read her Bible, let alone a novel.

Except for a group of photographs arranged on the top of the upright piano, the room was free of the stifling clutter of homes on the East Coast.

Branch hung his hat on the wooden hat rack next to the door and combed his mussed hair with his fingers. "You can sit here," he said amicably. "Or you can watch me make coffee. But I must warn you. Seeing me in the kitchen is not a pretty sight."

She laughed. "Since working at the restaurant I've come to feel very much at home in the kitchen." Odd but true. She once avoided the kitchen at all costs, leaving her sisters in charge of meals while she took on more masculine chores around the house.

"Very well, follow me." He led her into the next room and pulled out a ladder-back chair next to a wood trestle table and invited her to sit with a wave of his hand.

"Thank you." She suddenly felt self-conscious. She wasn't used to being waited on and had to curb the impulse to jump up and set the table.

The kitchen was small but efficient. An icebox stood in the corner next to a free-standing cupboard filled with gold-trimmed dishes.

Branch immediately set to work grinding coffee beans and pumping water into the coffeepot.

Her skin suddenly prickled with goose-flesh. Crossing her arms in front, she hugged herself.

"Are you all right?" he asked with a look of concern.

"I'm fine, thank you. Just a delayed reaction."

He studied her. "Was that your first tornado?"

She nodded. "Yes." And she hoped it was her last.

"We were lucky." He set the pot on the stove and lit the flame. "I thought for sure

287

it was heading straight for town."

"Thank God it didn't."

He vanished into the other room and returned a moment later with a knitted shawl. He draped it gently over her shoulders, his hand brushing against the nape of her neck. Chills of another kind shot down her spine followed by a wave of warmth.

"How's that?" he asked, stepping away from her.

"Much better, thank you." It would be better had he not left behind the tantalizing fragrance of bay rum hair tonic.

He reached for a plate of little cakes and placed them on the table along with two cups, saucers, and plates. She pressed her hands together. Nope, she would not rearrange the dishes to meet Harvey's standards, no matter how much she was tempted.

"Don't tell me you baked these," she said, helping herself to a cake.

"Not me. My housekeeper, Miss Chloe, keeps us in baked goods."

She bit into the chocolate confection and wiped a crumb off her mouth with her finger. "They're delicious."

He handed her a napkin and sat. "What you did for Andy . . . I'm mighty obliged."

She set the cake on her plate and wiped

her fingers on the napkin. "That's quite a boy you have there."

He nodded. "That he is." A smile of fatherly pride curved the corners of his mouth. "I'm afraid he's driving Miss Chloe crazy with all that restaurant talk you taught him. He won't touch milk or beans but can't get enough of moo juice and bullets."

She laughed. "I'm sorry."

"Don't be." His smile was as warm as his voice, and suddenly she had no need of the shawl.

"Never thought I'd be slinging hash," she said, hoping he didn't notice her reddening face. "With my job there's no telling what I'll be doing next."

"How long have you worked for Pinkerton?" he asked.

"Five years."

He arched his brows. "Ever meet the founder?"

"Allan Pinkerton?" She nodded. "And I have to say he's the most unusual man I've ever met."

"Unusual how?"

"He was the first to see the value of hiring female detectives." She only wished his sons had the same regard for women. Rumor had it that they wanted to disband the women's detective division. Fortunately, Allan Pinkerton would have none of it.

"I'm sure my wife would have approved of both of you."

She searched his face for signs of grief, but his expression remained as neutral as his voice. This gave her the courage to pursue the subject. "Oh? In what way?"

"She wanted to be a physician, but when her application to medical school was turned down, she became a midwife instead."

Katie felt for his wife. Few women had been allowed to enroll in medical schools. Elizabeth Blackwell had earned a medical degree decades earlier, but the medical establishment was still reluctant to let women enter the field.

Even as a detective Katie had to constantly prove herself. She'd helped capture some of America's most wanted criminals but still got less pay than male operatives. Even the new and inexperienced male detectives were compensated more handsomely than she was.

"I always thought midwifery a fine and noble profession," she said.

"Hannah certainly thought so. There was no keeping her away from a woman about to give birth. She said it was God's work."

"I think I would have liked your wife," she said.

His gaze met hers. "She would have liked you, too."

"Why? Because I'm doing God's work?"

His mouth quirked upward. "I don't know about that, but Hannah would have approved a woman doing a man's job."

"But you don't."

He pursed his lips as if trying to decide how to form his next words. "Yours is a dangerous job for anyone. Men included."

She couldn't argue with him there. "Forgive me for asking, but how did your wife die? I know she died in the tornado, but" — she glanced up at the ceiling — "your house was left intact." According to a recent article in the newspaper, most of the town had been destroyed, but Branch's neighborhood had escaped all but some minor damage.

"She was out that night. Delivering a baby."

Katie stared at him, confused. Had she heard him right? "On the same day she gave birth?"

"What?"

"Your son was born on the day of the tornado." The eight-year anniversary of the tornado had even been noted in the newspaper, with no less than three inches of space.

Color drained from his face, but before he could speak the back door flew open and Andy ran into the kitchen.

Branch jumped up to check on the coffee, and Katie sensed a change in the air, a change in him. Something like a winter chill had entered the room.

"Midnight all taken care of?" she asked.

Andy nodded.

She lowered her voice. "How would you like a mud brick?" she asked. "That's restaurant talk for little chocolate cakes."

Andy helped himself with a grin. Between bites he talked about everything that had happened to him that day, but even he couldn't fill the strained silence that stretched between her and his father.

Branch stared at his son as if he were talking a foreign language. "Dragon Breath?"

Andy laughed and explained.

While his father seemed attentive enough, she sensed his mind was elsewhere. He was simply going through the motions.

As if suddenly remembering his manners, he made every effort to be a good host, but the earlier rapport was now but a memory.

Taking her cue, she drank her coffee quickly and left. While passing through the parlor she stopped to gaze at the hand-colored daguerreotype on top of the piano.

Hannah Whitman had been a beautiful woman — no question. Katie couldn't help but notice the wide-set eyes and delicate features. His wife resembled her older sister Belle, now married to the man Katie once loved. Surprisingly, the usual anger and resentment that rose inside whenever she thought of her sister failed to surface. It felt as if all the pain and grief of the past had happened to someone else.

Is this what it's like to be healed, God? Or maybe it's forgiveness I feel. Certainly she no longer bore ill will toward her sister.

Puzzled, yet pleased by the welcome discovery, she let herself out of the house. She couldn't get the conversation with Branch out of her mind. *"She was out that night. Delivering a baby."*

How was that possible? What woman in her right mind would leave the house during a storm after just giving birth? Even more puzzling was Branch's response when she questioned him.

She glanced up at the angry clouds still hovering on the distant horizon and shivered. This time it was neither the cold nor delayed reaction that made her tremble. Instead, she felt a sense of foreboding.

CHAPTER 32

The restaurant was unusually quiet when Katie returned.

A movement under the table caught her eye. "Spook Cat! How did you get in? Better not let Chef Gassy catch you."

The cat meowed but made no movement toward her. The poor thing was trembling.

She walked into the kitchen. How strange to find the room deserted at this hour. Usually it hummed with activity. Finding a pitcher of milk in the icebox, she poured a few ounces into a dish and carried the bowl to the dining room. No sooner had she set it on the floor than the cat immediately lapped it up.

Curious as to where everyone was, she took the stairs to the second floor. Experience had taught her that people bonded during a crisis or emergency. Protective barriers broke down when life was at its most fragile.

A suspect once confessed to a robbery during a blizzard that had paralyzed St. Louis for days. Pinkerton detective Jeff Morley still boasted about a similar experience during the Great Chicago Fire of 1871 when an art forger, thinking the blaze was the wrath of God, confessed.

If anyone at the Harvey House was sufficiently traumatized enough to confess, gossip, or speculate, Katie wanted to be on hand.

Recalling that Miss Thatcher's photograph was still in her pocket, she decided the dorm matron was a good place to start. She knocked on the door.

"Who is it?"

"It's me, Katie." She waited for Miss Thatcher to tell her to go away, and when she didn't, she reached for the handle.

Miss Thatcher sat at her desk, the diary open in front of her.

"You dropped this earlier in the cellar," Katie said, holding up the photograph.

"Oh!" Miss Thatcher closed the leather journal and waved Katie over to her desk.

Katie crossed the room and handed her the photograph. "Is that a family member?"

"Fam—" The dorm matron shook her head. "It's a picture of my fiancé."

"You're engaged to be married?"

"Was." The woman heaved a sigh. "Matthew died during the war."

"I see." So she'd guessed right. The war had ended long ago, but Miss Thatcher looked as forlorn as if her fiancé had died only yesterday. "I'm so sorry."

Katie tried to visualize Miss Thatcher in her youth, before grief took its toll and the years left their mark. But the vision that came to mind was of her dancing in the moonlight.

"He was a handsome young man," Katie said.

Miss Thatcher's lips curved in a half smile. "He was indeed." She slid his photograph amid the pages of the diary.

"How did you two meet?" Katie asked, fully expecting Miss Thatcher to order her out of the room. Instead the dorm matron seemed to welcome the opportunity to talk about the past.

"We met at a revival." She fell silent as if reliving the moment. "I wasn't supposed to go," she said with girlish delight. "My father forbade it. He said we could get all the religion we needed at our local church and didn't need a bunch of strangers putting ideas in our head. But I went anyway, and that's when I met Matthew."

Miss Thatcher seemed to have forgotten

Katie's presence, her voice too low and whispery to be meant for another's ear. Intrigued, Katie leaned forward so as not to miss a single word.

"One night I sneaked out to be with him, and we danced beneath a full moon." She laid her hand on the leather book on the desk as if the memories written inside needed protecting. "That's when he proposed."

Katie listened intently and didn't dare move for fear of bringing the dorm matron out of her reverie.

"And then the war came," Miss Thatcher continued in a dreamlike voice. "He said he would only be gone for a short while. A couple of weeks at the most. Said he was going to 'whup those Yankees' and come straight home." She let out an audible sigh. "So I planned our wedding."

The light dimmed in her eyes as the memory faded away. Suddenly seeming to recall Katie's presence, she cleared her voice. "I'm sure you have other things to do beside listen to an old lady's ramblings."

"You're not an old lady," Katie said.

"I'll be thirty-eight next month."

Katie thought of Chef Gassy and the way he looked at Miss Thatcher in the cellar. "No one would think a thirty-eight-year-old man old. Or call him a spinster. Is there even a male word for old maid?"

Miss Thatcher surprised her by laughing. Without the usual dismal mask she looked surprisingly young and pretty. "I don't believe there is."

As if to catch herself, Miss Thatcher composed her features and tucked a loose strand of hair back into the tight bun. "I never expected my life to turn out this way. I was certain I would be married with a houseful of children by now. Not chaperoning a bunch of spoiled —" She cleared her voice. "You know what I mean."

Katie had hoped for just this kind of opening. "Did you think Priscilla and Ginger spoiled?"

Miss Thatcher frowned. "What kind of question is that? The poor women are dead. It doesn't matter what I thought."

"So you *did* think them spoiled."

"Well, now that you mention it . . . Not Ginger. But that Priscilla. Mercy. She was always sneaking out at night to be with her beau."

"She had a beau?"

"Not just one, but many."

"Really?" That was news to Katie. "Like who?"

"One night I saw her with Culpepper.

They looked like they were having a lover's quarrel."

That was surprising. Culpepper hardly seemed the romantic type. Or at least as far as Katie could tell. She was no expert on men, but Culpepper kept pretty much to himself and didn't strike her as a womanizer. At least she'd never noticed him flirt with the Harvey girls like so many of the other men did. Of course, employee romances were against the rules. Still, if he had taken a liking to Priscilla, the man could be grieving her death. That would certainly explain his withdrawn demeanor.

"You don't think that he —"

"Oh, no. I wasn't suggesting —" Miss Thatcher stood abruptly as if suddenly recalling her duties as a chaperone. She peered at Katie with narrowed eyes, her back ramrod straight. "You will not say a word to anyone about what you heard here today. Do I make myself clear?"

"Yes, Miss Thatcher. Not a word."

"Now go." As if to assure herself that she had regained her rightful position, she added, "You look a disgrace. Your apron . . ."

"I'll change." Katie quickly left the room, closing the door behind her.

She paused in the hall. Did Miss Thatcher kill the Harvey girls? She couldn't discount the possibility. Especially since at least one of them had given her trouble. The woman was an odd one to be sure, but somehow Katie couldn't help but think her bark was worse than her bite.

With this thought in mind, she scurried down the hall.

Chapter 33

Two days later, things had pretty much returned to normal at the restaurant. Some windows were still boarded, but the trains had started running again and the roads cleared of debris. Getting the restaurant back in shape had required a huge amount of work from everyone. Debris had to be hauled away from the property and the outside woodwork painted. Inside, everything was covered in sand and grit.

Katie stifled a yawn as she took her place behind the counter to wait for the twelve-twenty-five train. Her feet were sore; her back ached. What she would give for more sleep.

Branch strolled into the breakfast room and headed straight for her station.

She hadn't seen him since the day of the tornado. From what she'd heard, he'd been organizing cleanup crews and helping to round up stray animals. His bristled jaw told her he hadn't shaved, and he sure did look like he could use some sleep.

Oddly enough, his unkempt appearance gave him a dangerous edge that only added to his appeal. Strangely, her weariness lifted and even her aches and pains seemed to vanish at sight of him.

Without taking a seat, he leaned over the counter. "We need to talk," he said without preamble, his heated breath fanning her face.

"Not now," she said with a glance at Pickens, who was looking their way. Buzz had already sounded the alarm, and the chandelier overhead jingled like sleigh bells as the train neared the station.

Pickens rushed over. "Is there a problem, Sheriff?"

Branch tore his gaze away from her. "No problem. Just thought I'd stop by and get me some of that English pea soup everyone's talking about."

At mention of the soup, Katie almost laughed out loud. Orange juice was now a permanent ingredient. The new and improved soup had even earned an inch in the newspaper. Chef Gassy swore restaurant employees to secrecy. No outsider must know what gave the soup its unique zesty taste. He, of course, took full credit for the new recipe.

Pickens lifted his pointed nose. "We now refer to it as the chef's special."

Branch shrugged. "Well, whatever it's called, it's the talk of the town and I'll have some." He pushed away from the counter and sat at a table.

"Well?" Pickens gave Katie the eagle eye. "Are you going to stand there all day, or are you going to take the man's order?"

Katie wiped her damp hands on the side of her skirt and walked around the counter just as the door flew open and train passengers began streaming inside.

The dining room orders were taken in advance, but not in the breakfast room. Katie had a good memory for clues and anything pertaining to a criminal case, but a diner's order tended to go in one ear and out the other. However, she had discovered that if she talked up one specific dish and made it sound appealing, most if not all diners would order it. That sure did simplify things.

Today she talked up the pea soup.

As she hoped, all seven passengers — which included three men and four women — followed Branch's example and ordered the chef's special.

When she returned with their orders, she

noticed one of the men at her table whip out a photograph and hand it to Branch. The man was in his mid to late thirties. Hair the color of muddy water was parted in the middle and slicked down with grease. His thin nose and mouth were separated by a skinny mustache.

She set the tray down on the tray stand and picked up a bowl of hot soup.

"Name's Sam Fletcher," the man was saying, "and I need to find this woman."

Curious, she peered over the man's shoulder and caught her breath. He was holding a photograph of Abigail.

Just then Abigail walked into the breakfast room. Katie frantically waved her free hand to warn her and pointed to the man who she now suspected was Abigail's husband.

Her suspicion was confirmed by the look of horror that crossed Abigail's face just before she whirled about and fled the room.

Katie was so intent on warning Abigail that she forgot she was holding a bowl of soup until Fletcher jumped up with a curse.

Thick green broth ran down his arm and splashed across the photograph. He rubbed the picture against his trousers.

"You dumb dame!" he roared. The room fell silent following his outburst, and all heads turned toward her table. "Look what you've done."

"I–I'm sorry, sir," she stammered. "I'll get you a towel."

"Don't you come near me, you —" He drew back a fist as if to strike her.

Branch jumped up and shot a hand to Fletcher's throat. With one swift movement, he pushed him away from Katie. "There's no call for you to talk to her like that. It was an accident." He gave Fletcher a shove, and the man staggered backward against a chair.

Still Fletcher refused to leave and continued to berate Katie. His curses were met with shocked gasps from the other diners, and one woman covered her young daughter's ears.

Branch leaned toward Katie, his voice low in her ear. "What would your Pinkerton bosses advise under such circumstances?"

She'd told him he could learn a lot from her bosses, and apparently not forgotten.

"To reason with him," she whispered back. "And politely show him to the door."

Branch nodded. "Good idea." With that Branch stepped forward and threw his right fist into the startled man's face.

Fletcher flew back and hit the floor hard. Face purple, he glared up at Branch, hand on his bloodied nose. Branch yanked him to his feet, hauled him across the room, and tossed him out the door.

"The next time I see your ugly mug I'll lock you up." Slamming the door shut, he brushed his hands together and turned.

Applause greeted him. He acknowledged the crowd with an upraised hand and sheepish grin before taking his seat again.

"Is that what you call polite?" she murmured next to his ear.

"Absolutely," he said quietly, and she detected a touch of humor in his voice.

A matronly woman at Katie's table lifted her eyepiece to her face. "I must say, Sheriff, you certainly put that awful man in his place."

The diner next to her concurred. "I just wish we didn't have to travel on the same train as him."

Katie pasted on her most brilliant smile and hastened to pass out the remaining bowls of soup. She purposely engaged her diners in conversation and ignored Pickens, who looked ready to pounce on her at the first opportunity. Spilling soup on a diner was no less of a sin than eating a forbidden apple in the Garden of Eden.

Fletcher soon forgotten, the diners oohed and aahed as they ate, and everyone agreed that it was the best pea soup ever.

Just as the travelers rose to board the

train, Branch whispered in her ear. "Meet me tonight."

The whistle blew with a blast of steam. The cranks shifted, and the wheels turned. The train moved out of the station with a loud clank and gradually picked up speed.

"He's gone," Katie said from her place at the dining room window.

Abigail stood behind her, craning her neck. "Are . . . are you sure?"

"Saw him climb aboard," Katie said.

Abigail bit her lip. "It doesn't matter. He won't rest till he finds me."

Mary-Lou cleared the dirty dishes off a nearby table. "Who is he?"

Abigail hesitated before answering. "My husband."

"You're married?" Tully gasped, almost dropping a tray of dishes.

Katie hushed her. "You mustn't say a word." She glanced at Mary-Lou. "Any of you."

"But being married is against the rules," Tully persisted, this time in a lower voice.

Katie glared at her. Tully was the last person to talk about rules. "Yes, and so is spousal abuse. The Bible clearly states that a man must treat his wife with love and respect." Even with all her father's faults, she never knew him to be physically abusive. He had been thoughtless, emotionally distant, and, at times, even uncaring, but never once did he raise his hand.

Mary-Lou cast a look of sympathy Abigail's way. "I'm sorry. We didn't know."

Abigail looked close to tears. "I didn't want anyone to know."

"Maybe it's better this way," Katie said. "Now we can all be on the lookout for him."

Abigail shook her head. "I can't stay here."

Katie squeezed her hand. "You can't keep running. You must remain strong. Men like that prey on weakness."

"I don't know if I have it in me to be strong." Abigail's lips quivered. "He scares me, and I could be putting you all in harm's way." Tears flooded her eyes, and she let out a sob.

Tully discounted this concern with a wave of her hand. "We already have a killer on the loose. What's another?"

Katie glared at her and shook her head. This was no time for jokes. The tension in the house felt almost palpable. Everyone seemed to be waiting for the next shoe to drop.

Mary-Lou filled in the strained silence. "We won't let him hurt you or anyone else."

Abigail dabbed her eyes with a handkerchief. "I don't know that you can stop him."

"You'd be amazed what we can do." Tully put her arm around Mary-Lou's shoulder, showing surprising empathy. Tully could be kindhearted at times, but only when her protective armor slipped.

"Don't you know?" Tully asked. "We're the Harvey girls!"

CHAPTER 34

Katie waited for her roommate to fall asleep before slipping from beneath the covers and planting her bare feet on the floor. She quickly dressed in a blue skirt and matching shirtwaist set out in advance and then pulled on her shoes.

Not wanting to fuss with her hair, she let it fall down her back in a single braid. Moistening her lips, she let herself out of the room and tiptoed quietly down the hall to the stairs.

Branch was anxious to talk to her, and she had a pretty good idea it wasn't about the Harvey girl case.

He waited for her outside the dining room doors, his shadow falling across the glass as she fumbled with the lock. Heart pounding, she slipped outside and closed the door after her without bothering with the spoon-in-the-threshold trick.

"How are you getting back in?" he asked.

"Through a side window." Earlier she had unlocked not one but two windows. No sense taking a chance on being locked out again.

"Another Pinkerton trick?" he asked.

"Nope. Strictly my own."

They walked toward the bench outside the baggage room and sat.

It felt cool but not unpleasantly so. The night air seemed eerily still except for moths flitting around the gaslight globe. Overhead the stars glittered as brightly as Harvey's newly polished silver.

Branch sat with his elbows on his lap and rubbed his hands between his knees. Sensing his unsettling thoughts, she decided to make it easy for him.

"He's not yours, is he? Andy. He's not your natural child."

His intake of breath only confirmed what she already knew. "I messed up, didn't I? Telling you how Hannah died . . . If you figured it out, then —"

"You're worried that Clayborn might." It wasn't just a lucky guess; she had noticed the family resemblance when she saw them together at the restaurant, though it hadn't registered at the time. Andy and Clayborn had similar hair color and eyes.

"Yes, I'm worried. Now more than ever."

311

She let his statement hang for a moment before asking, "How did you end up with his son?"

He sat back as if bracing himself. "It happened on the night of the tornado." His voice was low, hesitant, and at times hoarse as he described how his wife had gone to the Clayborn home to deliver Dorothy's baby.

Even in the dim light she could see pain in the depths of his eyes as he related finding the newborn in the cast-iron oven. "I keep telling myself that God wouldn't give me a gift like Andy only to take him away."

She rested her hand on his arm. "God gives; He doesn't take." That's what her minister told her when she'd asked him why God had taken away the man she loved. For whatever reason, it had been easier to blame God than her sister or even the man who had dumped her, though in retrospect that made little sense.

"I used to believe that was true. But after I lost Hannah . . ." He leaned back. "Dorothy told everyone her husband was dead. It never occurred to me that she would lie about something like that."

"Why did she, do you suppose?"

"I don't know. Pride, perhaps. I imagine it's not easy for a woman to admit her husband ran off."

"I guess not," she said, thinking of Abigail's plight. It had been hard for her to admit to having an abusive husband. Thank God times were changing. Since Fred Harvey opened up his restaurants, women now had a legitimate means by which to support themselves. Staying in an abusive or unhappy marriage was no longer the only option left to women.

An owl flew overhead, the flapping wings breaking the silence that had settled between them.

"It must have been hard. Raising a child by yourself." She remembered how difficult it had been for her father to raise his daughters after her mother's death. That's when he'd started drinking.

"It *was* hard. The town was in ruins. My wife was gone. My transport business thrived for as long as it took people to leave town and then died." His voice broke. "Andy kept me going. I couldn't love him more if he were my own flesh and blood."

"Does Clayborn suspect Andy is his?" People didn't always recognize themselves in others, and he might not have noticed the family resemblance.

"I don't know."

"Why did he come back?"

"He wants me to sign a statement that his child died with his mother."

She frowned. "Why?"

"Dorothy's father left a substantial amount of money for his grandchild, and it's never been claimed."

"And your signature will help him claim the money."

"Andy's money," he said.

What a mess. She couldn't help but sympathize. "What do you think Clayborn would do if he knew his son was alive?"

"No doubt he'd want to claim him but only because of the money. As Andy's father, he'd have full control."

"Have you talked to a lawyer?" she asked.

"Yes, but I never legally adopted Andy. Never saw the need. That means I don't have much ground to stand on. The court almost always rules for the real parent."

"You *are* the real parent," she said. "I don't care what the court says."

"Thank you for that." He covered her hand with his own. "I didn't mean to get you involved."

"Isn't that what friends are for?"

The corners of his mouth tugged upward. "There aren't too many people I can talk to about this."

She moistened her lips. "You can talk to

God." Through all the trials and tribulations of the past, God had been the one constant in her life.

He nodded. "Believe me, I have. So far He hasn't given me any answers."

"He will," she whispered. God had been oddly silent of late in her own life. Usually when working on a case she felt Him leading her, but not this time. His lack of help left her feeling adrift.

"You sound like Reverend Bushwell. He told me I just have to trust the Lord."

"Sounds like good advice."

He studied her. "Would you?" he asked. "Trust God if Andy were your son?"

She thought for a moment. "I'd like to think I would."

He tilted his head. "But?"

She breathed a sigh. "You never really know how strong your faith is until it's tested." Hers had been tested through the years but never like Branch's.

He moved his hand from hers, and for a moment neither of them spoke, both in their own private thoughts.

She ached to wipe away the frown at his forehead. Instead she smiled up at him. "You'll do the right thing," she said.

His eyebrow lifted. "How do you know I will?"

"I have faith in human nature," she said. *I have faith in you.*

He laughed. "Do you now?"

"Yes and —"

He hushed her with a finger to his mouth and directed her attention to the alley.

It sounded like a door closing. "Do you suppose that's Miss Thatcher?" she whispered.

Shrugging, he left the bench and peered around the corner of the building. After a moment he gestured for her to join him in the alley.

Like two mischievous children, they ran between the buildings. Spotting Miss Thatcher, they stopped. Tonight she floated ghostlike along the deserted street, her white nightgown billowing around her.

She had already crossed the tracks by the time they reached the protective cover of the cottonwood. The dorm matron's body swayed, pivoted, and twisted beneath the diamond-studded sky and soft, waning moon.

"Holy smokes," Branch murmured, his voice low in her ear. "If I hadn't seen her with my own eyes I wouldn't have believed it."

"I feel sorry for her in a way," Katie whispered. "She's a prisoner of the past."

Miss Thatcher had caught Chef Gassy's eye but hadn't even noticed. "It's hard to reach for the future when you're still carrying the past in your hands."

"Is that what you think she's doing?" he asked.

"Maybe that's what we're all doing," she said. "To a certain extent."

"The past has a way of grabbing hold of you when you least expect it," he said after a while. "Mine certainly has. I didn't even know Clayborn was alive. It feels like I've been ambushed by a ghost."

She gazed up at his profile. Even the dim light couldn't hide his anguished look. If only she could think of something to say to ease his pain.

After a few moments, Miss Thatcher stopped dancing and drifted away like a lone cloud. Katie started to follow, but Branch stopped her with a hand to her wrist.

"Don't go." The low rumble in her ear made her pulse quicken. He swung her around, and just that quickly she was locked in the circle of his arms. "May I have this dance?"

A tingle of excitement rushed through her. "Here?"

"I have it on good authority that it's the perfect place to dance," he said.

"I–I'd like that." Suddenly she was having trouble breathing.

Taking her by the hand, he led her to the open field. He pulled her close and pressed one hand against the small of her back. The light that had seemed too bright for trailing the dorm matron now seemed woefully dim. His face was clear enough, but the depths of his eyes remained hidden.

He led her in a slow, graceful waltz. Around and around they danced, the tall grass brushing against the hem of her skirt.

For such a large man, he was surprisingly light on his feet. At first she followed his lead like a puppet on a stick, gradually relaxing until his every movement — even his breathing — became her own.

Their heartbeats provided the tempo as they danced beneath a canopy of twinkling stars. The past, the future — none of it existed. She closed her eyes and willed the present to last forever.

Steps quickening, he whirled her about until at last they were both out of breath and forced to stop. Even then he didn't release her. Instead he held her close, both hands at her waist, his touch creating a circle of warmth that radiated upward.

"I wish you could see what the stars look like in your hair."

Her heart sank. No one ever said anything nice about her hair.

"Don't talk about my hair," she said.

He tilted his head. "Why not?"

"Because I hate it and . . . never mind. I just don't want to talk about it."

His head drew back slightly, but his hands remained at her waist. "You hate your hair?"

"Don't sound so surprised. Anyone would."

"Not everyone," he said. Lifting a hand, he fingered her braid as if it were as precious as a baby bird. "Do you know what your hair makes me think of?"

"A red barn?"

"The roses that grew at my grandparents' farm," he said softly.

Her mouth parted, and something tugged at her heart. "Roses?"

He nodded. "I spent some of the happiest days of my childhood on that farm."

His words crashed over her like ocean waves, washing away every hurtful thing that had ever been said to her. A lump formed in her throat.

She pulled away from his touch but only to control the emotions inside. "You're the first person who ever said anything like that to me. Said anything nice about my hair . . ."

"Really?" He sounded genuinely surprised.

She nodded. "Really. As for my freckles . . ."

"I like freckles," he said. "I like counting them. I especially like counting yours. You have exactly eleven on your nose and twenty-eight altogether."

Her breath caught in her throat. He made her sound special. Beautiful, even. The knot of pain that she had carried inside for far too long melted away like the wax of a candle.

His hands slipped up her arms, and a shiver of awareness ripped through her. "I didn't mean to make you cry."

She was crying? Oh, for the love of Kansas, she *was* crying. Over freckles and hair, no less. In the light of his problems, hers seemed silly. Childish, even.

"It's not your fault," she said, swiping away a tear.

"I was kind of hoping it was."

Her eyes widened. "You wanted to make me cry?"

"Not cry exactly." He pulled a handkerchief out of his pocket and very gently dabbed at her tears. "But you must know it's hard to get to know a woman who masquerades as a Harvey girl one minute and a detective the next. I never really know for sure which one I'm with."

"Right now I just want to be your friend," she said. His loneliness was almost as tangible to her as the gaping hole inside she could never seem to fill.

He replaced his handkerchief, his gaze never leaving hers. "Do you mind if I ask a personal question?"

She wasn't much for answering personal questions, but her curiosity got the best of her. "If it's about my hair —"

"Have you ever been kissed?"

Had he punched her in the stomach she wouldn't have been more surprised. Of course she'd been kissed, not that she went around bragging about it. "W–what kind of question is that?" she stammered.

"A relevant one."

"Relevant how?"

Instead of answering, he pulled her all the way into his arms. Startled, she pushed against his chest with both hands, but this only made him tighten his hold.

"Don't pull away," he whispered. "I need you tonight. I need this. And I think you do, too." Crushing her in his arms, he brushed his mouth against her forehead before swooping down to capture her lips and even more of her heart.

Never had she felt so beautiful and desirable as she felt at that moment. Never had she felt so wanted. She now knew that no matter how many times she'd been in another's arms in the past, she had never truly been held. Nor had she truly been kissed.

CHAPTER 35

Katie stood behind the restaurant counter the next day struggling with confused feelings. One moment she was happy — thrilled, really — that Branch had kissed her; the next moment appalled. If her Pinkerton bosses so much as suspected she'd acted so unprofessional she'd be fired on the spot.

She spent most of last night and all of this morning trying to banish Branch from her thoughts, but it was no use. His kisses had burned into the depths of her soul like a branding iron, leaving his mark.

Land alive! A man complimented her hair and what did she do? She melted in his arms, that was what.

On the other hand, how could she not? The poor man was half out of his mind with worry. With the thought came a flash of understanding. Of course, that was it. She was just being kind and considerate. A true friend. Only a cold, heartless person would turn down a man's kisses under such circumstances.

If she could relieve his mind for a few minutes, what did it hurt? Except to make her want more . . . Not that anything more could happen between them. If she didn't come up with a suspect soon, her Pinkerton boss would pull her off the case and she'd be on the next eastbound train. Simple as that.

The thought sent her spirits spiraling downward. Funny how she had grown attached to the Harvey House in such short order. Odd as it seemed, there was a certain satisfaction in caring for weary travelers and sending them on their way with full tummies and happy smiles.

In contrast, tracking down bad guys made her feel more depressed than happy, but none more than her current assignment. Her next report to headquarters would be sadly lacking, indeed, but no more so than the last few reports.

Her thoughts were interrupted by Culpepper, who walked into the room and promptly had a sneezing spell.

"Bless you," she called.

His hay fever, as he called it, was always worse in the morning. Today his eyes were red as beets, and he made a funny hissing sound when he breathed.

He settled behind the reception desk by the door to prepare for the arrival of the first customers.

She took him a cup of coffee. "Maybe this will help."

"Thank you," he said and sneezed into his handkerchief.

As she set the cup on the desk, she couldn't help but notice the calluses on his hands. How did a man sitting behind a desk all day end up with the hands of a laborer?

Miss Thatcher had mentioned a possible lover's quarrel between Culpepper and Priscilla. If true, that raised more questions than answers. What would a young, beautiful woman see in a man like him? And how did Ginger fit into the picture?

She had queried him at length about both victims, but he gave no indication of a romantic attachment. She was just about to bring up Priscilla's name again when the chef interrupted her.

"Pssst." Chef Gassy motioned to her from the kitchen pass-through.

She was tempted to ignore him, but something in his manner suggested it was important. She left Culpepper and took her place behind the counter.

"What is it?" she asked, peering through the glassless window.

For answer he slipped a handbill through the opening. Big, bold letters heralded a May dance. She lifted her gaze to find the chef watching her. He'd acted like her best friend since the pea soup episode, but surely he wasn't asking her to a dance.

"Uh . . ." She didn't want to hurt his feelings, but neither did she want to encourage him.

"Do you zink she go vith me?" he asked.

She blinked. "Who?"

"Miz Zathcher."

"Oh!" Relief flooded through her. "Have you asked her?"

He held a finger to his mouth as he glanced over her shoulder at Culpepper. "You ask her."

Katie lowered her voice to a whisper. "You want me to ask her for you?"

He grinned. *Merci beaucoup.* He bowed. Thank you very much.

"Wait. I didn't say I would."

He nodded. "Oui, oui." He moved away from the wall that separated them.

"I didn't say yes," she repeated, this time louder.

He did a little jig in the middle of the kitchen, and she couldn't help but laugh.

His eyes shone like two black gems, and he pranced around as freely as a schoolboy. His toque flopped back and forth as if it couldn't make up its mind which way to fall.

She drew back and sighed. If this was what love did to a person, then she wanted some of it. Falling in love in the past had caused her more pain than happiness. Worse, she ended up berating God for not making her more lovable, like her sisters.

Blinking back a burning sensation in her eyes, she studied the handbill. The dance would be held Saturday night. That was only a couple of days away. How in heaven's name was she supposed to persuade a stubborn dorm matron to go out with a temperamental chef? What an odd combination. If God meant for those two to be together, He sure did have a funny sense of humor.

"You owe me," she called.

He puckered his lips and threw her a kiss. She shook her head. Only a Frenchman could get away with such a bold gesture.

A Frenchman and maybe even a certain handsome sheriff.

That Saturday evening after the train had left and chores were completed, Katie met Mary-Lou, Tully, and Abigail in the hallway in front of Miss Thatcher's room.

Mary-Lou held a pretty blue gown over her arm. The dress had been borrowed from the daughter of one of their regular customers. Katie hoped it would fit, but it was hard to know for sure.

As the designated hair person, Tully carried a heated curling iron. Over her arm hung a muslin sack containing brush, comb, and a wide selection of clips and ribbons. Harvey girls weren't allowed to wear jewelry, but Abigail contributed a cameo on a blue velvet ribbon and a pair of seed pearl drop earbobs belonging to her grandmother.

Tully shook her head. "This isn't going to work," she whispered.

"We won't know till we try," Mary-Lou whispered back.

"We could all be fired," Tully argued.

"If it works, maybe we'll get a bonus," Abigail said.

Tully rolled her eyes. "Yeah, and maybe one day women will get to vote and run for office."

"Shh." Katie pressed her ear to the door. Tully had every reason to be wary. When Katie told Miss Thatcher about the chef's invitation, the dorm matron made it clear that she wanted nothing to do with him or the dance. But Chef Gassy pleaded with

Katie not to give up. The poor man looked so heartbroken Katie couldn't say no.

"All right. On the count of three. One, two, three —"

Katie flung the door open with such force that Miss Thatcher let out a cry of alarm. "Surprise," Katie said, advancing toward her.

"What is the meaning of this?" Miss Thatcher rose from her desk, shaking with indignation. "I told you I'm not going to a dance."

Ignoring her protests, the four of them closed in on all sides like the drawstrings of a money bag and quickly got to work.

"We just want to see how you look in this dress," Katie said.

While Katie unhooked her skirt Mary-Lou started on the mother-of-pearl buttons on her shirtwaist. No sooner had the skirt fallen in a fabric puddle on the floor than the real battle began.

"What do you think you're doing?" Miss Thatcher squawked. She whacked at Mary-Lou's hands. "Leave me alone this minute!"

"You agreed to try it on," Katie said.

Miss Thatcher gave her head an indignant toss. "I agreed to no such thing!"

"Really?" Katie feigned a look of innocence. "I would have sworn . . ."

Miss Thatcher glared at her. "Just wait till Mr. Harvey hears about this. You'll all be fired. Do you hear me? Fired!"

While Katie and the dorm mother argued, Mary-Lou and Abigail worked quickly. Between the two of them, they managed to pull the dress over Miss Thatcher's head, and it slithered down the length of her, miraculously in one piece. The frock couldn't have fit more perfectly had it been made for her. Even the royal blue was flattering, the color turning Miss Thatcher's normally sallow skin to a lovely peach tone.

The neckline was modest but not prudish, revealing the dorm matron's long and graceful neck. The draped overskirt was caught in back by a bustle that gave Miss Thatcher's beanpole figure shape and substance. Lace-trimmed sleeves flared from her wrists, matching the lace at the slightly flared hem.

Miss Thatcher was too busy wagging her tongue to notice. "Never in all my born days have I seen such impertinence. . . ." On and on she went, threats flying out of her like bats from a cave.

Tully had a way with hair. Ignoring the dorm matron's rants and raves, Tully freed her tresses from their tight knot. Cautioning her to remain still or be burned, Tully coaxed the dorm matron's hair into a riot of curls with the hot iron.

The mass of chestnut ringlets was then pinned back to fall gracefully down to her shoulders. Tully left just enough tendrils loose to soften the angles of the dorm matron's face and hide her flyaway ears.

Abigail tied the cameo around Miss Thatcher's neck and clipped on the earbobs. Ignoring the visual daggers cast her way, Katie turned the mahogany-framed cheval mirror around so Miss Thatcher could see herself.

"Now, remember, if you don't like it we'll undo everything," Katie said. If this didn't work, they could all be out of a job.

"This is an outrage," Miss Thatcher sputtered. "This is —" Her gaze fell on the mirror and her eyes grew round as pie tins. Her mouth hung open as the last of her protests faded away.

Encouraged, Katie smoothed a touch of forbidden carmine dye to Miss Thatcher's lips, and for once the dorm matron didn't protest.

Katie and the others watched Miss Thatcher move her hands up and down the shiny fabric of her dress. She touched her hair and fingered the cameo. Outrage melted from her face, and a soft look of disbelief took its place.

Even Katie was surprised by the transformation. "You look pretty as a picture," she said, and she meant it. How could she not have noticed Miss Thatcher's pretty blue eyes? Or long eyelashes?

Nodding in agreement, Abigail clutched her hands to her chest. "You look beautiful."

"Like an angel," Mary-Lou added.

Tully shook her head. "By gummy, who would have thought it?"

"I don't understand," Miss Thatcher whispered. "Why are you doing this?"

Katie straightened the bustle at the back of Miss Thatcher's dress. "It's our way of thanking you for all the care you've given us." Tully rolled her eyes but mercifully said nothing. "And we thought you deserved to go to a dance."

Miss Thatcher shook her head. "I can't do that. Matthew —" She stopped and cleared her throat. "I have work to do."

Katie met the dorm matron's gaze in the mirror. "I think we can turn our own lights out just this once. And the best way to honor Matthew's memory is to be the woman he fell in love with. I have a feeling that woman wouldn't have thought twice about going to a dance."

Miss Thatcher lifted her chin. "You're

right. She wouldn't have."

Katie nodded. "Come. Chef Gassée is downstairs," she said, pronouncing his name the proper French way.

Miss Thatcher's cheeks turned a most becoming shade of pink. "Well!" She gave her head a slight toss. "What are we waiting for?"

CHAPTER 36

Branch snapped the book shut and placed it on the table next to his son's bed. They would have to rise early for church. That meant the further adventures of *Swiss Family Robinson* would have to wait for another time.

"Say your prayers, Son." Sitting up in bed, Andy pressed his hands together and closed his eyes. "God bless Pa and Miss Chloe and Miss Katie and . . ."

Since the tornado, Katie had become a regular addition to Andy's prayers. The boy was quite taken with her, and Branch couldn't blame him. Not even a little bit.

"Amen," Andy said and climbed beneath the covers.

Branch tucked him in but was reluctant to leave the room. Clayborn was still in town, and Branch felt like he was teetering on the edge.

Not only in his personal life, but professionally, as well. His investigation had hit a dead end, and his failure to bring the killer to justice was a heavy burden to bear. Sleep, if it came at all, offered little rest. Each morning he greeted the first light of dawn like a man waiting to be rescued at sea.

Maybe this . . . this thing with Katie was just his way of holding on to something not tainted by the past. When he kissed her it was as if the world had suddenly grown brighter. As if the troubles that plagued him no longer existed. As if the topsy-turvy planet had returned to its axis. What to call such a feeling he had no idea. Or maybe he was just afraid to call it by its real name.

After losing Hannah, he never thought he'd be interested in another woman. Work and Andy filled his life and that had been enough. It should be enough now. More than enough.

And yet . . .

Holding her in his arms felt like he'd been given a piece of heaven. And her lips . . . Her soft and yielding lips continued to haunt him. Kissing her had filled an aching need he hadn't even known he had. But, God forgive him, it had also triggered another need — a deeper need — the manly need to know her like he knew no other.

With a sigh he leaned over and kissed his

son on the forehead.

"You can turn the light off," Andy said.

Branch reared back. Andy always insisted he leave the light on until he fell asleep.

"I'm not afraid of muddy air anymore," Andy explained. "Not afraid of eight legs on the hoof, either."

"You were afraid of two cattle running?"

Andy giggled. "No, silly. Eight legs on the hoof are spiders."

"Ah." Branch grinned. "Sounds like you've been talking to Miss Katie."

He turned off the lamp. If only the fear of losing his son could be resolved with a simple change of words.

"Put your trust in the Lord," Reverend Bushwell had said. Trust God? Could he? Dare he?

"Night, Son. Sleep tight."

Leaving the room, he walked into the parlor and picked up the Bible. Sitting, he turned to the story of Abraham. Branch knew the story, or so he thought. God told Abraham to prove his faithfulness by sacrificing his son. What Branch hadn't known was that Abraham had not always been a man of faith. He'd made mistakes. Big mistakes. Eventually, Abraham learned the hard way that acting on his own and not trusting God only led to disaster.

Branch closed the Bible with a heavy heart. Since losing Hannah he hadn't allowed himself to trust anyone or anything. He'd surrounded himself with a shield of indifference. That meant not getting close to anyone. He was friendly to all, but friends to none.

Maybe that's the real reason he fought Katie so hard in the beginning. Somehow he knew that if anything could tear down his defenses it would be those big blue eyes of hers.

Now he felt like everything he cared about was about to slip through his fingers. Again. Trust God? How could he with so much at stake? He didn't even know *how* to trust God. And that was the most troubling problem of all.

Tully insisted upon following the chef and Miss Thatcher to the dance. "I still can't believe she agreed to go," she whispered as the four girls, including Katie, hurried along the boardwalk of Main.

Overhead the stars popped out through wispy clouds like shiny buttons on a general's uniform.

The couple was only a half block ahead, so they treaded lightly and followed at a discreet distance. Keeping their giggles under wraps was the biggest challenge.

The dance hall was four blocks from the Harvey House, so Chef Gassy thought it easier to go on foot than bother with horse and carriage. He and Miss Thatcher walked side by side at a respectful distance. Close to the same height, they made a surprisingly handsome couple.

Since Katie had no intention of letting the girls wander about after dark without protection, she agreed to join them, though secretly she longed for an early night and some much-needed sleep.

"I wish someone had asked *me* to the dance," Tully said.

Knowing that such flippant talk was Tully's way of keeping her interest in Buzz under wraps, Katie said nothing.

Abigail spoke up. "With all the marriage proposals you get, I'm surprised no one did."

"It's because of our blasted curfews," Tully complained. "Just when the fun begins, it's time to go home. It's a big pain, and most men don't want to bother."

The street in front of the dance hall was jammed with buggies and carriages. The screeching sound of fiddle music wafted from the open doors. Women dressed in colorful frocks were escorted inside by the town's most eligible bachelors.

Katie searched for Branch among the glittery crowd, but she didn't see him or his horse. The memory of dancing with him beneath a star-studded sky filled her with such a sense of longing that she literally ached inside. She'd felt beautiful in his arms, desirable even, and no one had ever made her feel that way. Certainly not Nathan Cole.

Is that how the chef made Miss Thatcher feel? His eyes certainly lit up when he saw her earlier, and he took as much care helping her into her wrap as he gave his pastry. *Oh, God, please make it so.* Miss Thatcher deserved some happiness.

They waited for the couple to enter the dance hall before turning back to the house. No longer worried about being overheard, Tully's voice rose but not her spirits.

"Next time there's a dance," she declared with a determined shake of the head, "I'm going. With or without an escort."

As they passed the sheriff's office, Katie kept her gaze focused straight ahead, but that didn't stop her heart from beating in triple time.

Her pace slowed as they reached the corner of Main and Sunflower, and she fell behind the others. This was the spot where

Ginger lost her shoe, and it still puzzled her. Nagged her, more like it.

Standing in the middle of the street, she visually followed the rooflines outlined against the black velvet sky. The shops and businesses located at street level were dark. Lights shone from the windows of second-story apartments where most of the shopkeepers lived. Mrs. Bracegirdle lived closest to the bank.

Branch had interviewed every resident living on the street and had come up empty. No one heard or saw anything suspicious.

Mary-Lou and the others were almost a block away, their voices fading. Anxious to catch up, Katie's gaze traveled over the upper part of the buildings again, and a flash of light caught her eye. It came from the vacant apartment over the bank.

The two rectangular windows were dark now, and she could just make out the FOR RENT sign in the corner of one. Had she seen what she thought she saw? Or were her eyes simply playing tricks?

Maybe she caught the reflection of the gas streetlamp from across the way. She backed up in an effort to test her theory, but the windows remained dark. Convinced she'd only imagined a light, she hurried to catch up to the others.

CHAPTER 37

The town was still deserted when Branch arrived at his office early that Monday morning to find Clayborn waiting for him.

Branch dismounted and tethered his horse to the hitching post next to Clayborn's brown gelding. He walked slowly, methodically, up the steps leading to the boardwalk. A walk to the gallows couldn't have taken more out of him.

Clayborn greeted him with a nod, his eyes dark and fathomless as two pieces of coal. He leaned against the building puffing on a cigarette, ankles crossed. Had he known the murderous thoughts going through Branch's head, he might have looked less casual and unconcerned.

Branch nodded in return. "What brings you here so bright and early?" As if he didn't know.

Clayborn dropped the butt of his cigarette on the boardwalk and ground it out with the heel of his boot. "Got a paper I need signed. Then I'll be on my way."

Stomach clenched, Branch unlocked the door. "Does that mean you're leaving town?"

Clayborn followed him inside. "Nothing keeping me here."

Stepping inside his office, Branch methodically hung his hat on the wall hook instead of tossing it. The keys he threw on the desk.

Woody and Scarface both looked up from their cots. Woody's gaze flitted from Branch to Clayborn and back again, but he said nothing.

Branch sat at his desk, the chair groaning beneath his weight. "Let's see what you got."

Clayborn reached into his trouser pocket for a folded piece of paper and handed it over.

Branch unfolded the document. The letterhead read ALFRED L. ASHFORD, ATTORNEY AND COUNSELOR AT LAW. Branch didn't recognize the name, which meant Clayborn hadn't trusted the local lawyers to handle the matter. The man was careless in manners, dress, and integrity but wasn't taking any chances with the trust fund.

Below was a line for the signature and date. In between were two tersely written sentences declaring the Clayborn infant and its mother deceased.

All Branch had to do was sign his name on the line and his troubles would be over. His signature would keep Clayborn from taking Andy away.

"It's all nice and legal," Clayborn said, as if sensing his hesitation.

The letter didn't waste words. It included only date and place of death and stated there were no other living relatives.

Branch stared at the document until his vision blurred and the ink seemed to dance across the page. He blinked to refocus and read the letter again.

Clayborn shuffled his feet. "Is there a problem?"

"No problem," Branch muttered. He reached for his fountain pen just as Reverend Bushwell's words came to mind.

"No one can have a relationship with God while living a lie."

His mouth twisted. *Sorry, Reverend, but I'm no Abraham.* He dipped the nib into the bottle of ink. This time Katie's voice echoed in his head, loud and clear. *"You'll do the right thing."*

He grimaced, and the pen slipped out of his clammy hand. Wiping his damp palm on his vest, he picked the pen off the desk.

It wasn't often that he was scared, but he

was today. Scared of losing Andy. Scared of losing the one thing that had kept him going these past eight years — the son his wife had died saving.

He was also worried about what it would do to the boy to be uprooted from the only home he'd ever known. Would Clayborn desert him as he'd deserted Dorothy?

Branch also feared losing his faith in God, imperfect as it was.

"I'm not afraid of muddy air anymore. Not afraid of eight legs on the hoof, either."

Brave words from a brave little boy.

A boy with a coward for a father.

The strong vibrant voice in his head left him reeling. Where had that come from? Surely not God . . .

Whether it was or not he didn't know. He only knew that signing that paper would be a coward's way out, and Andy deserved a better father than that. A lot better.

Tossing the pen on his desk, he sat back in his chair. "We're going to do this the right way."

"The right way?" Clayborn frowned. "What's that supposed to mean?"

"It means that I'm not signing that paper. I'd be breaking the law if I did."

"Whatcha talkin' about?"

Branch leaned forward. "Dorothy's infant

didn't die in that tornado. He's alive, thanks to my wife."

"He?" An incredulous look crossed Clayborn's face. "I have a son?"

Branch clenched his hands. "He's not your son. He's mine. And I'll fight you in every court of the land to prove it, if necessary."

Clayborn gaped at him, and only Woody's peg leg scraping across the cell floor broke the silence between them.

"Are you saying that the boy I saw you with —" He rubbed his chin, and his eyes grew wide as the implications sank in. "You have no right —"

"I have every right." Branch half rose out of his chair. "Eight years of being the only father he's ever known gives me that right. Now get out of here. It makes me sick just to look at your sorry mug."

Clayborn pointed a threatening finger. "This isn't over, Whitman. It won't be over until I get what's rightfully mine." With that he whirled about and shot outside. The door slammed shut with a bang, and Branch's hat fell from the wall hook, along with the newly posted sign forbidding both men *and* women from carrying guns in town.

"Whoo-ee," Woody called out, holding on to the bars. "That one's loaded to the muzzle. Better watch your back."

Scarface concurred with a nod. "And don't forgit to keep an eye on your front side, too. I don't aim on stickin' around if they bring in another sheriff."

The railroad workers were in especially good spirits that morning and lingered longer over breakfast than usual.

Seated at the counter, Okie-Sam shot a glance at the noisy group. "First of the month payday. They're always rowdier on payday." He folded his newspaper and flipped a coin onto the counter. "Thanks, sis," he said and sauntered off.

No sooner had he left than Long-Shot walked through the door.

One of the railroad workers called out, "Hey, Long-Shot! Whatcha running for next?"

Long-Shot tugged on his red suspenders and stuck out his chest. "How about I run for the school board?"

"How about you learn to read first?"

During the laughter that followed, Charley Reynolds arrived but sat by himself. He looked less forlorn today than he'd looked the night Katie questioned him outside the Harvey House.

She nudged Mary-Lou. "Go take care of

Charley. I'll take care of the others."

Katie enjoyed bantering with the boys, as she called them, but they were a demanding bunch and kept the Harvey girls hopping.

Finally they left, and Katie ducked behind the counter. She was anxious to talk to Mrs. Bracegirdle before the morning train arrived.

Sitting at the counter in her usual spot, the older woman greeted Katie with a smile and roll of the eyes. Today she wore a mauve skirt and shirtwaist with white hat and gloves. "These young whippersnappers don't know funny from hay. You should have heard my Harry. He could read the train schedule and make you double over laughing."

"I wish I could have known your husband."

"I wish you could have, too." Her eyes crinkled. "Right now you have to concentrate on finding your own man."

Katie blushed. "It's not that easy." It certainly hadn't been for her.

Mrs. Bracegirdle picked up the menu and perused it. "Actually, finding the right man is not the problem. Recognizing him is the real challenge. You'd be surprised at what's right there under your very muzzle."

Right now the only thing Katie hoped to

find under her nose was a sign pointing to the killer. She glanced around the room. *God, if there's a clue here, help me see it.*

Tully was in deep conversation with a cattleman. Buzz watched them as he polished the brass door handles, a look of uncertainty on his face. Poor man had his hands full with Tully.

Charley drained the last of his coffee. He said something to Mary-Lou, bringing a smile to her face, and left. Abigail refilled Long-Shot's cup and laughed at whatever he said. Next to the door Culpepper counted money.

Katie sighed. If there was a clue here, she certainly couldn't see it. She filled a cup from the coffee urn and set the steaming brew in front of the old lady.

"I'll have the usual." Mrs. Bracegirdle folded the menu and set it aside. She always read the entire menu even though her order never varied.

Katie smiled and called Mrs. Bracegirdle's order to the kitchen. Chef Gassy threw her a kiss before turning to the stove. Neither he nor Miss Thatcher mentioned the dance, but the dorm matron had been heard humming from time to time and just that morning failed to notice Tully was wearing face powder.

As for the chef, Katie swore she heard him whistling earlier when she stepped into the kitchen. He also failed to yell upon finding paw prints all over the chopping board. Instead, he surprised Katie by setting out a bowl of milk for Spook Cat.

She turned back to the counter. "Has anyone rented the apartment over the bank?" She spoke in a casual voice one might use to make small talk.

"No, and they won't, either."

Katie frowned. "Why do you say that?"

"The last couple who rented it moved in and out in less than a day. It's that darn cat. It thinks it's Jenny Lind or something."

Mrs. Bracegirdle added a dollop of cream to her coffee and stirred. "I spoke to the dogcatcher, and he told me it's not his job to catch cats."

"Did you ever see a light in the apartment?" Katie asked. "You know, through the window?"

"No lights. Just opera." Mrs. Bracegirdle blew on her coffee and took a sip before continuing. "Like I told you before, Branch checked it out but didn't find anything but a banging shutter." She set her cup down and added more cream.

Katie pondered this a moment before asking, "Do you remember Ginger?"

"Oh yes. Such a pretty little thing. She always served me breakfast. It's a terrible thing that happened to her. Priscilla, too."

"Did you know that Ginger's shoe was found in front of your place?"

Mrs. Bracegirdle set her coffee cup down with a clink. "My place?"

"Actually, on the corner in front of the bank. I believe she might have lost it the night she died."

Mrs. Bracegirdle pursed her lips. "That's the first I heard of a shoe. How do you suppose it got there?"

"That's a good question," Katie said.

"I'm telling you, there are some mighty strange things going on." Mrs. Bracegirdle leaned forward and lowered her voice. "Did I tell you about the time I found a strange man in my bed?"

CHAPTER 38

Katie waited for Branch to unlock the apartment over the bank. A horse and wagon passed on the street below, stirring up dust. The door to Mrs. Bracegirdle's place remained shut.

"I'm worried about her," Katie whispered. How was it possible to sound so lucid even when talking about singing cats and strange men in her bed? "I don't know that she should be living alone."

"Her son keeps a pretty good eye on her, but I'll talk to him."

She nodded. "Good idea."

The door opened with a creak of its leather hinges, and Branch gestured her inside.

"I don't know why I let you talk me into this," he said.

"I told you. I thought I saw a light."

They stood facing each other and a ripple of awareness rushed through her. Suddenly, she was in his arms again — or so it seemed — his lips on hers. The vision was so real it took her breath away.

Shaken, she turned away. Mrs. Bracegirdle wasn't the only one suffering from hallucinations. Time to concentrate on the investigation and not the man.

She might have done just that had he not stopped her with a hand to her wrist.

"The other night . . . ," he began, his voice thick with meaning. "We should talk about it."

She looked back at him, and her barely contained emotions took another perilous leap. "There's nothing to talk about," she whispered. "You needed a friend and it was me."

He released her arm. "Is that what you think?"

She nodded and waited for him to object. *No, no,* she wanted him to say. *The kiss meant much more than mere friendship. It meant the world to me. It meant I love you. . . .*

He said none of the words she longed to hear. Instead he stared at her long and hard before silently turning away.

She wanted to go to him. Lay her head on his chest and declare it all a lie. But fear prevented her from doing what her heart dictated. What if he rejected her like all the others? Her family. Nathan . . .

She'd managed to survive the rejections of her past, but she didn't think she could survive his. Already she had proof of that. The piercing pain in her chest could only come from a broken heart, pieces of which were lodged in her throat.

Swallowing hard, she forced herself to look around. Work. That's what she must concentrate on. It saved her in the past and she prayed it would save her now.

The room was empty and as forlorn as the void inside her. Flecks of wallpaper dripped from the wall like the tears she was too proud — or maybe even too stubborn — to shed.

Clamping down on her thoughts, she focused on the golden beam of sunlight streaming through the windows. Oddly enough, the cardboard sign she'd seen the night before was now on the carpet. She picked it up and placed it on the windowsill facing out.

Something bothered her nose and she sneezed. "What's that funny smell?" She glanced at him. Had he heard the tremor in her voice? She hoped not. She cleared her throat. "Smells like metal."

"Smells like dust to me," Branch said.

All three rooms were empty except for a

lantern in the kitchen.

Branch leaned against the kitchen door-frame with his arms crossed while she checked the cabinets and drawers. Even the light from the kitchen window failed to penetrate the darkness of his eyes.

"Satisfied?" he asked.

"Yes," she said, eyeing a tin cup in the kitchen sink. "For now."

She wiped her damp hands on the side of her skirt. "I just want to check the bedroom again," she murmured. There was nothing to check, but it allowed her an excuse to escape his scrutiny and get her rampaging emotions under control.

Moments later, she found him in the parlor staring out the window. The window shade had been lifted all the way up. He looked like he was a million miles away. Standing behind him, she rose on tiptoes to peer over his shoulder. The window over-looked the street where Ginger had lost her shoe.

"Sorry to waste your time," she said.

For the longest while he said nothing, and she hesitated to break the silence. She wanted so much to touch him. To bring him back to the present. To bring him back to her. But it was hard enough just being in the same room with him.

Finally he turned. "He knows," he said, and the look of devastation on his face nearly tore her apart.

She drew in her breath. She didn't have to ask who or what. His expression told her all she needed to know. "How?"

"I told him."

She frowned. "But why?"

"I decided to take the pastor's advice and put my trust in God."

She bit her lip. "That . . . that's good, isn't it?"

"We'll know soon enough. Judge Hendricks arrives on the midday train. He agreed to postpone Scarface's trial and hold a custody hearing instead." He cleared his voice. "I'd like you to be there. That is, if you can get off work."

"I'll try, but I'm not sure I can be of any help."

"You could say something nice about me to the judge. I'll need all the character witnesses I can get."

"I can do that." She wanted to kick herself for not realizing sooner that he was half out of his mind with worry. Here she was thinking about her own feelings, her own needs, while he feared losing his son.

"The hearing will be held at the hotel at two," he said and hesitated. "I don't want to get you in trouble with Pickens."

She discounted his concern with a shake of her head. "It doesn't matter. Working at the Harvey House has got me nowhere. I'd have done just as well staying at the hotel."

"I'm sorry, Katie. I know how much you want to find the killer. We both do."

She nodded. "Right now let's concentrate on the hearing. We could both use some good news."

A smile tugged at the corners of his mouth. "If you're done here —"

"I am." Turning, she walked to the door. She prayed she had better luck convincing the judge that Branch deserved keeping his son than she had in tracking down a killer. *God, please make it so. . . .*

CHAPTER 39

The hearing was held on the second floor of the hotel in a room set aside for just that purpose. Katie slipped into the room quietly and sat in the back row next to newspaper editor Clovis Read. He nodded a greeting, pen and paper in hand.

The circuit judge was a barrel-shaped man with a sweeping mustache and sideburns so furry as to look like earmuffs. He sat at the front of the room facing them, his head ringed with cigar smoke. Wire-framed spectacles teetered on the tip of his nose as he perused his notes.

No sooner had Katie seated herself than Branch glanced over his shoulder. He winked before turning back to the man next to him, probably his lawyer. Reminding herself to breathe, she pressed her hands together on her lap.

She wouldn't even be here had Chef Gassy not helped her sneak away and promised to cover for her. Ever since Katie had convinced Miss Thatcher to go to the dance with him, it seemed there was nothing he wouldn't do for her.

The clock on the wall indicated it was after two. Still there was no sign of Clayborn. Did that mean he had changed his mind about seeking custody of his son? *Oh, God, please make it so.*

The judge pulled the watch out of his coat pocket and flipped the gold case open. "We'll give Mr. Clayborn another few minutes before we get started."

The room was hot and airless, yet no one had thought to open the windows. In a front seat Reverend Bushwell swatted a fly away with his hat.

The judge clamped down on his cigar with his teeth as he dabbed at his forehead with a handkerchief.

A restless buzz filled the air like swarming bees. Next to her the newspaper editor doodled on his notepad.

If Clayborn failed to show, would the judge rule in Branch's favor through default? Now wouldn't that be an answer to prayer?

Just then the door swung open, and all heads, including Katie's, swiveled toward the back of the room. Only it wasn't Clayborn. Instead, a dark-skinned woman ran into the room, obviously in distress.

"Andy's gone!" she cried. "Andy's gone." She then collapsed to her knees, sobbing.

Branch shot out of his seat, ran to the back of the room, and stooped by her side. "What do you mean, gone?"

The woman could only manage one word, but it was enough. "Clayborn."

A collective gasp filled the makeshift courtroom, and Katie jumped to her feet.

"When?" The blood drained from Branch's face. "Tell me!"

"Just a while ago," the woman said between sobs. "Saw him snatch Andy and . . . and take off on his horse."

Branch straightened, hands clenched by his side. "Which way did he go?"

"West. He was travelin' west."

Katie ran down the stairs, through the hotel lobby, and out the door. "Wait!" she called. "Branch, wait!"

Already astride his saddle, Branch circled his horse to face her.

"I'm going with you!" she called.

"There's no time." He spun Midnight in the opposite direction and raced away.

Whirling about, she spotted Reverend Bushwell walking out of the hotel. She rushed over to him and whispered in his ear.

"I'm a Pinkerton detective and I need your horse."

His eyes widened and his eyebrows shot up, but he nodded.

"Thank you!" She quickly untied the minister's horse from the hitching post and jabbed her foot in the stirrup. Throwing her leg over the saddle, she'd barely settled astride before yelling, "Gid-up!"

The horse took off running.

A mule-drawn wagon blocked the road ahead while a farmer unloaded his crops. Katie caught up to Branch just as the farmer cleared the road.

"Did you see Andy pass by?" Branch called to the farmer.

The man's face was as dark and wrinkled as a prune. "Nope. Can't say that I did." The farmer started to say more, but already Branch had taken off, Midnight's thunderous hooves pounding the dirt road. The minister's mare was smaller than Branch's gelding, and Katie had a hard time keeping up.

Dogs barked, and chickens flew to the tops of fences, scattering feathers.

They saw no sign of Clayborn, but still they kept going, past fields of wildflowers and tall grass. Past herds of cattle and horses. Past acres of wheat and knee-high corn.

They rode for a good half hour before Branch reined in his horse. He twisted in his saddle and pointed to the side of the road. "That's Andy's!" he yelled.

She pulled up alongside of him and followed his gaze to the abandoned shoe — the first sign they were on the right trail. But that gave her little comfort. Between here and the cheerless prairie to the west was an abundance of hills and trees. Before Kansas became a state, this area flourished with outlaw hideouts. A person could get lost in those hills and never be found.

Branch slipped from the saddle and snatched the shoe off the ground. He held it to his chest before sticking it into his saddlebag.

Just as he mounted his horse, a gunshot ripped through the quiet, startling a flock of blackbirds. Squawking, the crows rose from the treetops, creating a swirling black cloud overhead. Branch raced away, clods of dirt flying from beneath his horse's pounding hooves.

Acting purely out of instinct, Katie spurred her mount and took off after him.

CHAPTER 40

Branch pressed his finger to his mouth. He and Katie lay on their stomachs side by side in a dry creek staring at the Connor cabin.

Branch pulled out his Colt. Katie already had her weapon in hand, though Branch was hesitant to put the ridiculously small derringer in the same category as his own.

He took the derringer from her and replaced it with his own revolver. "That's what I call a gun," he said, reaching into his holster for his second pistol. "Cover me. I'm going in."

She grabbed his arm. Surprised by the strength of her grip, he looked down at her hand before meeting her gaze.

"Be careful," she whispered. The concern in her eyes filled him with longing, and he inhaled sharply. It had been a long time since anyone looked at him like that. Too long.

He sucked in his breath. He hadn't wanted

her to come. Now he was glad to have her by his side — a selfish thought. Still, it felt like she belonged there. But should anything happen to her . . . *Oh, God, no!* Squelching the thought, he squeezed her hand.

"What would your Pinkerton bosses do under these circumstances?" he asked, hoping to tease the worried look from her face.

"They would try to negotiate with the hostage taker."

"Negotiate, eh?" Gaze riveted on the cabin, he jumped up and left the gully on the run. He was halfway to the cabin when a voice called out.

"Pa!"

For a split second he was confused by the still-closed cabin door. He then realized Andy's voice came from the woods, not the cabin. He spun around just as Andy broke away from Clayborn and ran.

"Pa!"

Clayborn was right behind him. "Come back here, you!"

"Watch out!" Katie screamed.

Branch's gaze shot to the cabin. The door was open a crack, and the sun glinted against the muzzle of a rifle.

"Don't shoot!" he yelled at the hidden gunman. He darted toward his son, but Clayborn reached him first and threw the startled boy down to the ground.

The sharp crack of a rifle was met with the heavy boom of a Colt pistol. Katie's blast did the trick, for the cabin door slammed shut.

It took only a second for Branch to reach his son's side, but it seemed like forever. Holstering his gun, he lifted Andy in his arms and ran into the woods for cover. He set Andy down in the middle of the thick grove of cottonwoods.

"It's okay, Son. It's okay." He didn't believe his own reassurances until he had checked Andy over from head to toe. Andy was still trembling, but there were no visible injuries. *Oh, God! If anything had happened to him . . .*

Andy stared up at him with eyes that seemed too old for his tender years. "I told that man I didn't want to go with him."

"I know, Andy. I know."

"I lost my shoe, Pa."

"I found it. It's in my saddlebags. We'll get it later. Right now you need to stay here."

Katie joined them, weapon still in hand, and fell to her knees by his side. "Is he all right?"

"Seems like it." He glanced over his shoulder. The cabin showed no sign of life, and Clayborn hadn't moved since falling to the ground.

"Stay with Andy," he said.

He heard her intake of breath. "Be careful."

Touched once again by her concern for his welfare, he was tempted to take her in his arms. But the sound of galloping horse hooves made him leave her side and dash into the clearing.

The horseman had a good head start, and Branch decided not to give chase. Was there only one gunman? The horse tied to a sapling was most likely Clayborn's, but he wasn't about to take a chance.

With an anxious glance at the cabin door, Branch knelt beside the fallen man and rolled him over onto his back. He'd been shot and his shirt was soaked with blood, but he was still breathing.

Hooking his arms beneath the injured man's armpits, he raised him to his feet. He grabbed hold of Clayborn's right arm and thrust him over his shoulder. Clayborn's head and arms trailed down his back.

Staggering away from the cabin, Branch entered the grove of trees, choosing a place away from Andy and Katie. The boy was scared enough without seeing all that blood.

He laid Clayborn down in a soft patch of leaves.

Clayborn's eyes flickered open. "Andy?" he whispered. He wasn't breathing as much as panting. "Is he . . . ?"

"He's fine," Branch said. He ripped Clayborn's shirt open and pressed a handkerchief against the wound on his chest in an effort to stop the flow of blood. "You saved his life."

The whites of Clayborn's eyes showed, and his lids came down.

"Hold on," Branch said, slapping him gently on the cheeks.

Clayborn's eyes flickered open, and his mouth moved silently before he was finally able to find his voice. "Done a lot of things I shouldn't have."

"Better save your strength till I get you in town."

But once started, Clayborn couldn't seem to stop. "Took money that didn't belong to me. Cheated at cards. Drank too much." His voice was so faint Branch had to lower his head to hear. "Shouldn't have left Dottie. Never should have done that. Maybe she'd still be alive if I'd stayed."

Branch shook his head. The man had enough reasons to feel guilty, but Dorothy's death wasn't one of them. "There was nothing you could have done. The tornado . . . There was nothing any of us could have done."

"Do you . . . think taking the bullet for . . . for Andy put me in good stead with G–God?"

"I'm sure it did," Branch said. His confession no doubt helped, too. "God's grace knows no end."

"Take . . . take care of him."

"You have my word."

Clayborn studied him from beneath half-closed lids, his pale face etched with the gray of impending death. "Dottie always said that special prayer when someone was sick or dying. Don't remember the words."

"Do you mean the Lord's Prayer?" Clayborn gave a slight nod, and Branch began, "Our Father . . ." He recited the prayer from beginning to end. "Amen."

"Amen," Clayborn whispered and coughed. He had a hard time catching his breath. "What . . . what are you gonna tell Andy about me?" he asked.

Branch pulled the kerchief from around his neck and wiped away the trickle of blood from the corner of Clayborn's mouth. "I'll tell him that in the end his father — his real father — gave himself to the Lord."

"That's good. Th–that's real good." Clayborn's body shuddered once, and his head fell to the side.

Branch checked Clayborn's pulse, but the vein told him only what he already knew.

CHAPTER 41

"Where's Pa?" Andy asked.

"He'll be here soon," Katie said. She craned her head around the trunk of a tree. Branch had disappeared in the woods with Clayborn and she hadn't seen him since.

Her legs trembled and her mouth felt dry as old parchment paper. The bullet had missed Branch, and that was a miracle. If something had happened to him . . . to his son . . .

The thought almost brought her to her knees, and she quickly banished it. Mustn't think about that. Have to stay alert. Protect Andy. That's what she had to do. The boy had gone through a terrible ordeal. She must remain calm for his sake.

The cabin was hidden behind the trees. Was the gunman still inside? She thought she heard a horse gallop away earlier, but it could have been a trick.

Her hand tightened around the Colt pistol.

Andy was occupied with watching a spider dangle from a tree branch on a silver thread. "I wasn't afraid, you know," he said. "I pretended — like you do."

"What do you mean?" she asked.

"You know how you pretend that beans are bullets and the dark is just muddy air?"

"And spiders are just —"

"Eight legs on a hoof." He giggled before growing serious. "Well, I pretended that I was brave like Mr. Robinson."

"Who is Mr. Robinson?"

"The father in *Swiss Family Robinson.*"

"Ah, yes, of course. I remember reading that book many years ago. I wasn't much older than you are now."

Andy abandoned the spider and picked up a stick. "Do you ever pretend to be someone you're not?" he asked.

She nodded. "Sometimes."

He gazed at her with curiosity. "Like who?"

"Let me think." She thought about all the disguises donned as a detective through the years. Each one had stolen a piece of her until she'd hardly known who she was. Then she met Branch, and somehow he put her back together piece by piece like a jigsaw puzzle. He made her aware of the woman inside, a woman who needed to love and be loved. The woman God had meant her to be.

Aware suddenly that Andy was still waiting for an answer, she said, "Once I pretended to be a pirate."

He laughed. "Next time someone tries to take me away I'll pretend I'm a pirate and make him walk the plank."

"What's all this talk about pirates?" Branch stepped into the small clearing, and Katie's heart leaped with relief and something else. Something she was afraid to name but that felt as deep and wide as an ocean. Her first instinct was to throw herself into his arms. She might have done just that had Andy not beaten her to the punch.

"Pa!"

Branch lifted Andy off the ground and whirled him around before setting him down again.

She held out his pistol, grip first. He took it from her and shoved it in his holster. His gaze locked with hers.

"Sure you don't want it?"

"Want it? I'm still trying to recover from firing it." The blood on his vest made her gasp, and she reached for his arm. "You're hurt."

"Not me," he said with a meaningful glance.

Andy waved his stick about like a sword. "Miss Katie pretended to be a pirate."

Branch put on a good show for his son, and no one could guess the ordeal he'd just come through.

"A lady pirate, eh?" Branch afforded her a wink.

"Clayborn?" she mouthed.

He answered her silent question with a shake of his head. That was one problem solved, but there was still the gunman to worry about.

As if to guess her thoughts, he said, "The cabin's empty. Whoever fired that shot is gone." He slanted a nod at her blood-covered hand. "Go wash off. We'll meet you at the horses. You and Andy can ride back to town while I finish up."

"I'll just be a minute," she said and started for the cabin.

Behind her Branch called to his son, "Come on, Pirate Pete."

The cabin door creaked as she pressed against it. She stepped inside, leaving the door open behind her.

The cabin was built from adobe brick, and a floor-to-ceiling rock fireplace commanded

372

one wall. The room was sparsely furnished. She walked through to the kitchen and primed the pump at the sink until rusty water trickled from the spout.

She rinsed off her hands and, having no towel, dried them on her skirt. A cup on the counter caught her attention, and the nine o'clock position of the handle made her think of orange pekoe tea. The Harvey House code had now become so ingrained that "reading" cups seemed as natural to her as reading tea leaves was to a medium.

Shaking her head at the incongruity of thinking of cup codes at a time like this, she glanced around.

Except for the cup and a dirty ashtray, the counters were bare. A quick check of the kitchen cabinets revealed a stash of neatly stacked tinned goods. The gunman had stayed in the cabin for a while but would probably not come back. Who or what was he hiding from?

Out of habit, she checked the bedroom. Rusty bed springs occupied one side of the room and an old chest of drawers the other. A window was open, and she leaned on the sill and peered outside. That must have been how the gunman made his escape.

She closed the window and returned to the front room. A bedroll was laid out flat and ashes piled up in the stone fireplace.

Since Branch was waiting for her to take Andy back to town, she walked to the door. Hesitating, she glanced around the room again. A strange sensation came over her. A thought tiptoed on the outermost part of her mind like a forgotten name or half-remembered dream.

Try as she might, she couldn't bring it to the fore. It continued to plague her as she walked outside to join Branch and Andy.

Something . . .

CHAPTER 42

The late-afternoon sun still felt warm as Katie rode back to town. Andy, seated behind her on the bay horse, held on tight, arms clamped around her waist as if to never let her go.

"We're almost home," she said.

Reverend Bushwell spotted them first. With a wave of his hand, he vanished inside the church, and seconds later church bells rang out the news of Andy's safe return. The pealing chimes brought people running from all directions to greet them.

Katie tugged on the reins, and the minister helped Andy from the back of the horse.

Just as Katie dismounted, Mary-Lou, Tully, and Abigail rushed up. "Thank God you're okay," Mary-Lou cried, throwing her arms around her.

"I'm fine."

Mary-Lou released her, and Katie looked around in bewilderment. "But what are you all doing here?"

"We heard about what happened to the sheriff's son," Mary-Lou explained.

"And we came to the church to pray for his safe return," Abigail added.

Miss Thatcher, Buzz, and Culpepper, along with at least half of the railroad workers, had turned out. Mrs. Bracegirdle stood leaning on her cane.

Even Okie-Sam was there, a knapsack flung over his shoulder. He slid a hefty arm around her shoulders. "Don't go scaring your brother like that, you hear?" He withdrew his arm. "If anyone hurt my sis . . ." He pounded a fist into the palm of his hand. "He'd have me to contend with."

She gave him a wan smile and tossed a nod at the canvas bag. "Going somewhere?"

"Just for a few days or so. My pa . . ."

"Hope it's nothing serious," she said, but already he had turned away and her attention was caught up by the other well-wishers.

Katie blinked away the burning in her eyes. Oddly enough, it felt like she was surrounded by family.

"What I don't understand is why you got involved," Tully said.

Mary-Lou frowned. "Really, Tully. This isn't the time —"

Just then Branch's housekeeper barreled up to them and Andy all but disappeared in her ample arms. "Lawdy, I never prayed so hard in all my born days. Whatcha taking off on me like that fur, boy? I swear, I've turned two shades lighter. My husband won't recognize me."

"I didn't take off," Andy protested. "That man stole me."

The housekeeper released him. "Well, let's get you home where you belong." She hustled the boy away, her mouth flapping like a broken shutter. "Looks like you could use some soap and water and . . ."

No sooner had Andy and the housekeeper departed than the crowd began to disperse.

Miss Thatcher gave her hands three sharp claps. "Come along, girls. We have less than forty minutes until the five-twenty-five." She hustled them back to the restaurant like a drover herding his stock.

Minutes later, Chef Gassy met them at the kitchen door. "Hurry, hurry, the zain due in soon."

While the others ran ahead, Katie stayed behind. Something snapped inside, and laughter bubbled out of her like water from a spring. Not mirthful laughter, but uncontrolled guffaws that brought tears to her eyes. Gassy stared at her as if she'd lost her mind, but she couldn't help it.

Andy had been kidnapped, a man had died, and Gassy's only concern was the next meal. Crazy as that sounded, she found it comforting.

"I love you!" she said through her tears and threw her arms around the startled man, knocking off his toque. And yes, it really did feel like she had come home.

Releasing him, she dashed from the kitchen and . . .

Crashed headlong into Pickens. Judging by his red face he was fit to be tied.

Andy fell asleep the moment his head hit the pillow that night. Smiling to himself, Branch set the unread book on the table next to his bed. It had been a long, hard day for all of them.

Thank You, God. Thank You for bringing my boy back to me. And forgive me for ever doubting You.

He reached over to turn off the light and quietly left the room.

In the parlor, Miss Chloe looked up from the rocking chair where she sat reading the Bible.

"How come you're still here?" he asked. "It's late. You should be home." His housekeeper closed the Bible. Giving the leather cover a loving pat with a large, capable hand, she set it on the table. "Wanted to make sure you and the boy had no need for me."

"Not tonight," he said and sat. He was too wound up to sleep. Maybe it would help to read for a while.

"You look like you fell off yer horse and was dragged to kingdom come," she said.

"Feel like it."

Miss Chloe hauled herself out of the chair and gathered up her gloves and hat. She then hesitated.

"Something wrong?" he asked.

"I feel bad about what happened. It's my job to take care of Andy, and I failed."

"You didn't fail." If anyone was to blame it was him. Fear of losing Andy had muddled his brain, and he'd handled the matter all wrong. He should have known Clayborn would pull a stunt like that. That's how he operated. Things got tough, the man took off.

Miss Chloe arranged her hat on her head and pulled on her gloves. Even a five-minute walk to her house required a certain ritual. "I promised Andy a treat in town if he done good on his schoolwork. He couldn't wait and ran ahead of me. I should have made him hold my hand."

"Andy's a big boy now." He hadn't realized how big and brave until today. He came out of the ordeal better than any of the adults involved, himself included. "He doesn't need us holding his hand. He just needs us holding him in prayer."

"That I do, Sheriff. That I do." Her forehead creased. "Just want you to know I've enjoyed workin' here. You're the best employer I ever did have."

He frowned. "You're not thinking of quitting, are you?" What would he do without her? What would Andy do?

"Not by choice," she said. "But it's been my experience that a home has room for only one woman at a time."

He pinched his forehead. He must be more tired than he thought, for suddenly she was making no sense. "What are you talking about? One woman."

"I saw how you look every time that boy of yours mentions Miss Katie's name." She gave her head an emphatic nod. "I sure enough did."

Branch moved his hand away from his face. Miss Chloe didn't know what she was talking about.

"Katie . . . Miss Madison was a big help today," he said. "I'm grateful to her."

"I don't have much in the way of school

learnin', but I know gratitude when I sees it and I know when a man sets his cap for a woman. I'd say you have it bad, real bad."

He stared at her. "You better go home and get some shut-eye. That's crazy talk."

"All I'm sayin' is that when the time comes, there's no call to worry about lettin' me go. I'll be fine."

"Far as I'm concerned, you can work here till the cows come home," he said.

Her teeth flashed white against her dark, glistening skin. "Those cows might not be as far afield as you think." She headed for the door. "Night, Sheriff."

"Night," he muttered as she let herself out. He reached for his book but, after rereading the same paragraph several times, finally gave up.

Was Miss Chloe onto something? He couldn't deny his attraction to Katie. One look into that pretty round face and he'd felt strangely alive, like he'd been walking around all these years half-asleep. He liked her — no denying that. Liked the way she walked and talked and even smiled.

He even liked working with her. He shuddered at what might have happened had she not been there to warn him of the rifle.

He couldn't make up his mind what affected him more: her strength or vulnerability. True, sometimes her willingness to put herself in danger made him want to wring her neck, but the other part — the vulnerable part — made him want to hold her. Hold her like he did the night they danced by the light of the moon. Hold her like he did that night in the alley.

But that didn't mean he'd set his cap for her. A lady detective, of all things. A *Pinkerton* detective.

A small-county sheriff like him had nothing to offer a woman like her. She lived a life of excitement and adventure. No one in her right mind would give up a life like that, especially for a man whose idea of adventure was settling down with a good book.

Miss Chloe was wrong. What he felt for Katie wasn't love. Couldn't be love. Because if it was, he was in a whole peck of trouble.

Katie stared at the paper in front of her, blank except for a spot of ink that had leaked from her pen. The house was quiet late that night. She sat at the kitchen table with only a lit candle by which to work.

The air hung thick with the smell of onions and wet cat fur. She'd let Spook Cat in earlier when a rain shower passed through town. After filling his belly with warm milk, the tom curled up by her feet.

Without the drops pitter-pattering on the windows to distract her, the blank sheet of paper seemed even more intimidating.

Two hours she'd sat there. It wasn't that she didn't know what to write. She knew exactly what had to be said. She'd failed in her duties. Two Harvey girls had lost their lives, and it looked like their killer would never be found.

Her cover was blown. The reverend now knew her identity, and so did Pickens. Confiding in the manager was the only way she could stay at the restaurant after he'd fired her. She had done the unforgivable and had left the restaurant without a word. Such an offense deserved no second chances. Nor would he listen to her explanations. He'd simply said, "You're fired. Pack your bags."

She either had to tell him the truth or leave on the next train. Her reasons for not wanting to leave were many. Branch . . .

No, mustn't go there. Branch had nothing to do with her not wanting to leave. Not a thing.

How dumb to think she could stay now that Pickens knew the truth. He'd promised to keep her secret, but whether she could trust him was another matter. Realistically, he was still a suspect. No one at the Harvey

House had been cleared. Any one of them could be the killer, though she hated to think it. She'd grown fond of the place and the people who worked there, even Gassy, and that was part of the problem. She could no longer be objective.

She closed her eyes. *God, why is it so hard for me to admit failure?* It happened to the best of detectives. Even Allan Pinkerton had known defeat in his attempt to capture the James gang. The attempt had ended in disaster and resulted in the death of a child. It had happened long before she joined the company, but some of the older detectives told her that Allan had taken it hard. Some even suggested that he hadn't fully recovered from the fiasco.

Is that what she had to look forward to? A lifetime of regret? Would she always be haunted by memories of Calico and everything that had happened here?

Her muscles ached from sitting so long. Yawning, she decided to get some sleep. The report would have to wait till tomorrow.

She jabbed the pen back into the penholder and reached for the paper. Her hand froze. Was it just her imagination, or did the blob of ink on the otherwise blank sheet of paper look like a shoe?

A woman's shoe.
Ginger's?

CHAPTER 43

Only Branch and Reverend Bushwell were at the small cemetery on that windy day in late May. Branch insisted on Clayborn having a proper Christian burial, and though others had tried to talk him out of it, he held firm. The grave site he'd picked was as far away from Dorothy's and Hannah's as possible. God's grace was infinite, but Branch's forgiveness went only so far.

Tattered clouds drifted across a deep blue sky, and the wind cooled Branch's brow.

The minister performed the simple ceremony and closed with a prayer. After the casket was lowered into the ground, he placed a hand on Branch's shoulder.

"It's a kind thing you've done," he said.

Branch arched an eyebrow. "Kind? Had I handled things better, Clayborn would still be alive."

"You don't know that."

He heaved a sigh. "I put my trust in God

and look what happened."

"What happened is, you have Andy and he's now safely in your care. I'd say that was a pretty good deal. As for Clayborn . . ." He looked down at the dull pine coffin. "His relationship with God failed, not yours."

Branch hadn't thought of it that way, and a weight lifted from his shoulders. "Thank you, Reverend."

"No need to thank me. I speak the truth." After a moment he asked, "Does the boy know it was his real father who kidnapped him?"

"Not yet, but he will." So far few people in town knew the real story behind Andy's kidnapping, but that was bound to change. Better for Andy to hear the truth from him. "When the time's right."

"Would that be his time or your time?"

"God's time," Branch said. Telling Andy about his birth mother posed no real problem, but he would need some heavenly assistance in discussing Andy's biological father.

The two of them fell silent. The quiet was punctuated only by the sound of the grave digger's shovel scooping up soil and dumping it into the hole.

After a while, Bushwell stepped back. "Don't know about you but I could sure use a cup of coffee."

"Joe," Branch said without thinking. "A cup of joe."

Katie stood at Abigail's station and gazed about the dining room, empty except for Tully and Mary-Lou putting last-minute touches on the tables.

Something Abigail had said about Ginger was still on her mind. *"She asked me to change stations with her. She seemed really upset."* Why would Ginger want to change stations? Both stations were similar except that this one had a better view of the front door. Was that the reason Ginger wanted to change?

Pickens entered the dining room with his trusty measuring tape and proceeded to work his way from table to table. Now that he knew her true identity his manner toward her had changed. He had been especially nice to her that day — too nice — even going so far as to ignore a poorly folded napkin at breakfast. Even now he greeted her with a pleasant smile.

"Looking good," he said, which coming from him was high praise.

His uncharacteristic behavior didn't escape Tully's notice. "No favoritism there," she said with a flick of her head. With a huff, she picked up a tray and stalked away.

The gong signaled the twelve-twenty-five train, and the chandelier bounced about like hail on a tin roof. Katie hurried to the breakfast room and took her place behind the counter. Soon both dining rooms were full of travelers.

Abigail leaned over the counter. "I need help," she said. "Could you take charge of the beverages?"

Katie placed an order of roast beef in front of one of the counter guests and nodded.

She quickly set pots of coffee and tea on a tray and carried it to Abigail's station. A quick glance at the cups told her that only one diner had ordered coffee. After filling his cup, she set the coffeepot on the tray stand and reached for one of the teapots. Like a gun going off in her head, a sudden memory came to the fore. Nine o'clock. Orange pekoe tea.

Startled by the thought, she stood there holding the teapot. *That* was what had bothered her at the cabin.

A bearded man held his cup aloft. "I'll take some of that tea, miss."

Shaking off the sudden inertia that rendered her helpless, she forced a smile. "Yes, of course." Her hand shook as she filled his cup. She quickly filled the other cups and moved away. That's when she noticed Branch at the counter.

Her pulse quickened as she hurried to greet him. "What are you doing here?" She set the tray on the counter. He knew this was her busiest time.

"Had a bad morning," he said. "Still no luck finding Clayborn's killer. Thought some of that pie you still owe me would hit the spot, along with a cup of your hottest and strongest."

She sympathized. Branch had the unenviable task of hunting down the man who shot Clayborn, but it couldn't be easy. Not after the trouble Clayborn had caused him.

As if to guess her thoughts, he added, "When the time's right I want to be able to tell Andy that his father's killer was found and justice served."

Nodding, she reached for his cup and saucer and turned to fill it from the large silver coffee urn. She then set the cup of steaming brew on the counter in front of him, careful to turn the handle facing his right hand in the proper Harvey House style.

"What about that pie?" he asked when she continued to stare at his cup.

She lifted her gaze. "I'll give you a piece on one condition."

"What's that?"

She glanced down at the cup again. She hated putting so much stock in a cup handle. Still . . .

"You agree to let me have another look at the apartment over the bank."

Branch was waiting for her that night when she slipped out of the house after curfew. Beneath the dense canopy of stars the air was still and the town quiet.

He held up a key ring and jiggled it. "Got the key from the bank president."

She let out her breath. "Good."

"So what's this about?" he asked as they walked around the building to Main.

"I just want to look around again," she said.

He glanced at her askew. "Why do I get the feeling there's more to it than that?"

"All right," she admitted. "I think the man in the cabin who shot Clayborn was in that apartment."

"Whoa, Nellie!" Stopping in his tracks, he turned to stare at her, pushing back his hat. "Where did that come from?"

She smiled mysteriously. "I also don't believe Mrs. Bracegirdle is off her rocker."

He hung his thumbs from his belt. "Sorry, but I don't see the connection."

"I'm not even sure there is a connection," she said. "But some things don't add up. Ginger's shoe for one. I could never figure out why her shoe was found so far away from where she was found."

"Granted, that's a puzzle."

"Suppose I really did see a light over the bank. And what if Ginger saw one, too. It might have scared her, especially with all that talk about the place being haunted."

"Makes sense," he said. "But what does any of this have to do with her death? Or even Clayborn's?"

She started walking again, and he fell in step by her side. "I'll get to Clayborn in a moment. First, let's focus on Ginger. What if she saw or heard something she wasn't supposed to?"

"Like what?"

"I don't know." Questions like that kept detectives pacing the floor. "We assumed she was killed in the alley. But what if she wasn't? What if she was killed right here?" They had arrived at the bank, and she stopped in the middle of the street.

He stopped, too. "I checked this area over thoroughly, but this is a busy part of town. By the time her shoe was found, the place had been pretty much compromised by wagon wheels and horses."

She glanced up. The windows over the bank looked dark and forbidding, and hair rose at her nape. An odd sensation put her on high alert, and she reached in her pocket for her gun.

A soft light shone from behind the curtains of Mrs. Bracegirdle's apartment. Even at this late hour it looked like she was still awake.

"You still haven't told me how Clayborn fits into this."

"I'll tell you." She slanted her head toward the stairs. "Inside."

CHAPTER 44

Branch inserted the key into the lock. Katie was acting especially mysterious tonight, even for her.

The door creaked open. He waited for Katie to step ahead of him before following. He quietly closed the door so as not to disturb Mrs. Bracegirdle.

The narrow shaft of light streaming through a dusty window turned Katie's hair into copper flames. Eyes bright, she surveyed the room like it was a museum filled with valuable pieces and not just empty space. The glint of metal drew his gaze to the gun in her hand.

"You like this, don't you?" he asked.

Her questioning eyes came to rest on him. "Like what?"

"This cloak-and-dagger stuff."

She slipped her gun into her pocket. "I'd be in big trouble as a detective if I didn't."

Somehow he'd hoped for a different

answer. "Ever think about doing something else?"

The question seemed to surprise her. "Like what?"

"I don't know. Marriage. Kids."

The brightness left her face, and a protective surge welled up inside him. Now why did he have to mention marriage? Evidently it was a painful subject.

"I thought about it," she said, her voice soft. "But it didn't work out." She turned abruptly and headed for the kitchen.

He gave her a moment of privacy before following. "What are we looking for?" he whispered.

"Why are you whispering?" she asked.

"I have no idea." The kitchen was dark and the air stale.

A match flared in her hand, and she held it over the sink. Standing behind her, he caught a pleasant whiff of perfume. It reminded him of the lilacs that grew in his grandmother's garden.

"See the tin cup." She was all business now, and he sensed her excitement as she pointed into the sink. "The handle is pointing left in the nine o'clock position."

"I see that," he said. "And the head of that dead fly there is lying at four o'clock," he teased.

Even in the dim light he could see her face close, and he immediately regretted his flippant tone. "Is that significant?" he asked, hoping to make amends. "The direction of the handle?"

"Only that the cup was probably put there by a left-handed person."

"Sounds like a reasonable conclusion."

"There was a cup at the cabin with the handle pointing in the same direction."

He raised an eyebrow. Her observation skills put his to shame. "So what you're saying is —"

"The same person could have left both cups."

He folded his arms. "I thought you brought me out in the middle of the night because of Ginger's shoe."

"First things first." She blew out the match before it burned down to her fingers. "Did you know that only ten percent of the population is left-handed?"

"Don't tell me you believe all that nonsense about a left-handed person being the devil's playmate?"

"Not me. Most criminals in the Pinkerton files are right-handed. I just think it's interesting to find two similar cups with left-pointing handles. Were you able to tell which hand the knifeman favored?"

He dropped his arms to the side and stared at her. As much as he appreciated what she was trying to do, linking two possibly unrelated coffee cups to the crime sounded like a leap in logic.

"Our killer is right-handed," he said and frowned. "Surely you didn't think there was a connection?"

"Maybe not with the Harvey girls, but possibly with Clayborn. Whoever was in that cabin didn't want to be found."

"I noticed that," he said. She moved away from the sink, and he caught her by the arm. "You're good," he said. "I never noticed the cups."

He heard her intake of breath. "Does this mean you've changed your mind about Pinkerton operatives?"

"Absolutely not," he said. *Only you.*

Gazing into her eyes, he knew a moment of reason. Kissing her would only make matters worse. It would be one more thing to haunt him the rest of his days, just like the other moments they'd shared. But knowing that didn't make the struggle between mind and body, reason and insanity, any less difficult.

Still, wisdom and good sense might have won had she not wrinkled her nose like she tended to do. Had she not slanted her head in that certain way and gazed at him with those big, bright, questioning eyes. Blue as the deepest ocean. Blue as the brightest sky. All at once rationale left him, rushing away like a speeding train.

Closing the distance between them, he circled her slender waist with his hands. She stiffened at his touch, and a look of dismay flashed across her face before her body relaxed in surrender.

"We shouldn't do this," she said, her voice soft. But even as she protested she slid her hands up his chest. "We're working."

"We're standing in an empty apartment."

"*Working,*" she repeated, her arms draped around his neck.

He sucked in his breath, but he could no sooner pull away from her than jump off a cliff. His hands explored the contours of her back, and the warmth of her body beckoned to him. Her delicate, sweet fragrance teased his nose, and her sweet, warm breath was like a beacon guiding his mouth to hers.

Just before his lips met hers a sound alerted him. "Shh. I hear something," he whispered next to her silky skin.

She pulled out of his arms, and he immediately felt a void. Somehow she had taken something of him with her.

"I hear it, too."

She showed no sign of resenting the intrusion. Instead, she was all business as she pulled out her gun, ready for action. Evidently, his kisses were a poor substitute for the excitement of her job, but now was not the time to think about that.

"Sure you don't want my Colt?" he asked, keeping his voice low.

"I'll stick with this." He felt her gaze on him. "And if you laugh —"

"Wouldn't think of it."

He moved quietly into the front room, and she followed close behind. Beneath the carpet the floor creaked like a rickety old bridge.

"The superintendent should have the building checked for termites," she said, her voice hushed.

"My thoughts exactly."

"Get ready," he whispered, hand on the doorknob. "One, two —" He yanked the door open and something flew out of the dark. The object hit the floor with a bang, missing him by mere inches. It looked like a stick of some sort.

Grabbing hold of it, he reeled the attacker into the room.

"Mrs. Bracegirdle!" He stared at her in horror. Only then did he realize he was holding on to her walking cane. Had he pulled her off her feet she could have been seriously hurt.

He holstered his gun. "Confound it! What are you doing here?"

In the dim light from the window, the older woman's face looked pale as a wintry moon. "Branch!" she gasped when she was finally able to find her voice. She pressed the tip of her cane onto the floor and held on to it with both hands. "You nearly scared me into my grave!"

"Sorry." He closed the door.

"Are you okay?" Katie asked, her voice soft with concern.

"Other than having aged ten years in thirty seconds, I'm fine." Mrs. Bracegirdle glanced at Branch before turning her attention back to Katie. "So what are you two doing here?"

"I thought I saw a light up here the other night," Katie explained, "and we were just checking it out."

The widow gave a self-righteous shake of her head. "It's about time someone took me seriously."

"I do take you seriously." Branch felt bad for scaring her. "But you still haven't told us what you're doing here."

"I heard someone coming up the stairs

earlier. I decided to take matters into my own hands and find out once and for all what's going on here."

"All you heard was Katie and me."

Mrs. Bracegirdle shifted her gaze from him to Katie and back again. "You mean all this time the noise I heard was just the two of you making like a married couple?"

Katie's mouth dropped open. "No, no!" she hastened to explain. "Just tonight. I mean —" She looked to Branch for help, but something made him angle his head to the side.

"Branch? What is it?"

"Shh," he cautioned, finger to his mouth. He pressed his ear to the door. A footfall was followed by the sound of a key entering the lock.

He jerked back. "Quick!" he whispered. "In the bedroom."

The three of them barely had time to reach the next room when someone entered the apartment. Senses on high alert, Katie held her breath. Whoever entered the apartment had a key. The question was, why would anyone come here so late at night?

Branch held the bedroom door open a crack and peered out with one eye.

"Can you tell who it is?" Katie whispered.

"Too dark."

"Man or woman?" Mrs. Bracegirdle asked.

"Can't tell that, either."

For several moments no one spoke. Creaking boards were followed by an odd thumping sound.

Puzzled, Katie strained her ears. "It sounds like he's moving furniture," she said, her voice low.

"In an empty room? That would be a trick," Branch whispered back.

The intruder sneezed, and Katie grabbed hold of Branch's arm. She would recognize that sneeze anywhere.

Branch's hand rested on hers. "What is it?"

"Culpepper," she whispered.

He glanced back at her. "What?"

"That's Stanley Culpepper. The restaurant's accountant."

"Are you sure?"

For answer Katie nodded. The three of them didn't move for several moments. The strange thumping sounds continued.

"What in the name of Sam Hill is he —"

A high screech cut him off, and Mrs. Bracegirdle tugged on Katie's sleeve. "That's the cat I told you about. The one who sings opera." She turned her ear to the door. "*Il Trovatore,* if I'm not mistaken."

"I don't think it's a cat," Katie said. Neither was it opera. The high-pitched grinding noise sounded like metal grinding against metal.

Branch whispered, "How would your Pinkerton boss proceed at this point?"

"He would caution us to wait and observe." With that Katie pulled out her pistol and darted out of the room.

CHAPTER 45

A flickering light greeted Katie. Culpepper was facedown on the floor, head and shoulders in a hole. Wooden boards and the carpet had kept the hole hidden, and both had been moved aside.

She exchanged a glance with Branch before stepping over what looked like a log but was really the rolled-back carpet.

Branch followed and nudged the man's leg with the toe of his boot. The grinding sound stopped, and Culpepper's head popped out of the hole. "It's about time you —"

Seeing Katie, he reached for his hammer. She pointed her gun at him and kicked the hammer aside. "I wouldn't do that if I were you."

Culpepper stared at the gun, and panic crossed his face. "You! But you're nothing but a Harvey girl."

"And you're nothing but a thief and a killer."

Branch grabbed Culpepper's hands and pulled them behind his back. "And I'm the sheriff."

After Branch snapped the handcuffs around Culpepper's wrists, Katie called to Mrs. Bracegirdle. "It's safe to come out now."

Mrs. Bracegirdle entered the room cautiously, stabbing the floor with her cane. "Would you folks mind telling me what's going on? What is Mr. Culpepper doing here?"

Branch nudged a chisel and hammer with his foot. "I'd say by the look of things, he was trying to work his way to the bank vault below." Mrs. Bracegirdle inched forward and stared down the hole in disbelief. "You mean that's what's been keeping me awake all this time?"

"You try grinding through two feet of reinforced concrete," Culpepper said and then sneezed.

Katie waved a hand in front of her nose. "Maybe you don't have hay fever after all. Maybe it's all this dust." It also explained his battered hands and dirty nails. "What I don't understand is why? You have a good job."

"You call working at the Harvey House a good job?" Culpepper's eyes took on a feverish glow. "Do you know how much money is down there? It would have made me a rich man and I'd never have to work again."

"Don't feel bad," Branch said. "You won't have to work in jail, either."

Culpepper sneezed again but said nothing.

"So why'd you do it?" Katie asked. "Why'd you kill Ginger and Priscilla?"

Mrs. Bracegirdle gasped. "*He* killed the Harvey girls?"

"I didn't do it." Sweat beaded Culpepper's forehead. "You can't pin their deaths on me."

Katie studied the tools Culpepper had dropped. "He's right-handed," she said. But that wasn't all. There were two sets of tools. Two hammers, two chisels.

"So who's your partner?" Branch asked.

"Who says I have one?"

"You better have one," Katie said. "Otherwise you and you alone will be charged with a lot more than trying to rob a bank."

Culpepper suddenly seemed to have trouble breathing. "I didn't kill nobody," he said between gasps. "You can't prove that I did."

"I think we can make a pretty good case," Branch said. "Ginger found out what you were up to and you couldn't let her get away."

"So you chased her," Katie added. "All the way back to the Harvey House where you killed her."

"You don't know nothing from Adam," Culpepper groused and sneezed.

"If you didn't do it, then your partner did." The edge to Branch's voice matched the dark look on his face.

"I told you. I don't have a partner."

Culpepper stuck to his guns and no amount of questioning made him change his tune.

"I think I've heard enough for tonight," Branch said. He pushed Culpepper across the room and out the door.

Katie let out a sigh and closed her eyes. *Thank You, God.* She'd prayed for a clue but never expected it to come in the form of a cup handle.

A movement reminded her she wasn't alone. She opened her eyes and slipped her arm around the old lady's stooped back. "Come on, let's get you home."

"Does this mean I'm no longer off my rocker?" Mrs. Bracegirdle asked.

Katie laughed. "I never thought you were."

CHAPTER 46

Pickens called everyone into the dining room following the morning rush, and all stood in a straight line, equal inches apart as customary.

Katie had gone to the restaurant manager with her plan, and now she said a silent prayer that it worked. Was Pickens up to the task? She would know soon enough.

Hands behind his back, he paced before them with an air of such unbearable importance it was a wonder that the buttons didn't pop off his overworked shirt.

"Ladies and gentlemen, I have an announcement to make."

"Maybe he's quitting," Mary-Lou whispered to Katie.

Katie shook her head. "Don't hold your breath." Though Pickens insisted that the line be perfectly straight, she inched forward where she could observe the others. Nothing was more revealing than an unguarded look.

Pickens cleared his throat. She had told him exactly what to say, but his arrogant bearing was clearly his own.

"Thanks to Katie here, the killer of our Harvey girls has been caught and is now behind bars."

His announcement drew gasps of surprise and appreciative applause.

"Praise God." Mary-Lou clutched her hands to her chest, and her eyes glistened with tears.

"Now we can all rest easy," Abigail said, her voice choked with emotion.

Tully, as usual, looked more suspicious than pleased. "What did Katie have to do with it?"

"Katie," Pickens began, "is actually a Pinkerton operative."

A stunned silence followed his announcement, and all eyes turned to her. Chef Gassy's mouth dropped open, and Howie Howard's peepers nearly popped out of his head. Miss Thatcher's hand flew to her mouth, and Buzz did a double take. The Mexican cooks looked at each other and shrugged.

"No entiendo," one murmured.

Cissy did understand but showed no surprise. Instead she kept her head lowered, as if the floor was of prime interest.

Tully rolled her eyes. "I always knew there

was something strange about you."

Mary-Lou shook her head in disbelief. "You mean I've been rooming with a real live detective?" She glanced around as if seeking confirmation from the others.

"But who was it?" Abigail asked, rubbing her bare ring finger as she tended to whenever she was nervous, upset, or anxious. "Who was the killer?"

Though she asked the question of Katie, Pickens answered. "Why, Mr. Culpepper, of course," he said, as if he'd known it all along.

"Culpepper?" Chef Gassy slapped his forehead with the palm of his hand. "But he vas one of us."

Pickens shook his head, and his jowls wobbled. "Not anymore."

Abigail glanced from left to right. "Personally, I never cared much for the man,"

Miss Thatcher nodded in agreement. "He was an odd one, all right."

"Look who's calling the kettle black," Tully said under her breath.

"How did you know it was Culpepper?" Buzz asked.

Katie quickly explained how she and Branch found him in the apartment over the bank.

"You mean he planned to rob it?" Buzz

shook his head. "Incredible."

Everyone started talking at once. Pickens silenced them. "Quiet! Katie has something she wants to say."

Katie stepped forward. "It's important that no one reveals who I am." Asking a room full of people to keep a secret was like trying to sneak daylight past a rooster, but she had to try.

"What difference does it make?" Tully asked. "The killer's been caught."

"An undercover agent mustn't reveal his or her identity," Katie explained. Given the number of people passing through the restaurant daily, she could easily bump into someone who recognized her in the future. More than one agent's cover had been blown by some well-meaning acquaintance. "Pinkerton rules."

She hoped the detective agency's rules commanded as much respect as Harvey's.

Pickens looked at his watch. "The train's due in fifteen minutes."

"What about our checks?" Tully asked. "I mean now that Culpepper's gone."

"Your paychecks will be issued on Friday as usual," Pickens assured them. Noticing Katie out of line, he paused and glared at her until she stepped back. "Buzz, you can handle the money at the door until we find a replacement for Culpepper." He clapped his hands, signaling the end of the meeting. "Now back to work, all of you."

Katie made a beeline for her station, and Mary-Lou hurried to catch up to her. "You, too?"

Katie shrugged. "The restaurant's under-staffed. May as well make myself useful while I'm waiting for my next assignment."

Mary-Lou's face softened into a wistful smile. "A Pinkerton detective. Wow. If I were you I'd never serve another meal."

"I thought you liked it here."

"I do. It's just that your life is so much more exciting."

Katie smiled. She really liked Mary-Lou and would miss her. Miss all of them — even Pickens. And the regulars — she would miss them, too. Mrs. Bracegirdle, Okie-Sam, Long-Shot, the railroad workers and cattlemen.

Mostly she would miss Branch. Her heart felt heavy as a lead balloon. "Trust me," she said. "A detective's work is dull and te-dious."

A dubious look crossed Mary-Lou's face. "If you say so." With a wave of her hand, she hastened away, and Katie strode to her own station.

The tables were set with every plate and

piece of silverware in perfect alignment. What would her sisters say if they could see her now? Plain, undomesticated Katie now knew how to set a table that would put a Boston socialite to shame.

Oddly enough, her station behind the counter seemed as comfortable and familiar to her as an old pair of shoes, and her spirits dropped even more.

Her job was complete except for writing the final report. Once she turned it in, she would be assigned to another case. The paperwork should have been completed by now.

But something held her back. True, she felt sorry for the other girls who were already overworked and would have to take up the slack when she left, but that wasn't the only reason she procrastinated. There were simply too many loose ends and unanswered questions for her peace of mind.

Culpepper refused to implicate anyone else, but it was hard to believe he worked alone. Not only did the double set of tools suggest a partner, but Culpepper hardly seemed physically capable of pulling off such a labor-intensive job by himself. Not with his breathing problems.

It seemed that arresting Culpepper had raised more questions than it answered.

■ ■ ■ ■

Branch walked through the door, and her thoughts scattered like little mice. Even the sun streaming through the windows appeared brighter with his presence.

He strolled across the room toward her with purposeful strides. Mouth drawn in a straight line, his eyes narrowed as if guarding a secret.

She chewed on her bottom lip. She thought she had memorized his every expression, but this one was new. "Everything okay?" she asked.

He slid onto a stool. "I just wired the circuit judge. Hope to have the trial as soon as next week."

"That's good," she said and tried not to think of how close they had come to kissing yet a second time. Feeling warmth climb up her neck, she looked away. "I — I think I figured out why Ginger asked to change places with Abigail."

"Oh?"

She met his gaze, determined to think about the case. Nothing else. "Something must have made her suspicious of Culpepper. Maybe she suspected he had something to do with Priscilla's death and decided to watch him. She could only do that from Abigail's station."

Branch rubbed the back of his neck. "If that's true, I wish she had come to me and not acted alone."

"Maybe she felt she needed proof or something."

"I guess we'll never know, will we?"

"Guess not." She studied him, still puzzled by his serious expression. "Were you able to get any more out of Culpepper?"

He shook his head. "He still maintains he worked alone. I checked his room at the boardinghouse but couldn't find a knife. Nothing there to indicate a partner, either."

"Such loyalty between criminals is rare," she said. No one liked taking a rap by himself, not if someone else could be implicated.

"Give him a couple of days. He'll sing."

"And if he doesn't?"

"We'll cross that bridge." He hesitated. "How long do you plan on sticking around?"

She swallowed the lump in her throat before meeting his gaze. She'd spent a restless night trying to convince herself that his kisses and near kisses meant nothing — that *he* meant nothing. But in the light of day she saw her lies for what they were.

"A day or two. I'm waiting for my next assignment." Her voice drifted off.

A muscle at his jaw quivered, but he said nothing. For the longest moment they locked eyes. *Don't look at me like that,* she wanted to scream. *Don't make me want you more than I already do.* Mercifully, their gazes slid away to the counter, the floor, the walls, the ceiling. Safer ground.

She cleared her voice. "Anything else?"

He drew in his breath. "I decided to tell Andy tonight about his mother. Father, too, if he asks."

That wasn't what she'd wanted to hear, but it was foolish to think that the worry on his face was about her. About her leaving. "That's probably a good idea."

"Just hope I know what to say when the time comes."

"Knowing you, you'll do just fine." Never had she known a more caring or loving father.

He gave her a sheepish smile. "If that business with Clayborn taught me anything, I have to put my trust in God. Right now I'm trusting that He'll put the right words in my mouth."

"I'll pray for you," she said softly.

He nodded. "I'm counting on it." He slanted his head, and a double line formed

416

between his eyebrows. "Did you ever have to tell someone something you dreaded?" His voice was so low she had to lean forward to catch his words.

"No," she said softly. "I never did." But that was about to change. For the one thing she dreaded more than anything in the world was telling Branch good-bye.

He opened his mouth to say something more, but just then the train pulled into the station and the tension between them snapped. Rising, he tapped the counter with his knuckle and left. But upon reaching the door, he took a long, hard look at her before ducking out through the crowd of newly arriving passengers.

CHAPTER 47

"Once upon a time," Branch began as Andy nestled by his side, "there was this lady about to give birth." They sat in the parlor in front of a slow-burning fire, and his words were punctuated by crackling logs.

Andy gave him a knowing look. "This is a story about baby Jesus, isn't it?"

"Not exactly. This lady's name wasn't Mary. It was Dorothy."

"Was Dorothy in Bethlehem, too?"

Branch chuckled. "Actually, Dorothy lived right here in Calico. Just as the baby arrived a terrible tornado hit the town." His voice remained strong with only an occasional pause as he searched for the right words. He'd prayed long and hard before sitting down with his son, and so far God was doing a pretty good job of guiding him along.

Andy giggled upon hearing that the baby had been put into an oven. "Like Moses," he said.

Branch arched an eyebrow. "Moses was put in a basket."

"I know, but his mother wanted to save him. So she put him in the basket."

Branch thought for a moment. "You're right. His mother did want to save him. Just as Dorothy wanted to save her son."

Andy listened with rapt attention as Branch continued. His eyes grew big and round as Branch described digging him out of the debris. Enough time had passed so that he could now relay the story without getting all choked up. Only an occasional catch interrupted the flow of words.

"I like that story," Andy said when Branch fell silent.

"That's just it, Son. It's not a story. Every word of it is true. That's how you came to be my son. I dug you out from underneath that house with these very hands." He held up both hands and turned them over.

Andy frowned as if trying to make sense of it all. "What happened to the lady who put me in the oven?" he asked at last.

"She was my wife, and she died and went to heaven. That's her picture on the piano."

"Do you have a photograph of the other lady?"

"The other lady was your mother. I'm sorry to say, I don't have a picture of her."

Andy thought about this for a moment. "Too bad there wasn't room in the oven for them, too."

Branch hugged his son close. "Yeah, too bad."

Andy laid his head on Branch's chest. "I wouldn't fit in the oven now."

"Nope. You sure wouldn't."

"Clarice just got a new mother." Clarice was one of Andy's schoolmates.

"So I heard." Branch was as surprised as anyone when old man Anderson remarried. Got himself one of those mail-order brides.

"Do you think I could get a new mother, too?"

The question was like a knife to his heart. Or maybe the thought of Katie leaving was behind the stabbing pain.

Branch stared at the red cinders in the fireplace and thought of moonlight and roses and sweet ruby lips. "You'll have to talk to God about that."

"I want Miss Katie to be my ma."

Another twist of the knife. "We can't always have what we want, Son." Even if one could, there was no guarantee of keeping it.

Katie waited for Cissy to climb the stairs that night. The others were still downstairs

420

eating supper, and so the second floor was deserted.

Cissy reached the landing and, upon spotting Katie, paused. Worry fleeted across her face . . . or maybe it was guilt.

"We need to talk," Katie said.

Cissy shoved her hands into her apron pockets. "What . . . what about?"

Katie held up the note found on her pillow. "This. You left it, didn't you? In my room."

Cissy glanced at the stairs as if to make certain they were still alone. Or maybe she was looking for a way to escape. "How'd you know that?"

Katie hadn't known for certain until that moment. "You were the only one who didn't seem surprised to learn my identity." She regarded the girl with narrowed eyes. "How'd you know I was a detective?"

"I didn't. I only knew that . . ." Cissy's voice faded away.

"Go on."

"I had a dream that someone would come and find the killer."

Katie reared back. "You had a dream?"

Cissy nodded. "And the person in my dream had red hair."

Katie stared at her. The girl was kidding, right? But she sure did look serious. "And you thought I was the one in your dream?"

Cissy gave her a look of curiosity. "You're the only one working here with red hair."

"Why didn't you tell me who the killer was instead of writing in riddles?" They were just lucky Culpepper hadn't killed again. "Had you told me from the start it was Culpepper, that would have saved us all a lot of trouble."

The girl looked confused or maybe just scared, but Katie was of no mind to let her off the hook. Instead, she wheeled about and headed for the stairs.

"Oh no, Miss Katie," Cissy called after her. "The killer ain't him."

CHAPTER 48

Branch couldn't believe how well his talk with Andy had gone. He still hadn't told him about his father. Andy didn't ask, and Branch didn't volunteer. But the questions were bound to come and when they did, he would, with God's help, be ready.

He was just about to lock up and hit the sack when a rap sounded at his door. A night visitor was never a good sign. It almost always spelled trouble, but the last person he expected to find on his doorstep this late was Katie.

His heart lurched at sight of her. Even in the dim light she looked soft and desirable. Beautiful. Had she come to say good-bye? The thought filled him with such anguish he clenched his hands by his side in an effort to maintain control.

He finally found his voice. "Come in," he said hoarsely, before realizing she wasn't alone.

The two women stepped inside, and Katie introduced him to her companion. "This is Cissy. She's the Harvey House pantry girl."

The dark-skinned girl stared at him, the brown irises of her eyes swimming in a sea of liquid white. He remembered seeing her after Ginger's death. Had even questioned her, but she denied knowing anything. He nodded at the girl before turning back to Katie.

"What's this about?"

For answer Katie turned to Cissy. "Tell him what you told me."

Lowering her gaze to the floor, the girl mumbled something. Branch leaned forward to catch the last of her words. Startled, he pulled back.

"Did she say Culpepper is not the killer?"

Katie nodded. "That's exactly what she said."

"Then who?"

"That's the problem. She doesn't know his name but thinks she might be able to identify him if she saw him again."

He frowned. "How does she know it's not Culpepper?"

"She saw the man who killed Ginger, and it wasn't Culpepper."

"Saw him?"

"Her bedroom window overlooks the back

of the house. She didn't see the actual murder, but she saw a man leave the alley around the time of Ginger's death."

He fixed his gaze on the girl. "Why didn't you say something about this before now?" He didn't mean to sound harsh, but neither did he have patience with people who held back information or claimed to see things they didn't.

Katie touched his arm and beseeched him with a slight shake of her head. "She's scared," she whispered.

The girl was shaking. Either she was scared of the killer or scared of him. Could she be telling the truth? Hard to know.

Katie moved her hand away, and he shifted his gaze back to Cissy. "The man you saw . . . Is he a restaurant customer?"

For answer Cissy shrugged her shoulders, and he frowned.

"She's not allowed to leave the kitchen during restaurant hours," Katie explained.

"Can you describe him?" Branch asked.

Cissy shook her head. "I only saw his face for a second. He had a beard."

Branch rubbed his chin. "That narrows it down to ninety percent of the men in this town. What about his hair color?"

Cissy's gaze dropped to the floor. "It was too dark."

"She thinks she'll recognize him if she sees him again," Katie said. "That's why we need your help."

"My help?"

"I've arranged for her to work in the dining room tomorrow. If she recognizes anyone, she'll point him out to us."

It sounded like a wild-goose chase. Still, he'd bet his life that Culpepper didn't work alone, and he was willing to do anything to prove it. "I'll be there."

Katie nodded. "Thank you."

Cissy walked outside, but Katie hesitated. She obviously had something else on her mind.

He slanted his head. "Katie?"

She lowered her voice to a whisper. "I thought of something earlier. About the cups. Long-Shot is left-handed, and he was friendly with Culpepper. He also has a beard."

"Long—" He frowned. He'd known the man for several years and never noticed he was left-handed. Still, that didn't mean he was Culpepper's partner. The man was a loser, but a killer? "You don't think — ?"

"I don't know. We'll see if Cissy recognizes him." She turned and joined Cissy outside.

Her gaze softened as she glanced back at him, and his heart responded with a jolt.

"You better get some shut-eye."

He nodded, though he doubted he'd sleep any better tonight than he had the other nights. "Be careful."

Katie hooked her arm around Cissy's and waved with her free hand.

Stepping onto the porch, he watched the two of them slip away into the folds of the night. *"If she recognizes anyone, she'll point him out to us."*

It sounded like a simple enough plan. There really was no reason for him to worry. Or was there? He turned to the house. *Long-Shot?*

CHAPTER 49

Katie met Cissy behind the counter that morning. It was early, and not even the locals had arrived yet. Dressed as a Harvey girl, the pantry girl looked every bit the part. She even had the smile down pat. She really was a pretty girl when she didn't look scared or insecure.

"Perfect," Katie said, clasping her hands to her chest.

Cissy's smile grew even wider. "I dreamt about being a Harvey girl." Today she held her head high, and her eyes shone with newfound confidence.

Katie smiled but didn't say anything. Cissy did a lot of dreaming, that was for sure.

Tully stopped in front of the counter. "What's *she* doing here?"

"I'm training her to take over for me," Katie said.

"That's ridiculous. Everyone knows that

Mr. Harvey would never allow a blackie —"
She broke off as Branch walked in the door.
Tossing her head, she moved away.

Branch greeted Katie with a finger to the
brim of his hat. Instead of his usual place at
the counter, he opted for a table with a full
view of the room. Once seated, he opened
up his newspaper.

Katie filled a cup with coffee and set it on
a tray. "Here, take this to the sheriff." She
handed the tray to Cissy. "And don't forget
to smile."

The locals started arriving just after seven.
Buzz sat by the door collecting money. During each lull his gaze followed Tully. Katie
sighed and dug her fingers into her palms.
Tully had no idea how lucky she was. Buzz
was smitten with her, but Tully hardly
seemed to notice. Was she really so heartless as to taunt him? Or was there some
deep-rooted reason why she so shamelessly
flirted with all the other men?

Maybe she was afraid of Buzz abandoning
her as her mother had. Was that why she
was so reluctant to commit to him and him
alone?

Pickens snapped his fingers, bringing her
out of her reverie, and she immediately set
to work.

Chair legs scraped the floor as railroaders

gathered around the tables. One of the men was telling a joke about two drunks who were walking upgrade on a railroad track and complaining about the banisters being too low.

The punch line brought uproarious laughter from his audience. Even Mrs. Bracegirdle chuckled as she took her usual place at the counter.

"I can't tell you how much better I slept last night without all that racket next door," she said.

Katie smiled. The woman did indeed look more rested. Perhaps the lack of sleep had caused the occasional mental lapses. Katie certainly hoped it was true.

Cissy returned with an empty tray.

"Is this a new girl?" Mrs. Bracegirdle asked.

"Yes, this is Cissy. Cissy, this is Mrs. Bracegirdle and she likes her coffee hot and strong."

"Yes, ma'am." Cissy reached for a clean cup and saucer.

She was a fast learner and seemed to have no trouble keeping track of orders. Since she normally worked in the kitchen, she was familiar with the lingo and could yell out menu dishes like she'd been doing it all her life. Even Gassy looked impressed.

Surprisingly, none of the locals objected at having a black girl work behind the counter, and this pleased Katie. Times, they were a-changing.

Katie moved to Cissy's side. "See anyone who looks like our man?" she whispered.

Cissy's brown-eyed gaze swept the room. "No, no one."

"What about that man over there?" She inclined her head toward Long-Shot, who was joking with the railroad workers.

When Cissy shook her head, Katie didn't know whether to be disappointed or relieved. She really liked Long-Shot but was hoping for a quick resolution.

Branch left with the locals just before the train arrived. There was no reason for him to stick around for a bunch of strangers, but Katie hated to see him go.

"Now what?" Cissy asked.

"Go work in the pantry and come back at noon. Oh, and don't forget to put on a fresh apron."

The midday crowd came and went, and still Cissy recognized no one. Same for the supper hour.

Cissy helped Katie clear away the tables and set them for breakfast.

"Sorry." The girl looked so upset Katie

felt sorry for her.

"Not your fault." Katie straightened a plate. "We tried. That's all we can do. We'll give it another shot tomorrow."

Cissy bit her lip. "You mean I get to be a Harvey girl for another day?"

"Looks that way."

"Do you think Mr. Harvey will ever allow a blackie like me to be one for real?"

Katie hated to get the girl's hopes up, but neither did she want to discourage her. "You never know. Not that long ago he hired only males." He soon discovered his mistake. Women were more dependable and didn't imbibe on the job. "Maybe when I tell Mr. Harvey what a good job you did, he'll reconsider his policy."

Cissy smiled, though she didn't look all that convinced.

Cissy didn't recognize any of the locals the next day or even the following, but Katie wasn't ready to give up. Detective work could be so frustrating at times, but patience often paid off, and she was counting on that.

On the fourth day, following Branch's departure, Okie-Sam walked in and sat at the counter. Today, his hair looked more orange than red. "How come so serious looking, sis?" he asked.

She smiled. "No reason." She filled his cup. "Haven't seen you around for a while." Come to think of it, she hadn't seen him since the day Andy had been kidnapped.

"Just got back to town last night. Funeral."

She frowned. "Your father?"

He nodded. "His heart."

"I'm sorry," she said.

"Yeah, well. You know what they say. No one leaves this world alive." After a beat he added, "I'll have the usual."

She called his order of scrambled eggs and bacon to the kitchen. Abigail reached behind the counter for clean napkins. With a flick of her eyes, she indicated Katie's apron.

Katie looked down and groaned. Somehow she had spilled syrup on her bib. "Take over for me while I change, will you, Abigail?"

"Will do."

Katie ducked from behind the counter, crossed to the hall, and took the stairs two at a time. Reaching her room, she lifted the apron over her head. In her haste she knocked over a perfume bottle. The glass atomizer bounced against the wall and shattered.

A sickly perfume smell wafted upward, but Katie hardly noticed. Her gaze was riveted on the shards of glass at her feet.

Snatches of dialogue ran through her head, and she thought about those cups with the handles turned to the left.

"What happened to you?" she'd asked Okie-Sam.

"Cut it on some glass."

She held her hands up. Right hand or left? Which hand had he cut? Right. She was pretty sure he'd injured the right hand. That would force him to use his left, even while drinking from a cup, wouldn't it?

Forcing herself to breathe, she checked the weapon in her pocket. *Could this be it, God? Is this what You've been trying to tell me all this time?* Heart pounding, she raced from the room.

Abigail and Okie-Sam were deep in conversation when Katie returned. Abigail leaned over the counter to stare at the watch in his hand.

"Pa was an honest man. Worked his fingers to the bone, he did. And you know what happened? His wife took off with a Bible salesman, people stole his cattle, and the bank foreclosed on his farm. All he had to his name on the day he died was this here cheap watch."

Katie took her place next to Abigail and willed her heart to stop pounding. "That

434

must have made you angry," she said, watching his face.

Okie-Sam slipped the watch into his shirt pocket and picked up his fork. "Anger doesn't begin to describe how I feel." He stabbed at the bacon on his plate and lifted the fork to his mouth. She studied his hands. Today he wore no bandage, but a jagged red mark from a recently healed scar sliced across the top of his right hand. Could glass have made a wound like that? Or had he cut it while working his way to the bank vault?

"I can take it from here." Katie nudged Abigail away.

Abigail gave her a puzzled look but didn't argue.

Katie had no intention of doing anything rash or overplaying her hand. Okie-Sam suspected nothing, and she meant to keep it that way. Branch would make the arrest. No need to hurry.

Okie-Sam watched as she made a fresh pot of coffee. "Guess you had some excitement while I was gone," he said.

She glanced over her shoulder. "Excitement?"

"Heard they arrested the killer. Heard he worked here."

"You heard right," she said, as lightly as

her ragged breath allowed. "Guess we can all breathe easy now."

"Guess so." His eyes narrowed. "What's the sheriff say?"

"Say?" she asked, feigning innocence. So he was probing for information. Was he worried about Culpepper implicating him?

"Is the case closed?"

"Far as I know," she said. "The circuit judge is due to arrive at the end of the week."

He finished the rest of his breakfast in silence then reached for his rawhide hat and set it atop his head. "Any use for a cheap watch?" he asked.

She shook her head. "Since it's your father's, you should keep it."

"Guess I should at that." He swung around on the stool and stood. "See you later, sis."

She considered trying to stall him but thought better of it. He might leave town now that his partner was behind bars, but that was the chance she'd have to take.

"You, too, brother."

Just then Cissy walked in the breakfast room. She jerked to a stop, her face contorted in horror. "That's him," she cried, pointing at Okie-Sam. "That's the killer!"

CHAPTER 50

Branch walked into his office and, with a flip of his wrist, tossed his hat against the wall. He hit the wooden peg maybe once out of twenty-five tries, but today he was lucky. His hat held, but that was as far as his luck went.

He'd spent practically four days at the Harvey House and had nothing to show for his time except frustration. Cissy hadn't recognized any of the regulars. Not that he was surprised. He hadn't really expected anything from her.

Woody had finished his breakfast and sat on his cot whittling on a piece of wood. Chips flew to the floor like chicken feed.

"Not a very friendly type," he complained. He slanted his head toward Culpepper, who lay on his cot facing the back wall, wheezing. The breakfast tray sat on the cell floor, untouched.

Scarface made a rude sound from the next

cell over. "You can say that again. I've known friendlier corpses. Bank robbers like him give the rest of us a bad name."

Ignoring their gripes, Branch grabbed a chair and set it in front of Culpepper's cell. He wasn't much for making deals with prisoners. *But if all else fails . . .*

He straddled the chair and rested his arms on the back. Some lawmen were known to use physical or mental abuse to gain a confession, but Branch was against such methods.

"You admit to trying to rob the bank," he began.

Culpepper turned over on his cot and glared at him with red eyes. "I didn't admit to nothing."

"Not in so many words. But you find a man digging within the vicinity of a bank safe and well . . . I'm no whiz in math, but I know how to put two and two together."

Scarface shook his head in disgust. "Why go to all that bother? That's what I want to know. It's easier to just walk up to the clerk and demand the money up front."

Culpepper glared at Scarface. "What do you know? You're in jail same as me."

"Yeah, but only because I had a run-in with a pie."

Branch rubbed the back of his neck. Just

hearing the word *pie* reminded him of Katie, and right now he had a job to do.

"Attempted bank robbery will get you at most . . . what? Six or seven years at Lansing." The Kansas state prison was originally called Petersburgh but underwent a name change a few years back.

"Four or five with good behavior," Woody called from his cell.

"Seven at the most," Scarface concurred.

"Ah, there you go." Branch let Culpepper chew on that for a moment before he continued. "Murder? Now that's a whole different ball of wax. That'll buy you a prime piece of property in the criminal graveyard."

"Yeah, but only after they throw you a bow-tie party," Woody said.

This got a rise out of Culpepper. "I didn't kill no girls, and you can't prove that I did. I'm innocent."

Branch shrugged. "Claiming to be innocent is one of the prerequisites of a good hanging. Never knew a condemned man claim otherwise."

Culpepper glared at him but said nothing.

"Ow!" Woody yelped and stuck his finger in his mouth.

"You okay?" Branch called over to him.

"Yeah. Just cut myself. You don't happen

to have somethin' I can wrap around this, do you?"

Branch stood and crossed to his desk. He reached into the top drawer for gauze, tape, scissors, and a bottle of iodine.

He handed the iodine through the bars. "Put that on your wound."

Woody did as instructed. "Ouch, that hurts."

"Not as much as hanging from the gallows," Scarface said as if he were talking from experience.

Branch cut a strip of tape and stuck it to a metal bar. "Stick out your hand."

Woody reached through the bars, and Branch applied gauze and tape. "This is what I get for letting prisoners use a knife."

"I'm not a prisoner," Woody said. "I'm the resident cell dweller. 'Sides, that knife's so dull, you could ride to town on it."

Branch secured the bandage on Woody's hand. "That should do it."

Woody held up his hand to inspect the bandage. "At least it's my left hand and not my right."

Branch turned to replace the medical supplies. Stopping short of his desk, he whirled about. "What did you say?"

Something in his voice must have alerted Woody, because his forehead wrinkled. "I was just saying I'm glad it's my left hand."

"That's what I thought you said." Dumping the gauze and other items on the desk, Branch grabbed his hat and shot out the door.

Cissy's screams brought an immediate reaction from Okie-Sam. Pouncing like a lion, he grabbed Tully and held a knife to her throat. For such a large, awkward man, he moved surprisingly fast.

Katie reached for her gun but quickly changed her mind. Okie-Sam didn't know she was armed, and right now she intended to keep it that way.

Others ran into the room, including the entire kitchen staff. Gassy slid to a stop, and Howie Howard plowed into him. The Mexicans avoided the pileup but just barely. Chef Gassy righted himself, but he looked deathly pale, like he had just stepped off a storm-tossed boat.

Abigail dropped a stack of napkins. Behind her, Mary-Lou's hand flew to her mouth.

"Do what he says," Katie said, though none of them looked in any condition to give Okie-Sam trouble.

Only Cissy's quiet sobs broke the silence. Katie was stunned by Okie-Sam's transformation. He looked nothing like the man who had called her sis. How could she have missed the vacant stare? The grim set of his mouth? The hateful expression?

Pickens was the last to walk into the room, voice first. "Who screamed? Don't tell me it was another mouse. And why are all these napkins on the floor?" Seeing Okie-Sam, he jerked back. "What the —"

"Don't move." Okie-Sam's gaze darted around the room, but he held the knife steady at Tully's throat.

Katie silently ran through everything she knew about dealing with hostage situations. She had to keep him talking. Make him think she was on his side.

"Okie-Sam just got back from burying his pa." She spoke in a natural, conversational voice. "The poor man is half out of his mind with grief." She moved ever so slowly from around the counter. "Tell them, Okie. Tell them how hard your poor daddy worked."

"He worked hard, all right. All his life. And you know what it got him?"

"Tell them, brother. Tell them."

And he did. He seemed all too eager to talk about his father's hardscrabble life, and she'd counted on that, though the knife never wavered from Tully's neck. As he droned on, the small but attentive audience remained rooted in place like a grove of dry oaks.

Tully's face was deathly white and her eyes wide with fear, but she didn't move.

Ever so slowly, Katie pulled out her gun and held her arm by her side, hiding her weapon beneath her apron. Despite its small size, derringers were lethal at close range. Still, with Tully in the way, firing a gun would be tricky no matter the distance.

Without warning, Buzz lunged at him. Gripping Tully with one arm around her neck, Okie-Sam sliced his knife through the air with his free hand, ripping the sleeve of Buzz's shirt.

Tully cried out, and Buzz fell back, holding his arm.

Okie-Sam shouted to the others, "Don't any of you move!"

Katie froze in place. The distraction allowed her to advance, but she was still four tables away. So close and yet so far.

She swallowed hard. "Tell them about the watch. Tell them, Okie."

Okie-Sam was breathing hard, and beads of perspiration dotted his forehead. "I know what you're doin', but it won't work." He stepped back, pulling Tully with him.

A movement beneath the table drew Katie's gaze downward. Spook Cat! Only the tip of his tail was visible beneath the white tablecloth, indicating he faced the right direction for her purposes. *Do what I want you to do, cat, and I promise you all the pie you can eat.*

Katie gave the chair a good hard kick. The chair didn't touch Spook Cat, but it sure did scare him. Screeching like a barn owl, the tom shot out from under the table in a furry streak. Startled, Okie-Sam jumped back, and the knife flew out of his hand, along with something else. His hair. What turned out to be a red wig fell on the cat, and the animal raced around the room blindly, screeching all the way.

Tully pulled free and ran into Buzz's arms.

Okie-Sam retrieved his knife, but it was too late. In the confusion, he failed to notice Branch had entered the restaurant and now stood directly behind him.

Branch pointed his gun at Okie-Sam's now-bald head, and Katie pointed hers at his chest. Okie-Sam was bookended between two muzzles.

"Drop the knife," Branch said.

The knife fell to the floor with a clunk.

While Pickens, Gassy, and the others watched slack jawed, Branch calmly snapped the handcuffs around Okie-Sam's wrists.

Only Tully's low murmurings broke the silence as she tended Buzz's wound. It didn't look like a bad cut, but one would never know it by the way Tully fussed over him like a mother hen. She had wrapped a clean napkin around his arm to stem the bleeding.

Branch grabbed Okie-Sam by the arm. "You're under arrest for the murder of Priscilla Adams, Ginger Watkins, and Gable Clayborn."

Mary-Lou gasped, Miss Thatcher fanned herself with her handkerchief, and Abigail swayed as if about to faint. Gassy crawled under a table where Spook Cat was hiding and pulled the wig off the poor tom's head.

Pickens's face puckered. "Would someone tell me what's going on? I thought Culpepper was the killer."

Branch shook his head. "Nope. This is the culprit."

"Why did you do it?" Katie asked, pocketing her gun. "Why did you kill those girls?"

Okie-Sam's beady eyes bored into her. "Wasn't my fault. Priscilla insisted we make her a partner. She wouldn't take no for an answer."

Katie raised her eyebrows. So that's what Priscilla and Culpepper had argued about. "And Ginger?"

"She got it into her dumb head that Culpepper had something to do with Priscilla's death. She followed him up to the apartment, and when she saw what we were doing, she ran."

"And you ran after her," Katie said. Had Charley not discovered Ginger's shoe, they might never have thought to check the apartment over the bank. By the time anyone discovered the money missing, Culpepper and Okie-Sam would have been long gone.

Katie felt like a load had lifted from her shoulders. At long last, the Harvey girl case was closed and they could all breathe easy.

Branch looked at her with warm approval. "I thought the pie-in-the-face thing was something. But the cat trick . . ." He shook his head and grinned. "That sure takes the cake."

Katie felt a warm glow. "What's this I hear? Praise for a Pinkerton detective?"

The corners of his mouth lifted. "You made a believer out of me." He jerked Okie-Sam toward the door.

No sooner had they left than the train slid into the station with a low, long whistle.

The train never failed to spur Pickens into action, and today was no different. He flapped his arms like a farmer chasing birds out of a newly planted field. "To your stations, everyone. Now!"

Tully looked about to argue, but Katie shook her head. "Take care of him. I'll cover for you."

Tully nodded her thanks and led Buzz out of the room. She clearly loved him and no longer cared who knew it. Life-and-death situations almost always changed people, mostly for the good. It certainly opened up Tully's heart. Maybe now she and Buzz could start building a future together.

Katie rushed to Tully's station. Suddenly the whole chain of events struck her as funny, and she giggled. No matter what happened around here the rule was business as usual. None of the passengers would have a clue as to what had just happened.

My stars, how I love this place!

CHAPTER 51

Mary-Lou watched Katie through the bedroom mirror as she brushed her hair. "I wish you didn't have to leave."

"I wish I didn't, either. But I have to be in Houston by Friday to start a new job."

"How exciting." Mary-Lou worked a knot out of a strand of hair. "I so envy you."

She could have knocked Katie over with a feather. No one had ever envied her. She was the one who'd envied others. Her sisters . . .

"Don't say that."

"It's true."

Katie blew a strand of hair away from her face. Not only had envy made her miserable, it separated her from her heavenly Father. Instead of thanking Him for giving her good health and a curious mind, she cursed her red hair. She might as well have come right out and said, "God, You made a mistake."

"You have a wonderful life here."

"I know. It's just . . ." Mary-Lou tossed down her hairbrush. "Seeing how happy Miss Thatcher and Tully are makes me wonder if there will ever be someone special for me."

"Oh, Mary-Lou, you're the nicest and kindest person I know. The right man will come along. I'm sure God has someone special in mind for you. You just have to be patient."

"What about you? I thought maybe you and the sheriff . . ."

Katie shook her head. "He loved his wife dearly, and I don't think there's room in his heart for anyone else."

"You can't be sure of that."

"Perhaps not, but I'm not sure I can trust a man again." She explained how the man she loved ran off with her sister.

"That's terrible," Mary-Lou gasped. "You must have been heartbroken."

"I was. But now I realize God had other plans for me. If Nathan hadn't wed my sister, I would never have become a detective and we would never have met."

Mary-Lou frowned. "How can you be so sure what God's plan is? I have a hard time figuring it out, myself."

"My minister back home said that God's

plans fill us with hope for a bright future. That's how I felt when I applied for my job as a detective."

"I kind of felt that way when I was hired as a Harvey girl."

"See?" She spread her hands. "It's God's will." She didn't feel hopeful whenever the possibility of a future with Branch came to mind. Such thoughts always made her feel nervous and confused. Maybe even a little bit scared.

A knock sounded at the door, and Tully poked her head in the room. "The sheriff's downstairs. He asked for you, Katie."

Katie's stomach knotted. There it was again: nerves and confusion. No hope there.

Katie spotted Branch through the glass doors, and her breath caught. She stepped around Spook Cat, stretched out on the floor enjoying the sun. The cat had been officially adopted by Chef Gassy and was allowed to roam freely, providing he stayed out of the pies.

Branch greeted her with a grin, and her heart did a flip-flop. All that talk about not trusting another man went out of her head. *Dear God, if there is the slightest chance that this man could love me . . .*

"Thought you might like to know that

Okie-Sam was found guilty and is on the way to the gallows as we speak." He paused for a moment. "When the time's right I'll be able to tell Andy that justice was served."

Pressing her hands together, she took a deep breath. "What a relief." After what Okie-Sam had done to those girls, hanging was probably too good for him. "What about Culpepper?"

"Heading to Lansing where he'll be locked up for a good many years."

Music to her ears. "What I don't understand is why Culpepper kept quiet about Okie-Sam. Why take the blame for something he didn't do?"

"I think I can answer that question," he said. "The Calico Bank isn't the first bank they robbed or tried to rob, and both have aliases a mile long. They tried robbing a bank in Kansas City, but Culpepper was caught and Okie-Sam busted him free."

"And Culpepper was hoping that history would repeat itself," she said. "Now we know why Pinkerton had no record of a redheaded criminal." Why anyone in his or her right mind would choose a *red* wig was beyond her. "But Culpepper wasn't wearing a wig. Why didn't they have a file on him?"

"Probably because he's really blond."

She slapped her forehead with the palm of

her hand. "The shoe polish. I should have known. And to think both men were under my very nose."

"Don't feel bad. They were under my nose, too. If it hadn't been for your crazy cup theory, they might have gotten away."

"I'm just glad it all worked out." A detective never knew how a case would break. But a cup code? That was a new one.

"It worked out all right. I'd say the two of us make mighty fine partners."

"Partners?" She laughed. "What happened to the man who preferred working alone?"

His mouth curved in a sheepish smile. "I guess you could say that a certain lady detective taught me a thing or two. See? Even an old dog like me can learn new tricks."

She smiled. "Old dog?" Hardly.

He rubbed the back of his neck and cleared his throat. "I've been thinking." He hesitated. "How do you feel about making the partnership permanent?"

Catching her breath, she gaped at him. Something stirred inside — an opening of a door. Warmth flowed through her like a summer breeze, sweeping away any lingering doubts. She had been afraid to admit to her feelings. Afraid to think that true love really existed. But looking into his open, honest face it suddenly seemed that loving him — trusting him — was the right thing to do.

Shaking with emotion, she could hardly get the words out. "Are . . . are you saying —"

He nodded, his eyes filled with warm lights. "Say yes, Katie. And you'll make me the happiest man alive."

Her mind scrambled. She felt all at once weak and strong. Dazed and alert. One moment they were talking about criminals and the next making a future together.

"So what do you say?" he prodded.

She struggled to find her voice. "Th–this is all happening so fast."

"Maybe this will help." He pulled something out of his pocket, and her mouth went dry. A ring? Her eyes stung, and she blinked. This wasn't just a dream. He was actually serious about marrying her. Joy bubbled up inside. Had this been God's plan all along? She certainly felt hopeful and happy and . . .

He held out his hand, and the sun glinted against the object in his open palm. Her jaw dropped, and her heart sank to her knees.

It wasn't a ring. It was . . .

"A badge?" she said, her voice barely above a whisper. The shiny object winked in the sunlight as if enjoying a joke at her expense.

He nodded. "An undersheriff's badge. The town's growing in leaps and bounds, and I'll need a lot of help. You know how lousy I am at paperwork. I talked to the mayor, and he approves."

He paused, and when she said nothing, a shadow of uncertainty crossed his face. "It's not as exciting as your current job. The pay's lousy. So are the hours, but you and I would make a great team. We've already proven that."

Pulling her gaze away from the badge, she looked at him with burning eyes. "You're offering me a j–job?" she stammered, feeling like the world's biggest fool.

His eyebrows rose. "So what do you say?"

"A job doing paperwork?"

He frowned. "I'm not doing a very good job of explaining myself, am I?"

"Oh, but you are." She shook her head. "You're doing an excellent job." Whirling about, she yanked open the restaurant door and dashed inside.

CHAPTER 52

Branch tossed the badge on his desk and kicked his chair.

"Temper, temper," Woody called from his cell. He and Scarface sat facing each other through the bars of their cells playing cards. "What's got you so riled up?"

"Women!"

"Would that be women in general?" Woody asked, reaching into Scarface's cell to play a card. "Or one in particular?"

"I offered Katie a job, and she didn't even give me an answer. Instead she shot off like a cannonball."

"Katie?" Woody drew a card and arranged it in his hand. "Is that the pie-in-the-face gal you were hankering to kiss?"

Scarface grimaced. "Better watch it with that one. I wouldn't put it past her to charge the gates of hell with a bucket of ice water."

Branch gripped the back of his chair. "That's the one, all right."

"Your turn," Woody said to his cellmate. In a louder voice he said, "Guess you don't know."

"Know what?" Branch asked.

"She's actually a Pinkerton operative sent here to help solve the Harvey case. That's what that Culpepper fella told us."

Scarface made a rude sound with his mouth. "I shoulda known from the git-go that the lady was a Pink."

"Yeah, and a good one at that," Branch muttered.

Scarface shook his head. "It's getting so you can't trust anyone, anymore. Females included."

Woody set his cards on his cot. "Let me get this straight." He rose, straightened out his wooden leg, and hobbled to the front of his cell. "You offered her a job?"

"Yeah." He couldn't think of any other way to keep her in town without getting hurt in the process. He wanted to keep her close but not too close. Keep her safe while protecting his heart.

Not that he blamed her for turning him down. Compared to her Pinkerton job, his offer was almost laughable. If only . . .

He clenched his teeth. No sense going down that road. She would never give up her job. She was like Hannah in that regard.

Why couldn't he fall in love with a more traditional woman? One who would be content just to be his wife?

"I offered her a job as undersheriff."

Woody rolled his eyes. "Congratulations. You just proved that it takes no brains to be a lawman."

"What's that supposed to mean?"

"It means you're dumb as a lamppost," Scarface said, throwing down his cards.

"I made a good offer," Branch said in his own defense. "Do you know how many men would jump at an offer like that? Even you."

"Not me," Woody said. "Not on your tintype. It's safer on this side of the bars than out there."

Scarface nodded. "Yeah, and room and board is free."

Branch pushed his chair against the desk with a bang. "She acted like I'd told her to jump in front of a train or something."

"I'm surprised she didn't tell *you* to jump," Woody said.

Branch frowned. "You sure do know how to make a fella feel like a heel."

"Yeah, well, it's no less than you deserve." Woody gripped the bars tight. "Listen to me and listen good. I'm a busy man, so I'm only gonna say this once. She has a job, and it probably pays a whole lot more than what this here town can afford to pay. If you want her to stay, then you better figure out something she don't already have."

"Like what?"

Woody rolled his eyes. "Now I gotta think for you, too?" He lumbered back to his cot. "Like I said, I'm a busy man. It's time to get me some shut-eye. Wake me when that fool head of yours figures out what to do with its brains."

"A job! He offered me a job?" Katie tossed a pair of bloomers into her carpetbag and bit down on her lip. "He wants me to do paperwork?" She groaned. Now she was talking to herself.

"What this town needs is a good under-sheriff, and I think you're the right person for the job."

The memory shot through her like a bullet, tearing her apart. She imagined hearing a ripping sound from within — some vital organ pulling away from its moorings.

She closed her eyes. *Oh, God. Why do I always fall for the wrong man? I'm trying to accept Your will, but it's hard.* It was in fact the hardest thing she ever had to do.

The door flew open, and Tully rushed into the room, scattering Katie's thoughts.

458

"Abigail's husband is here. You better come quick!"

Springing into action, Katie raced from the room, reaching the dining area behind Tully. Abigail was nowhere in sight.

Sam Fletcher stood at a table showing a photograph to one of the train passengers. Katie recognized the passenger as Mr. Thumper, a Bible salesman who traveled through Calico regularly and knew all the girls by name.

Nodding, Mr. Thumper handed the photograph back and said something.

Abigail's husband straightened and slipped the picture into his shirt pocket. He glanced around before taking his place at the counter. His slow, methodical movements indicated he was in no particular hurry. He would wait till after the midday crowd left.

Mary-Lou cast an anxious glance at Katie before handing him a bill of fare. Katie lifted her gaze to the clock. The clock indicated it was almost time for the train to leave. The train she was scheduled to leave town on . . .

Outside, Buzz stood ready to strike the gong. Intent on telling Buzz to hold off, Katie started for the door, but it was too late. The gong sounded and right on cue, the diners rose like a choir ready to burst into song.

Buzz held the door open with his one good arm and wished the passengers Godspeed as they streamed past him and onto the waiting train. His other arm was wrapped in a bandage and held in a sling.

The breakfast room was soon empty except for Abigail's husband and the regular staff. For several moments no one said a word. Buzz, sensing something was wrong, walked over to Tully. Silently she tossed a nod at the man on the stool. Mary-Lou looked close to tears.

Katie stepped behind the counter. "I'll have some of that berry pie," Fletcher said. His face was as white and puffy as unbaked dough, and his skinny mustache teetered up and down like a child's seesaw.

Katie sliced a piece and carried the plate over to him. He grabbed her by the wrist, surprising her. His fingers pressed into her flesh like an iron clamp.

"I know Abby's here. I'm her husband, and I want to see her now."

Katie glared at him. "Take your hands off me."

He jerked her arm before releasing it and picked up his fork.

She rubbed her wrist. "You better leave."

He took a bite of pie and chewed before answering. "This a public place. That means I have the same right to be here as anyone else."

Katie glared at him. "Buzz, go fetch the sheriff."

"That won't be necessary." All heads swung to the archway where Abigail stood, looking very much alone and vulnerable.

Her husband dropped his fork and pushed his bulk off the stool. "That's more like it. Get your things. We're going home."

Abigail shook her head. "I'm not going anywhere. This is my home now."

Katie moved from behind the counter. The Pinkerton agency never worked on cases involving marital problems and for good reason. Most detectives would rather walk into a den of thieves than a domestic dispute.

Fletcher's eyes glittered, and the tension in the air was palpable. "You're my wife, and you belong with me."

Abigail lifted her chin. "Not anymore. You'll be hearing from my lawyer. It's over, so you better just leave." Somehow she managed to put on a brave front, and only the most discerning eye would notice the slight tremor of her lips.

Fletcher took a step forward, his hands

knotted into fists by his side. "Who's gonna make me?"

"I am," Katie said, stepping next to Abigail.

He snickered. "You don't think I can take on the two of you?"

"Make that three," Tully said, surprising Katie. Surprising Buzz, too, who quickly took his place by Tully's side.

"Th–that's f–five of us," Mary-Lou stammered, hastening across the room to stand next to Buzz.

Fletcher glowered at the small group. "You better tell your four friends to move before someone gets hurt."

Pickens joined them, crowding in next to Mary-Lou. He crossed his arms in front of his ample chest and glared back at Fletcher. "Make that *five* friends."

"Six!" Chef Gassy squeezed between Tully and Buzz. He was followed by Howie Howard and the other kitchen staff, along with Miss Thatcher and even Cissy. What the group lacked in muscle they made up for in numbers.

Fletcher appeared confused or maybe bewildered. The pupils of his eyes shifted back and forth like little black marbles. "You better make sure this is what you want, Abby. 'Cause when I walk out that door I ain't never coming back."

"Staying here with my friends is what I want," Abigail said, her voice now strong with conviction.

Seeming to shrivel in defeat, Fletcher no longer appeared menacing. Instead, he looked about as harmless as an empty potato sack. Without another word, he stalked across the room and paused in front of the door. With one last glance at the group, he left the building.

No sooner had the door slammed shut behind him than Abigail burst into tears.

Katie handed her a handkerchief and put an arm around her. "It's over."

Abigail's body shook beneath her touch, but for the first time since Katie had known her she didn't look afraid.

"I can't believe it." Abigail blew her nose. "I never thought I'd have the nerve to stand up to him."

"But you did," Mary-Lou said. "We're so proud of you."

Abigail dabbed the tears away from her cheeks. "I saw the way Katie stood up to Okie-Sam. I decided it was time to take a stand of my own. But . . . I couldn't have done it without all your help."

"You know what they say," Katie said. "Two are better than one."

"And there were twelve of us," Mary-Lou said.

Chef Gassy lunged forward, thrusting a wooden spoon as if battling a dragon. "He come back, he answer to great chef."

"I'm trembling in my shoes," Tully whispered.

Abigail smiled through her tears.

Pickens clapped his hands. "All right, men. Ladies. Back to work." He pointed his finger at Katie. "You, too."

Katie sighed. She'd missed her train. If she didn't know better, she'd think God didn't want her to leave. But what possible reason could He have for wanting her to stay?

CHAPTER 53

The dining room was packed that night, and everyone was in good spirits.

Everyone except Katie. She played her role as a Harvey girl to the hilt, right down to a sparkling smile, but that didn't prevent her heart from aching.

Abigail couldn't stop smiling, even when she was in the kitchen. "Come here, I want to show you something," she whispered and led Katie to the dining room door. "Look over there."

Katie followed her finger to the coatrack where Mary-Lou was helping Charley Reynolds pick out a coat. The two of them were deep in conversation.

Abigail sighed. "I know it's too soon. Charley is still grieving the loss of Ginger. But Mary-Lou is the only one who can make him smile. Do you suppose . . . ?"

Katie nodded. "Oh, I do hope so. You must write and let me know how it all works out."

Pickens came up behind them and addressed Abigail. "It's time for dessert."

Promising to write, Abigail turned and hurried to the kitchen.

Pickens cleared his voice and ran a hand down his ample chest. "Sure I can't talk you into staying?" He looked as awkward as a young man asking a girl out to a dance. "Thought maybe you might consider trading in your gun for a tray."

Katie laughed. Only Pickens would think such a trade-off comparable. "You've got three new girls. You don't need me."

The new Harvey girls had arrived on the morning train.

Pickens lifted his shoulders and splayed his hands. "If you ever change your mind, you know where to find us."

His offer touched her deeply. "Thank you."

She picked up her carpetbag. She wanted to board the train before the crowd. Earlier she had said her good-byes, and there was nothing left to do.

She turned, and one of the new girls bumped into her, tray first. The Rhode Island chicken took off in one direction and the Long Island oysters in another. A look of horror crossed the poor girl's face, and she looked as frantic as a mouse in a trap.

"It's okay." Katie set her carpetbag down and helped the girl scoop up the food. Her name was Suzanne, and she was a pretty blond with a Southern drawl. "At least you didn't set the kitchen on fire like I did."

The girl looked up. She couldn't be more than eighteen or nineteen. "You did that?"

"Sure did."

"And you weren't fired?"

"Nope."

"But Mr. Pickens looks so mean. And so does Miss Thatcher. And the chef . . ."

"You can't always tell what people are like until you see into their hearts. Just wait. You'll be amazed. Meanwhile, just remember to keep smiling, no matter what." She spread her lips to demonstrate, and Suzanne smiled back. "That's it. The right smile can hide anything."

Even a broken heart.

The sun had dipped low in the afternoon sky by the time Branch raced back to town. He would have made it back a whole lot earlier had his horse not thrown a shoe.

Shadows stretched and yawned across his path as he galloped down Main. Midnight's flying hooves hammered the road, stirring up dust and curiosity.

Pedestrians turned to stare before dashing out of his way. Horses neighed and pawed the ground. Dogs barked.

The train was still in the station when he reached the Harvey House, and that was a relief. He quickly dismounted, tied his horse, and ran. *God, don't let that be the whistle.* But it was; he knew it was. Racing along the alleyway, his feet barely touched the ground. He took a flying leap onto the platform, but the train had already pulled away.

"Stop, stop!" he yelled, waving his arms over his head, but it was no use.

The train quickly picked up speed as it rushed away from the setting sun. Soon only a speck remained, no bigger than a period at the end of a sentence.

Turning, Branch surveyed the deserted platform, and his heart sank. Despair washed over him in angry waves. The train had taken his whole world with it, and he had no one to blame but himself.

He should have told Katie how he felt when he had the chance. Should have told her how much he loved her. Instead, like a coward, he'd held back out of fear of losing her like he'd lost Hannah. Like he'd lost almost everyone he'd ever loved. Had almost lost Andy.

Too late he realized his heart was beyond protecting. He was already hooked. Already head over heels. Already past the point of no return.

He debated what to do. He couldn't go to the office. The last thing he needed was his know-it-all jail occupants telling him what he already knew. He was a dang fool. Nor was he in any condition to face Andy or Miss Chloe.

He stalked into the restaurant. Big mistake.

Everything inside reminded him of Katie. The coatrack where first they'd met. *"If you'll step over to that rack, I'll help you pick out a dinner coat."*

The table where he celebrated Andy's birthday. *"Would you rather another waitress serve you?"*

The counter. *"Anything ever mess up your game, Sheriff?"*

Coffee. He needed coffee. Maybe that would clear his head. He staggered over to the counter, but even that offered no escape from the hundreds of memories that clawed at him.

He sat, elbows on the surface, and held his head in his hands. His misery cut him off from everything else like blinders.

"Looks like you could use a cup of joe,

Sheriff."

He dropped his hands, not sure he'd heard right. He blinked. "Katie?" His heart practically leaped out of his chest. "I . . . I thought you'd left."

She filled his cup. "I almost did, but then I realized that there were too many unanswered questions." She peered at him through lowered lashes. "A Pinkerton detective never rests until all the loose ends have been tied up."

Loose ends? Unanswered questions? What was she talking about? The case was closed. But even if it wasn't, he didn't want to think about it. Not now, at least.

He inhaled. Never had she looked more beautiful than she did at that moment. Never had he felt at such a loss for words. "Is that the only reason you're staying?"

Her eyes flashed. "If you think I have any intention of accepting your job offer you better think again."

"I'm withdrawing the job offer."

She regarded him with wary eyes. "Is that so?"

"Yeah, that's so." He blew out his breath. *God, don't let me mess this up. Not this time.* "I told my . . . uh . . . someone you'd turned down my offer. Know what he called me? Dumb as a lamppost."

"Did he now?"

He nodded. "Said you had a job. If I wanted you to stay I had to offer you something you don't already have."

She set the coffeepot down and smoothed her hands over her apron. "Don't know what that could be. Got everything I need right here."

"But you don't have this." He reached into his pocket and pulled out a small box. "Traveled all the way to Topeka to purchase it." He lifted the lid. Hands shaking, he pulled out a slim gold band set with a mine-cut diamond.

Placing the box on the counter, he held up the ring until her pretty round face was framed by the gilded circle.

Her eyes grew wide, softened, and slowly turned to liquid, and he heard her intake of breath.

He lowered the ring. "And you don't have this." He thumped his chest. "But if you'll let me, I'll give you all the love this ol' heart has to offer."

"Oh, Branch, I —"

"Wait. Hear me out." He wasn't one for putting his feelings into words, but he intended to give it his best shot. "I tried not falling in love with you. Never worked so hard at anything in my life. But every time

471

you looked at me a certain way or made me want to wring your neck, I was a goner." His voice trailed off, and he cleared his throat. "I was afraid of loving you for fear of losing you. I know it sounds crazy —"

"Not to me." Her lips trembled, and her eyes filled with tears.

"I guess what I'm trying to say is that God tested my faith once, and now He's testing it again. I can't love you without trusting the future to Him. That's what I'm trying to do here. So what do you say?"

Katie swallowed the lump in her throat, but even then she was having a hard time finding her voice. She'd told the new girl Suzanne that you couldn't always tell what people were like until you saw into their hearts. Right now the view into Branch's heart was spectacular, and her own heart was about to burst with joy and, more than anything, love.

"I love you, too," she whispered. She'd asked God why He had made her the way she was and at long last had her answer. God made her this way — red hair, freckles, and all — just so she could love and be loved by Branch.

He tilted his head. "So? Does that mean you'll marry me?"

"She says yes," Abigail said.

"Yes, she'll marry you," Mary-Lou called from where she was setting a table.

"She better," Tully added.

"Oui, oui," Chef Gassy said from the other side of the kitchen pass-through. *"N'est pas l'amour grandiose?"*

Even the new girl Suzanne gave an enthusiastic smile.

Pickens threw up his arms. "Hurry up and tell the man what he wants to hear. We got to get this place ready for tomorrow."

An eager look shone from Branch's eyes. "One more yes and it'll be unanimous."

Katie could hardly get the words out fast enough. "In that case, I say . . . yes! Yes, Branch Whitman. I'll marry you!"

Grinning from ear to ear, he surprised her by leaping over the counter. Mercifully he landed on his feet. He reached for her hand and slipped the ring on her finger. Before she knew it, she was in his arms. He hugged her so tight that their hearts seemed to beat as one.

"I love you, Katie Madison Jones and soon to be Whitman. God willing, if we're blessed with children, I hope they all have your crazy red hair and cute freckled nose."

The love shining from his eyes took her breath away. "I love you, too," she said with meaning, but no words could adequately express what was in her heart. "And I hope those children you mentioned will all be as tall and handsome and as stubborn as you." Something occurred to her and she drew back. "Andy . . ."

"No worry there. He's already said he wanted you to be his mom."

She sighed with happiness, and fresh tears sprang to her eyes. *Thank You, thank You, God.*

"About those loose ends . . ."

She shook her head. "All the loose ends have been cleared up. Case closed."

"Well then . . ." He inclined his head. "What would your Pinkerton bosses suggest we do at a time like this?"

She didn't even have to think up an answer. "I believe they would say that no betrothal is valid without a kiss."

He grinned. "That's one thing we can agree on."

No sooner had his mouth found hers than applause broke out. Pulling his head back, he groaned. The whole gang stood on the other side of the counter, and each and every one had a full Harvey smile, even Pickens.

Branch whispered in her ear, "What would your Pinkerton bosses say about one of their operatives making a public spectacle?"

She grinned up at him. "They would say, 'Miss Katie Madison Jones and soon to be Whitman, you're fired.' "

"Hmm. Maybe the Pinkerton National Detective Agency isn't as bad as I thought." And with that he kissed her again.

DEAR READERS,

Have you ever wondered what Sherlock Holmes would have thought had he somehow landed in a modern crime lab?

Crime solving in his day was no walk in the park, that's for sure. Can you imagine having to track down criminals without benefit of DNA, fingerprints, security cameras, social media, cell phones, or computers? But that's exactly what those early gumshoes had to do.

This posed an interesting problem when I set out to write my Undercover Ladies series.

It seems that years of watching *Castle, CSI,* and *Rizzoli and Isles* taught me a lot about modern-day forensics (and how to solve a crime in an hour). However, the shows left me clueless when it came to plotting my own story. It took a lot of research to come up with answers, and I now have only the greatest admiration for those early sleuth-hounds. With little more than wits and determination, they almost always got their man — and in some cases, their woman. How did they do it?

Detectives Worked Undercover

Some, like real-life Pinkerton detective Kate Warne, were masters of disguise. Kate was hired by Allan Pinkerton in 1852 and could change her accent as readily as she could change her clothes. If you haven't yet read books one and two in the Undercover Ladies series, you'll never guess how the heroines in those stories disguised themselves.

Detectives Shadowed Suspects (aka Surveillance)

This was a tiring but necessary part of crime fighting. The Pinkerton organization had a long arm and would follow a criminal to the ends of the earth if necessary, and occasionally did.

Detectives Resorted to Trickery

It's hard to believe, but the Federal Bureau of Investigation didn't get its first forensic crime lab until 1932. It's no wonder that Pinkerton operatives resorted to some interesting (and probably illegal, by today's standards) tricks to solve crimes.

Kate Warne had more than one trick up her sleeve and actually saved president-elect Abraham Lincoln's life. After verifying a plot to assassinate him, Kate wrapped Lincoln in a shawl and passed him off as her invalid brother, thus assuring his safety as he traveled by train to Washington, DC.

Detectives Pounded the Pavement
Questioning witnesses was and still is an important part of solving any crime. But witness testimony isn't always that reliable, and Pinkerton detectives relied on facts.

Detectives Were Experts at Body Language
(Even Before Anyone Knew What Body Language Was)
Detectives of yesteryear were only as good as their observation skills, and the best ones could read a person's personality at a glance. You think social media raises privacy concerns? Just be glad that you never had to walk past Sherlock Holmes.

I hope you enjoyed reading Katie and Branch's story. If you missed reading about Jennifer and Tom, and Maggie and Garrett, books one and two are still available.

Until next time,
Margaret

DISCUSSION QUESTIONS

1. Branch didn't think his faith was strong enough to pass God's test, but that turned out not to be true. Name a time in your life when your faith was tested. How did it change you and your relationship to God?

2. Katie hated her red hair and freckles and often struggled with feelings of envy. Have you ever envied another's looks or circumstances? The Bible says that the way to handle envy is to see yourself how God sees you. If you were to look at yourself through God's eyes, what would you see?

3. Katie and Branch were both afraid to commit to love because of past losses. The same was true for Miss Thatcher and Tully. Have you ever been afraid to do something because of a past experience?

4. Which character did you most identify with and why?

5. The Bible says there's strength in numbers. Abigail stood up to her husband with her friends' support. Name a time that a friend or friends gave you courage to do something you dreaded or were afraid to do.

6. In what ways did working at the restaurant help Katie overcome her feelings of inadequacy?

7. What do you think was the turning point in Katie and Branch's relationship?

8. Woody preferred living in a jail cell to facing real life. Other characters in the book lived in less obvious prisons. Fear of loss, fear of another person, and fear of failure were just some of the challenges they had to overcome. Katie, Branch, Andy, Abigail, Cissy, and Miss Thatcher all had to break through the chains that kept them from following God's plan for them. Name a challenge or fear in your own life and make a list of ways to conquer it.

9. The Bible doesn't mention tornadoes, but it does mention whirlwinds. God even spoke to Job from a whirlwind. The tornado struck when Branch was going through a whirlwind of troubles. What message do you think God was sending?

10. There's an old adage that it's better to have loved and lost than never to have loved at all. This makes perfect sense until you lose someone close. In what ways did Branch and Katie try to protect themselves from future losses? Have you ever been tempted to do likewise?

ABOUT THE AUTHOR

Margaret Brownley loves hearing from her readers and can be reached through her website. The author of more than thirty novels, she was a former RITA finalist and INSPY nominee. For more love and laughter in the Old West, check out Margaret's latest books at www.margaret-brownley.com.

The employees of Thorndike Press hope you have enjoyed this Large Print book. All our Thorndike, Wheeler, and Kennebec Large Print titles are designed for easy reading, and all our books are made to last. Other Thorndike Press Large Print books are available at your library, through selected bookstores, or directly from us.

For information about titles, please call:
  (800) 223-1244

or visit our Web site at:
  http://gale.cengage.com/thorndike

To share your comments, please write:
Publisher
Thorndike Press
10 Water St., Suite 310
Waterville, ME 04901